Praise for the novels of Heather Graham

"Graham wields a deftly sexy and convincing pen."
—*Publishers Weekly*

"A fast-paced and suspenseful read that will give readers chills while keeping them guessing until the end."
—*RT Book Reviews* on *Ghost Moon*

"If you like mixing a bit of the creepy with a dash of sinister and spine-chilling reading with your romance, be sure to read Heather Graham's latest."
—*Miami Herald* on *Unhallowed Ground*

"*The Keepers* is original and exciting. Constant tension—both dangerous and sexual— will keep readers on the edge of their seats."
—*RT Book Reviews*

"The paranormal elements are integral to the unrelentingly suspenseful plot, the characters are likable, the romance convincing and...Graham's atmospheric depiction of a lost city is especially poignant."
—*Booklist* on *Ghost Walk*

"Graham's rich, balanced thriller sizzles with equal parts suspense, romance and the paranormal— all of it nail-biting."
—*Publishers Weekly* on *The Vision*

"Great writing and excellent characters make *Wicked* a terrific read.... The undercurrent of mystery and suspense will keep readers riveted."
—*Romance Reviews Today*

"Graham's tight plotting, her keen sense of when to reveal and when to tease... will keep fans turning the pages."
—*Publishers Weekly* on *Picture Me Dead*

Also by HEATHER GRAHAM

THE UNHOLY
THE UNSEEN
AN ANGEL FOR CHRISTMAS
THE EVIL INSIDE
SACRED EVIL
HEART OF EVIL
PHANTOM EVIL
NIGHT OF THE VAMPIRES
THE KEEPERS
GHOST MOON
GHOST NIGHT
GHOST SHADOW
THE KILLING EDGE
NIGHT OF THE WOLVES
HOME IN TIME FOR CHRISTMAS
UNHALLOWED GROUND
DUST TO DUST
NIGHTWALKER
DEADLY GIFT
DEADLY HARVEST
DEADLY NIGHT

THE DEATH DEALER
THE LAST NOEL
THE SÉANCE
BLOOD RED
THE DEAD ROOM
KISS OF DARKNESS
THE VISION
THE ISLAND
GHOST WALK
KILLING KELLY
THE PRESENCE
DEAD ON THE DANCE FLOOR
PICTURE ME DEAD
HAUNTED
HURRICANE BAY
A SEASON OF MIRACLES
NIGHT OF THE BLACKBIRD
NEVER SLEEP WITH STRANGERS
EYES OF FIRE
SLOW BURN
NIGHT HEAT

* * * * *

Look for Heather Graham's next novel
The Uninvited
Available from Harlequin MIRA
in September 2012.

HEATHER GRAHAM

THE
UNSPOKEN

HARLEQUIN®
entertain, enrich, inspire™

Recycling programs
for this product may
not exist in your area.

ISBN-13: 978-0-7783-1361-8

THE UNSPOKEN

For questions and comments about the quality of this book, please contact us at
Customer_eCare@Harlequin.ca.

www.Harlequin.com

Printed in U.S.A.

In loving and grateful memory of my mom, Violet, who came from Dublin to the amazing city of Chicago.

And for Aunt Amy, Katie and my Irish side of the family, especially my great-grandmother who, when watching my sister and me, would warn us that the banshees "be gettin' us in the outhouse" if we didn't behave. (She issued this threat so well, we were teenagers before realizing we didn't *have* an outhouse!) Granny, however, had a touch of magic about her, and told wonderful stories. She, my mom and all those who believed in (or pretended they believed in!) banshees, leprechauns, pixies, ghosties and all else gave me my love for what might be in the darkness or in realms we have yet to discover—and for reading.

A book, they taught me, could give me a new world or adventure to explore every day of my life.

What a gift to give a child. I am grateful to them all.

Prologue

The midnight hour

Austin Miller loved his comfortable home. Built by his grandfather in 1872, after the ravages of the Great Chicago Fire of October 10, 1871, it had the grace—and even opulence—of the mid-Victorian era. The staircase was carpeted in deep crimson, a shade picked up in the period furniture. Swirling drapes in black and cream adorned the parlor, and the windows were etched glass. He had changed little since his grandfather's day.

It boasted a true gentleman's den with bookshelves that lined the walls, filled with wonderful tomes, old and new. It also boasted some of his fabulous collections, the most impressive of which was his collection of Egyptian artifacts. They were legally obtained, since Austin's grandfather had been on the dig when Tut's tomb was discovered; he had lived much of his life prowling the sands of the Sahara in pursuit of discoveries. Canopic jars were kept in a temperature-controlled display case, along with funerary statuettes that were gilded and bejeweled. A real sarcophagus—that of a king's illegitimate son, of little import to Egyptians at the time—stood open in a corner of the room. It had been arranged in a display case of its own, built by his grandfather in the mid-1930s. He'd exhibited his collection of mummified snakes and cats behind glass, as well. On one side of Austin's beautiful desk was an exquisitely crafted statue of the god Horus, adorned with gold paint and fine jewels. On the other side was a carafe, where he kept his finest brandy and glasses for when the need arose.

Yes, Austin loved his den. He held his most important meetings here, with business associates and with fellow members of the Egyptian Sand Diggers, the Society of Chicago and scholars who loved and appreciated all things Egyptian.

He felt the need for a brandy arise at that moment. Tonight, he was happy. So happy. After more than a century of being at the bottom of Lake Michigan and her shifting sands, the *Jerry McGuen* might well be on her way to twenty-first-century discovery!

He knew he should go to sleep. His doctor had warned him that he had to rest and that he had to avoid sleeping aids, that he needed to take his heart and blood pressure medications and stick to a healthful regimen. He was, after all, eighty-three years old.

But…

They were on the brink of knowledge. Nothing had hit the papers yet, but come morning, divers and documentarians would, at long last, discover the *Jerry McGuen*.

And, with the ship, untold treasure.

His cat, Bastet, a beautifully marked Egyptian Mau, also seemed restless that night. Bastet meowed and sidled along his leg.

"Tomorrow, Bastet, tomorrow!" He had changed for bed and wore his pajamas and a smoking robe, although he'd long ago given up the cigars he'd once enjoyed so much.

But a little brandy wasn't a bad thing.

He poured himself a snifter and rolled the tawny liquor against the sides of the glass, smelled it and finally sipped. He let out a soft sigh. "Tomorrow, Bastet, tomorrow," he said again.

But the cat leaped atop his desk with a screech that was frightening.

"Bastet!" He frowned. He tried to stroke the cat, but Bastet vaulted from the desk and disappeared behind the standing sarcophagus. What could be bothering the creature? Mrs. Hodgkins, his housekeeper, was long gone for the day.

The massive grandfather clock behind him began to toll the midnight hour.

He swallowed another sip of his brandy.

A cool breeze blew from the patio beyond the den; the curtains wafted.

The clock chimed three times, four, five.

And then…

He saw it. Moving in from the patio.

He sat completely still and blinked. He had to be seeing things. But, as if compelled by his vision, he rose, swallowing down the rest of the brandy. He wanted to scream. He *couldn't* scream, but somewhere in his mind he knew that even if he could, no one would hear.

The clocked chimed six times, seven, eight.

It was coming...coming...coming for him.

His heart! Instinctively, he clutched his chest and felt the thundering of his heart. He groped in his pocket for his nitroglycerin pills, but just as he reached them, *it* reached him. The pills were knocked from his hand.

The clock chimed nine times, ten, eleven.

He felt as if he'd been struck by a sledgehammer. The pain was overwhelming. The *thing* before him was enveloped in the black of his vision.

The clock chimed the hour of midnight.

And he fell down dead.

The wee hours

Kat Sokolov slept deeply, and in that sleep, she dreamed. It was a lovely dream. She was sailing somewhere. She stood on the deck looking out at the darkness of the water and watched the stunning display in the sky overhead. The moon was full, but clouds drifted in and out, and the world seemed beautiful.

She listened to the music from the ship's grand salon, where someone was playing a Viennese waltz. Attracted to the sweet sound of the music, she turned.

She wore a gown as elegant as those she saw around her. Silk and velvet, it swept gracefully as she moved. There was a celebration going on, and she could hear delighted laughter along with the enchanting strains from the piano. At the doors to the grand salon, she felt the breeze and pulled her fur stole more closely around her shoulders. It couldn't be about to snow! The moon had been too bright, too visible. The breeze had seemed so gentle....

But now it touched her like a blast of ice. When she opened the door to the salon, she felt the wind snatch it from her. It banged hard against the wall, and she was embarrassed for losing it and creating such an awful sound. But before she could apologize to anyone, the ship suddenly pitched and rolled. Glass shattered; people screamed. She thought she heard the blast of a horn, or a high, loud whistle. Then people were shouting, screaming. A voice of authority boomed out, warning people that a storm had come in, that they needed to go to their cabins immediately.

A couple pushed past Kat as if she wasn't even there. "It's cursed! The ship is cursed!" the man said to the young woman at his side. "Oh, God! What they should do is cast out the cargo, clear us of the curse!"

"You're scaring me!" the young woman cried.

"I'm so sorry, my darling!" the man said.

Then the woman seemed to see her. She looked at her with wide, desperate eyes. "It's the curse," she said. "It's the curse!"

"No, no, it's a storm, that's all," Kat heard herself say reassuringly. She smiled at the young woman. But then she turned. There appeared to be something out on the water. Something huge coming toward them.

She felt another blast of cold. Wet cold. The lovely night had become treacherous. It wasn't snow rushing at her; it was ice. They had sailed into an ice storm.

And still, that thing was out there, mammoth, a dark shadow that couldn't quite take shape because of the raging elements.

The wind picked up again and seemed to strike her in the face.

Then she awoke, frozen.

Kat blinked. She was still in her room in the lovely California hotel where her Krewe was staying.

She almost laughed aloud. She was cold because she'd kicked away her covers. Jumping up quickly, she hurried over to the thermostat. Somehow, sometime, either she or the maid had set the temperature down to the fifties.

She reset the thermostat to eighty-five.

She was much fonder of heat than cold.

That done, she dragged the extra blanket from the closet, grabbed all her covers again and curled back into bed. She'd practically forgotten the dream, she'd been so cold.

As she lay down, she thought it had been quite absurd. But then, of course, dreams often were.

Next morning
9:00 a.m.

The water of Lake Michigan was eerie, with different shades of gray shadows and darkness, as Brady Laurie plunged into the chilly depths. Only near the surface could anything that resembled natural light or warmth be found; the lake had always been a place of darkness and secrets. Motes seemed to dance before his eyes as the dive light on his head illuminated his journey, ever deeper into the water. Tiny bits of grasses, sand, orts from the meals of the lake's denizens swirled like dust particles, shimmering as his light hit them.

It was a world of silence down here, making every little noise sharp. The sound of his breathing and the throb of his regulator, the expulsion of his air bubbles, the very pulse of his heart.

It was a world he loved, but today he was on a mission.

He was so anxious. He shouldn't have been diving alone; he knew that. It was against every rule of scuba and salvage, but people often did it, anyway. In fact, he'd met enough he-man types so sure of their own prowess that they ignored the rule all the time. He didn't usually—just today.

He knew exactly what he was looking for, and the sonar on his boat seemed to have proven his theories and calculations right.

At long last, he'd found the sunken ship—the *Jerry McGuen*.

He believed in his heart that he'd found her, the freighter that had carried sixty men and women to their graves, doomed along with the treasures they'd brought from Egypt. The ship had sailed faultlessly all the way across the Atlantic Ocean and up the Saint Lawrence River, only to be lost on December 15, 1898, a day before the journey's end, battered and buffeted by a sudden, fierce storm. She had disappeared so close to her destination, just east-northeast of Chicago.

People had speculated then, as they still did, that a curse had lain upon the ship. The explorer who'd made the Egyptian discovery, Gregory Hudson, had been aboard. And, of course, there'd been a threat, etched into the stones of the tomb, warning that any man who disturbed the final resting place of Amun Mopat would soon know misery and death. Surely the passengers and crew of the *Jerry McGuen* had known both—almost able to see Chicago, but storm-tossed in violent, winter-frigid waters, finally succumbing to the brutality of the lake and disappearing.

Yes, the ship had disappeared, never to be seen again.

Until today. He would see her again. He, Brady Laurie, would see her again!

Salvage crews had hunted for her soon after she'd sunk—to no avail. And through the years, time after time, historians and divers had sought her, but like many a ship lost in the murky waters of the massive lake, she was simply not to be found.

Brady had been certain all his life that she had to

be there. And he'd excitedly put forth his theory to his coworkers that, following their recent wicked summer storm, there was a chance she could now be discovered. Violent storms altered a lake bed, just as they could alter the seabed in the Atlantic. He had seen what storms could do. A ship sunk in Florida had gone down on her side; one of the storms that had torn apart the Florida Straits had set her up perfectly again. He believed the same strength and force of that phenomenon was going to reveal the *Jerry McGuen*.

Storms moved sand and dirt. Storms had tremendous power—enough power to right a multi-ton ship. Even one lost for more than a century, a true shipwreck. His calculations had been off, but not by much. Not if what the sonar had shown him was true.

Through the dark, mystic water of the lake, he saw her.

There she was. The *Jerry McGuen!*

She lay at an angle, starboard hull lodged into the lake bed, as majestic and visible in the glow of his dive light as if she were at dock.

His heart beat fast, and pride surged through him. *They'd done it! They'd found her.*

No—*he'd* found her!

His theory was sound, his calculations making adjustments for time, weather conditions, the power of the recent storm and the earth's rotations. It couldn't account for the various unknowns, but he'd been so close. And now, as he saw it looming before him, his time had come. While that kind of storm usually sank ships, this one had removed layers of sand and almost righted the *Jerry McGuen*.

Yes, there she was, her massive hull tempting and seductive…

Even righted as she was, she had *suddenly* seemed to loom before him. The lake bed made the water so dark at eighty feet.

Just eighty feet! She'd been there all along, so damned close to Chicago!

He didn't feel any cold through his dive suit, but he was numb. A shiver of excitement reverberated through his limbs. All around him, the water danced in the wavy shadows of the eighty-foot depths, and he became intensely aware of the sound of his own breathing again, the pump and flow of his regulator. He wanted to shout with happiness and share his discovery with the world. Of course, he would do that soon enough, and if any of his team had followed him out today, they'd already know that he'd been right. *Everyone* would know that he'd been right, including every salvage diver who had ever dreamed of finding her.

He laughed inwardly, smiling around his regulator. He was pretty sure *someone* had been behind him. Not that everyone on Lake Michigan had to be following him, but he thought he'd seen a research vessel in the distance when he'd come down.

His coworkers might be angry that he'd jumped the gun, but Amanda had already sold the story of their search to a film producer, who was going to document and *finance* their historic discovery. He'd supplied money for the search based on Brady's theory. Now they could begin to chart out and rope off the ship and show the world the remains of the *Jerry McGuen*. Others interested in pursuits far less esoteric than theirs would be stopped at the gate. No more worries about Landry Salvage or Simonton's Sea Search beating them to the punch!

He could imagine the treasures in the hold. Priceless Egyptian artifacts, the still-sealed coffin of the high priest known as the Sorcerer of Giza, the sarcophagi, the army of golden figures, the canopic jars, the ancient stones…

Underwater for more than a century, he reminded himself.

But even the Egyptologists of the nineteenth century had known about preservation. Sure, they hadn't reckoned on toxins and gases, but they knew all about waterproofing—gunpowder and the pursuit of war had certainly furthered man's knowledge of that!

Of course, the hold might have been compromised, a zillion things might have happened and still…what they might find!

He—*they*—didn't seek treasure or the fortune it could bring. The treasures they discovered always went to museums, and he felt a thrill rush through him as he imagined the headlines when they returned the jeweled sarcophagus of Amun Mopat to the Egyptian people.

Amun Mopat would be back where he rightfully belonged, and the name Brady Laurie would be revered in Cairo's museum. Yes, yes, yes!

The *Jerry McGuen*.

She lay there—exposed! He was so elated his heart seemed to stop.

He checked his air gauge. He had at least another ten minutes to take a quick look at his momentous discovery, another ten minutes to explore, and then time to decompress at thirty-three feet and safely reach his research vessel on the surface.

The *Jerry McGuen* appeared huge, her forward section still pitched slightly into the lake bed, as if she'd taken a dive while sinking. Parts of the hull were broken, exposing staterooms and a passenger lobby, and what had been the purser's office. Brady knew the ship; he had studied her plans time and time again. She was a steel-hulled ship, built by the American Stuart Company of Chicago and launched on October 2, 1888. One hundred and eighty-six feet long, thirty-two feet wide, and twelve feet in depth. Her gross tonnage was four hundred and eighty-six, and when she sailed the seas, she'd been powered by a triple-expansion steam engine and two Scotch boilers. There had been fifty-two cabins for guests, captain's quarters, first mate's quarters, four cabins for officers and a bunk room, down in the hold, for crew. The ship, chartered by the very rich Gregory Hudson, had been a state-of-the-art beauty.

Her ballast for the trip had been stones—great stones

taken from the tomb of Amun Mopat. Before Howard Carter's discovery of King Tut's tomb, the discovery of Amun Mopat's tomb *right in the Valley of the Kings* had been one of the most important events in the annals of Egyptology. But the treasures had come aboard the *Jerry McGuen,* and just a few months after that, those treasures and their history had been lost to the ages. They were soon forgotten by the world at large as new findings occurred and the age of Egyptology moved on.

But now…

He eased himself slowly along the hull, fumbling at his dive belt for his underwater camera. As he began to snap photos, the sound of the shutter whirred softly in the water. The flash illuminated bits and pieces of the ship. There it was—the grand salon, exposed by a gaping hole in the port side, encrusted in weeds and grasses, occupied by fish, large and small. The treasures would be down below.

Yes!

The hull was ripped open belowdecks, as well. He didn't have much time. Just minutes left now, but he could slip through the great tear in the port side, move along the length of the ship….

It was dark within. Eerie. Time had stolen any vestiges of life that might have remained; the cold and the elements would have eaten away at organic fabric—and human bodies.

He found the hold and moved past giant crates, some protected by tarps that had withstood the years. Before him was a door, which swung open when he pushed it. The door hadn't been sealed, which might have aided in the flooding that had brought about the ship's demise, he thought, distracted. He didn't care at that moment how the ship had sunk. He'd nearly reached the treasure....

As he kicked his flippers and swam through, the dive light strapped to his head suddenly went out.

He muttered to himself, tapping the light. It came back on.

He saw the boxes—huge crates, really, wrapped and sealed in waterproof tarps!—and in the midst of them, he could see the giant box with the label peeling and nearly gone, and yet…he could still read the name on it.

Amun Mopat.

There it was! The box containing the sarcophagus holding the inner sarcophagus and then the mummy. It had survived; the men who'd discovered the treasure had stolen it away carefully sealed....

Over there, boxes of jackals and sphinxes and funerary artifacts, bows, quivers—

His light went out again. Cursing silently, he tapped it. As he did, he heard a curious sound. A noise so deep in the water was different from what it would be on the surface, and yet…

It sounded like the hold door was closing on him!

The light came back on.

He stared in horror.

He opened his mouth to scream. Losing his regulator, he sucked in air, and his scream was silent.

He was stunned, terrified....

The curse! The curse, silent, unspoken in these depths...

It was real!

Yes, he had found the *Jerry McGuen*.

But he would not live to tell the tale.

1

"*Amun Mopat,*" Katya Sokolov said to Logan Raintree. "You're kidding me, right?"

The heat that had been shining through the skylight seemed to disappear, as if the sun itself had lost some energy.

The name made her shudder. They'd just finished investigating a death in Los Angeles at Eddie Archer's special effects studio—a death based on an old film noir remake. The original movie had been titled *Sam Stone and the Curious Case of the Egyptian Museum.* The new one, fittingly, was called *The Unholy.*

"No, I'm not kidding," Logan said.

He had a fascinating face, the result of Native American and European parents, handsome and filled with character. She had learned to read it well, and she knew—he was not kidding.

Amun Mopat.

It was the name of the insidious ancient Egyptian priest who had supposedly come back to life to perpetrate murders. He was a character in a *movie.*

A character used in the very recent tragedies that had taken place.

And now…*Amun Mopat?*

"Amun Mopat, yes," Logan said, almost as if she'd spoken aloud. He leaned back, looking around with a sigh. They sat in the beautiful little lobby-café of their boutique hotel, surrounded by wrought-iron lattice work and art deco design. The past weeks—although somewhat traumatic in the final resolution and cleanup—had still contained some nice upswings. They'd seen tapings of half a dozen TV shows, including Kat's favorite comedy, spent days at the beach in Malibu, visited the Magic Castle and other attractions, and actually experienced something that resembled a vacation.

This meeting didn't bode well. She'd received the call to meet Logan while she was enjoying a visit to the La Brea Tar Pits. It had been an urgent call, and she'd known it meant she wouldn't be seeing a retro performance of the *Rocky Horror Picture Show* that night with Tyler Montague and Jane, two of the six in their special FBI unit.

She'd wondered if the others were going to be involved, but she was sitting here alone with Logan.

She had all but forgotten her strange dream of the night before. And now, even as it seemed to come crashing down around her, she wondered what a storm at sea could have to do with Amun Mopat.

The curse. She'd heard the words in her dream. Egyptian entities always seemed to come with curses!

"Go figure. After all this—Amun Mopat. In Chicago," Logan said in a dry voice.

"Yeah, go figure. Chicago," she repeated blankly.

Logan Raintree was her superior, the head of their team. Their actual *boss* was the elusive Adam Harrison, who had begun this excursion into the unknown—and the known—combining FBI technology and certain… unusual talents. Logan worked loosely with the head of the first team, Jackson Crow, evaluating information from those who sought help and deciding which cases truly called for their unique abilities. Since the original group of special investigators had become known as the Krewe of Hunters, they'd unofficially been dubbed the Texas Krewe. Their first case had been in San Antonio, home to many of them. Working with Logan and the other team members was thrilling and gratifying at once; it felt as if they spoke an ancient and secret language, and had come together as nationals from the same foreign country.

At the moment, she wasn't feeling especially thrilled. Or gratified. She wished she was back at the Tar Pits.

"And you want me to go out there *now?*" Kat asked. She didn't add *alone*.

Logan glanced at his watch.

"Yes. It could be nothing." He shrugged. "And it could be something. But we're talking about a dead body, and the autopsy is probably being performed as we speak."

"Chicago is a big city, and I'm sure they have a fine staff of medical examiners and pathologists," Kat said.

"I'm sure they do, too. But before too much time goes by, I want you in on it. Even the best people in their fields can miss little signs and clues, especially when they're convinced by the circumstances that they're looking at an accidental death."

Everyone on the Krewe had his or her technical or "real world" specialty.

Hers was forensic pathology.

"Amun Mopat," Kat said again. "In Chicago."

Logan leaned forward. "As I said, this *could* be nothing—nothing at all. That's why I need you there first. Sean is still out in Hawaii, but he's been alerted," he said, referring to another of their team members, Sean Cameron, who had been most heavily involved in the recent occurrences. "And we still have a few loose ends here—the last of the legal documents, another deposition—so I'm keeping Kelsey, Jane and Tyler with me. If it's a tragic but simple case of drowning, there'll be no need for the whole team. In that case, we'll meet back at headquarters. But if it's something else…"

Kat nodded dully. There was a dead body. She was a medical examiner. The dead body, of course, wasn't an ancient Egyptian priest. It was a historian and diver.

Who had died. Searching for a sunken ship in Lake Michigan.

"I dreamed I was on a ship last night," she told Logan.

"Really?"

"And the passengers were talking about a curse."

His expression was serious. "Maybe you'll be able to use that," he said.

She smiled. "Maybe it was to warn me I was about to head off—to Chicago. And a sunken ship. And a curse."

"I think in our line of work," he said, eyebrows raised, "we've learned that curses are pretty much things people invent when they want to do something evil for their own gain. And you may only be there a few hours. Who knows? The situation might just be that this diver went overboard in his excitement when he should have waited for the other researchers. The entire discovery was supposed to be filmed. But, like I said, he didn't wait. His excitement might have led to carelessness, which is probably what happened. And there's always competition to salvage the treasure on a sunken trip. But because we've been helped by the documentary crew in question, I feel it's important that we help out in return."

"Who's doing the documentary?" Kat asked.

"Alan King. We barely saw him when we were in San Antonio, but he had a bad time with the documentary there, especially losing his star. Apparently the Chicago Ancient History Preservation Center—where our dead man worked—is struggling like the rest of the world. They need funding." He studied his papers. "One of the staff, Dr. Amanda Channel, sent out queries to various film people and hit upon some friends of ours—you remember Bernie Firestone, right?"

"Of course," Kat said.

"Yes, well, he's frequently hired by Alan King, who can make films whenever he wants because he has billions—no, he didn't make his billions in film. He's able to do documentary films because he *does* have billions. Bernie approached Alan, who loved the idea, and there you have it."

"Sean should be available soon," Kat murmured. "He's worked with them before."

"If he's needed, he'll be there. Remember—we don't know if this is anything at all. Anyway, if you do end up staying, you've at least met Alan and you know Bernie and his cameraman, Earl Candy. Right now, you'll take a look at the deceased, read the autopsy report, talk with a few people—and, if there's nothing, we'll all meet back in Virginia. Requests for our expertise are already piling up back at headquarters." Logan paused. "But like I said, I feel we're in debt on this one. There's also the fate of a historical institute on the line, not to mention an incredible discovery."

"I still say..."

"That it's ironic?" Logan asked. "I thought that, too, but then, not so much. Not really. When the original *Sam Stone* was filmed in the early forties, the sinking of the ship in Lake Michigan had occurred half a century earlier. A writer, one who was fascinated by Egyptology, would readily have seized upon a real priest for his story. I looked into it and found out that the original screenplay was by a man named Harold Conway—who was born in Chicago. He grew up going to the Field Museum and hearing stories about the *Jerry McGuen.* The priest's actual mummy, with the inner and outer sarcophagi, as well as other treasures, went down with the ship. So our screenwriter would definitely have known about Amun Mopat, and he was obviously interested enough in the historical character to use him in a movie."

"Great," Kat muttered.

"Hey, it could be an M.E.'s dream," he said.

"A mummy? An anthropologist's dream, not mine," she retorted. "But…all right, so I'm to examine the body and try to discern if he died by natural means, or…"

She let her voice trail off.

They dealt with the unknown, the world that lay beyond the veil. Their "sixth sense."

But Logan had a point. In her experience, and in that of the others, they'd never come across a ghost or a curse that *killed.*

It was human beings who killed other human beings.

"They're not expecting to find much left of the people who went down with the ship," Logan was saying. "According to the records, there were no survivors, and no bodies rose to the surface—or none that were found or recognized. But I've read that time would have destroyed even their skeletons by now. Is that true?"

Kat nodded. "Unless someone was caught in a sealed

area, it's unlikely that there'd be any remains. Time and sea creatures take their toll. They may find skeletal remnants, but only once they're into the bowels of the ship."

"So, it really is one big watery grave."

"It does seem respectful to salvage what might be important to history and the living, and then let the ship itself stay where it sank, a memorial to those who were lost."

"I believe that's the eventual plan." Logan flipped a page in the file that lay before him on the table. "You won't be alone," he told her, grinning as if he'd read her mind. She wasn't afraid of being alone, nor was she unaccustomed to the strange and unusual.

"Oh?"

"A member of the original Krewe is out there now. He happened to be visiting an old buddy in Chicago when this came down. You'll meet up with him. His name is Will Chan. He'll stop by to see Alan, Bernie and Earl this afternoon, and he has an appointment with the people at the Preservation Center bright and early tomorrow morning. He'll meet you at the morgue at 10:00 a.m."

"Okay, but do I need to reach him first?"

"No. Head straight to the morgue. Will's going to catch up with you there." Logan handed her the folder. "His contact information is in here. Between the two of you, we'll have a good sense of what's going on, be it too much enthusiasm by a diving historian—or a

predator with an enthusiasm for murder. Oh, and Alan
King has hired private security to guard the dive site."

"You can guard a dive site?"

"I thought you were a diver?"

"Yes, but I dive because I love it, not because I'm
looking for lost treasures." Kat offered him a wry smile.
"I've *seen* salvage from the *Titanic* and the *Atocha* in
museums. I never went looking for them. And I usually
dive in nice warm water in the Caribbean or the Gulf."

"Salvage rights are complicated. Federal law says
that all wrecks belong to the state that claims the waters. Depending on what's found, ownership of artifacts and the wreck itself may wind up in court for
years. But the Preservation Center did file papers for
the right to dive and work on the wreck. However, it's
not the legal aspect that people worry about as much
as the black market."

"Other divers stripping the site and selling salvage
illegally?" Kat asked.

"You can't begin to imagine what can be bought and
sold on the black market."

"Still…it's got to be tricky, raiding a dive site."

"Yes, but it's been done. Hence, the security."

"I guess so."

"You have gone diving in cold water, right?" he
asked next.

"Well, yes."

"Make sure you pack a good dive suit. I understand
the water temperature ranges between fifty and sixty at

this time of year, and I believe that's kind of cold when you're down there."

"I've never been in Lake Michigan." Kat frowned. "And I've never been involved with the discovery of a wreck."

"See, you're all excited now."

"Excited. Well...I'm not sure that's the best word to describe how I'm feeling, not after we nearly lost Madison Darvil to Amun Mopat—or his look-alike!"

"We knew that Amun Mopat wasn't the killer. And we know that mummy isn't swimming around planning to kill anyone who discovers the ship."

"We don't know that anyone is killing people at all yet," Kat said. "We've probably been asked in because Alan King is feeling a little worried—since his luck with documentaries hasn't been so good lately."

Logan looked up at the skylight. Then he looked back at her. "No, we won't know anything until you examine the body and get more information. Since Alan has hired private security near the site, hopefully no one else will be exploring the area and ending up dead while the situation is investigated. You're booked on a 5:40 p.m. flight out of Burbank. You should be in a nice cozy room by midnight, and then tomorrow... I'll be waiting to hear what you have to say."

"What if I can't find the answer in the autopsy?" Kat asked him. "Or in anything else we're able to examine?"

"Then we'll join you—and figure out where the answer does lie."

Kat nodded and sipped her coffee. The sun seemed to come out again and stream through the skylight overhead.

"You have information on the ship, the sinking, the discovery of the tomb—all kinds of stuff—in the folder," Logan said. "Along with info on all the principle players working on the discovery and preservation of Egyptian antiquities."

"Anything else?"

He grinned. "Be glad it's not the dead of winter?"

There was no keeping down a true scholar.

Will Chan hadn't come for a lesson in Egyptology, but it seemed to be part of the interview.

Senior researcher Jon Hunt grew animated as he spoke, saying, "Amun Mopat lived and died during the reign of Ramses—Ramses II, the most powerful ruler of the New Kingdom and the nineteenth dynasty and perhaps the most powerful of all the great pharaohs or god-kings of Egypt. Ramses ruled from 1279 BC to 1213 BC, and it appears that Mopat, reputed to be a shady character, was born in the same year and the same month, which seemed to be a great oracle to people at the time. Ramses was first drawn to him, believing in the power of sorcery. Amun Mopat lived a life of luxury, respected and consulted on most important matters of state. Ramses, you'll remember, was a warrior king. He's the one with Moses in all the movies—the villain, you know."

"Except," Amanda Channel—also a senior researcher—interjected, "historians have argued constantly over the true factual dates of 'the time of Moses.' And whether or not he eventually expelled the Hebrews from Egypt, Ramses II was a builder and a soldier and a peacekeeper. In short, a remarkable ruler. Living in a world with a totally different belief system, of course. Must have been nice to be a god, huh?"

Will sat in a conference room at the offices of the Chicago Ancient History Preservation Center as he spoke with—or, more accurately, listened to—Jon Hunt and Amanda Channel. Both of them were trying to explain everything at once, or so it seemed. More than three thousand years of ancient Egyptian history, Brady Laurie's tragic death and the story behind the *Jerry McGuen.*

Apparently neither of them needed to take a breath very often. And they switched from Egyptian history to Brady and then to the *Jerry McGuen* with record speed.

But then, Egyptian history, Brady and the ship were now joined for all eternity.

"Brady loved anything that had to do with ancient Egypt," Jon said. "He could rattle off every pharaoh in every dynasty in the Old Kingdom, the Middle Kingdom and the New Kingdom more quickly than your average high school kid could come up with all fifty states."

Will wasn't sure most high school kids *could* rattle off all fifty states.

"But," Amanda jumped in, her voice almost a fluid continuation of Jon's thoughts, "Brady especially loved the New Kingdom, and everything that's been learned from excavations in the Valley of the Kings."

"Howard Carter's discovery of King Tut's tomb happened after the discovery of Amun Mopat's. Since the treasures of Mopat's tomb—a good portion of them, anyway—went down with the *Jerry McGuen,* a lot of important artifacts and information were lost to history," Jon explained. "And Amun Mopat, much as he *wanted* to be a god, was only a priest. Tut had been a pharaoh."

He actually paused for breath and Amanda remained silent. Will took the opportunity to survey the conference room; there was an excellent bust of Nefertiti on a counter that stretched out from the back wall. Next to her were a dozen or so canopic jars, all copies, according to Amanda and Jon.

He assumed they were telling the truth. Next to the canopic jars was a large coffee urn, and the usual collection of paper cups, sugar, creamer and whatever else one might desire for a cup of coffee. Nothing truly valuable would have been kept so casually and haphazardly where coffee could spill at any time.

He'd only had a quick glimpse of one of the workrooms. It was sterile in appearance except for a piece Amanda had been working on, a funerary statue that had been dug out of a pit in the city—property of someone who'd lost everything in the Great Chicago Fire.

The fire had occurred in 1871, before the sinking of the *Jerry McGuen,* but collectors had been avid about ancient Egyptian pieces for a hundred years by then, and there'd been those who'd coveted Egyptian art even before Napoleon's soldier had cracked the code in 1799 and translated the Rosetta Stone.

"Brady was being an ass," Amanda said mournfully.

Jon Hunt immediately looked offended, and Amanda softened her words.

"An ass in the way we can all be asses. Jon, please, I'm not insulting him. I'd say the same thing about us. We get too excited about a discovery like this." She sighed. "Brady grew up hearing his great-grandfather talk about the disappearance of the *Jerry McGuen.* Maybe that's when he fell in love with Egyptology. Or maybe it started with the visits to the Field Museum. And you can imagine how he felt, considering what he knew about both Egyptology *and* the *Jerry McGuen.* We can't help it. I guess we're real nerds— oh, my God! Who would've thought that being a nerd could be dangerous? We think we know what we're doing, and then…"

"He was brilliant." Jon shook his head as if he still couldn't accept that his friend and coworker was dead.

"Brilliant—and, this one time, so foolish!" Amanda said. "Yes, I admit the rest of us hadn't totally believed in his theory. I mean, we believed—we just weren't as insane about it as Brady. That's how we work. Even when we're not convinced that someone else is right, we work with them to find out. And all of Brady's calculations did make sense. We were scheduled to start looking together. If they hadn't been sound theories and calculations, we wouldn't have approached the film director—Mr. Firestone. Oh, if Brady could just have waited…"

"We would have been right with him," Jon said. He gritted his teeth. "I was the one who found him," he whispered.

"*We* found him," Amanda corrected.

"Yes, well, I was the first to see him…floating there."

"We have two boats," Amanda said. "He took one out ahead of us. We have a small, exploratory dive boat, and then our larger vessel. It was Saturday and—"

"Yes," Jon interrupted. "If only it hadn't been a Saturday!"

"We were supposedly off work, but Brady called both of us that morning. He said he was going to take the boat out and use sonar," Amanda said. "Seriously, finding anything actually salvageable on the *McGuen* was always a long shot, but Brady believed that the treasures taken from the tomb had been so carefully packed, there was a real chance. I thought we were going to start on Monday, but he called me. I called Jon, and we agreed we'd go out with him, but he'd already taken the smaller boat. We let him know we were on our way, but I think he ignored us because he had to prove it to himself first. He shouldn't have gone down to the wreck. He shouldn't have gone down alone—he knew that. I was furious with him. Before we found him, of course." She paused, looking at Jon and then at Will and added, "I was afraid. We didn't want to lose our funding." She glanced at Jon again, as if feeling guilty about something she'd done while trying to rationalize it at the same time.

"We brought out our second boat—the big one, *Glory*—and found the *Seeker* at anchor. There was no sign of Brady. And it was wrong of him, because Mr. King, the producer, said from the beginning that he'd finance us as long as we let him document every step— right or wrong—along the way," Amanda told Will.

"I think Brady was afraid we'd start work, and there'd be no ship," Jon said. "And if that was the case—"

"We'd already taken money," Amanda broke in. "It's also really competitive, diving for salvage. It can be confusing, too, with U.S. laws, state laws, international laws…except that we're not in it to make a fortune. A 1987 federal law says the states own all wrecks found in their territorial waters, but there's still money in salvage. There's another law about disturbing a grave site, but really, there can't be anything left of the people…. Except if the mummy itself was properly sealed… The thing is, we believe in returning antiquities. What we'd earn would be a percentage of what Mr. King makes in IMAX films and the like. Of course, he gave us a hefty sum as a down payment."

"I knew something was wrong when the boat was empty, and Brady's dive flag was still out," Jon said.

"So, anyway," Amanda continued, "Mr. King's director, Bernie Firestone, and some of his crew came out with us, taking their boat—nice and fancy, all kinds of great stuff on it—and two of his underwater cameramen followed us down. And…and we found Brady." Tears welled in Amanda's eyes.

"Yeah. It was great. He'd found the *Jerry McGuen*," Jon said bitterly. "And we found him."

Amanda let out a little choking sound. They both stared at Will, their eyes soulful and wet.

Amanda was thirty-two, a pretty woman, reed-thin and passionate about her work. Jon, her coworker, was a few years older. His brown hair was graying at the temples and he wore bottle-thick glasses and was also thin. He was wiry and seemed fit as the proverbial fiddle.

Their attempt to explain everything to him at once seemed to point to their clinical and obsessive pursuit of knowledge. They both spent hour upon hour—day upon day—in their little cubicles or labs, painstakingly dusting or chiseling away the dirt and dust of the ages. Sometimes, they got to go on a dig or a dive, but most of the time, they were in their offices and labs.

Will liked everything he'd read about the Chicago Ancient History Preservation Center. He'd always been intrigued by history himself, especially by the way many societies—including the ancient Egyptians—used mysticism and magic.

As Amanda had said, the center kept none of the antiquities it discovered or worked on; its sole purpose was to preserve historical artifacts, delve into their secrets and pass them on to their homelands or an institution worthy of guarding and displaying them. It had been founded in the latter part of the nineteenth century by Jonas Shelby, an avid Egyptologist. In the years since, grants and private donations had added to Shelby's legacy, and while the "treasures" came directly from ancient Egypt, they might also have been discovered in a Chicago backyard.

Amanda suddenly frowned at Will. "I'm not really sure why you're here, Agent Chan," she said. "It's fine, but..."

"We brought Brady right up. He was dead by then. Obviously dead." Jon grimaced. "When I radioed in the emergency the guy kept telling me to give him artificial respiration. I would've done anything for him— but Brady was dead when we brought him up. Like Amanda said, the filmmakers followed us down, so there's actually footage—" he broke off "—footage of us finding Brady. The film crew has it. And the police have a copy, too."

Will listened gravely. He knew that already. He'd spent yesterday with Alan King, Bernie Firestone and Earl Candy. Alan didn't dive, but Bernie and Earl did. Alan was deeply worried about his future in film; it was not a good thing if people kept dying on the films he produced. Will had seen the footage of the two divers coming upon their dead coworker. Luckily, neither of the men was the kind of person to leak such footage to YouTube or any other site.

He didn't tell Jon or Amanda that he'd seen the film. He wanted to hear their version of everything that had happened.

"And he was taken right…right to the morgue," Amanda said. She appeared stricken, as if she'd begin crying again. "He drowned down there, and it's tragic. To us more than anyone else, but…"

"He drowned," Jon said flatly. "Why is the FBI investigating?"

"Your filmmaker." Will smiled and leaned across the conference table to pick up a copy of the Sunday paper, lying there. The headline read Historian Dies Tragically During Greatest Discovery—Accident or Victim of Ancient Curse?

"Oh, please!" Amanda said. "Seriously, oh, please! That's just a reporter scrambling for headlines. I saw Brady. He drowned!" She sighed. "Listen, I loved him like a brother. But we have to keep going on this, and quickly. We've gotten the rights to dive her first and salvage what we can. And Brady was absolutely correct. The precious cargo down there was carefully—*carefully!*—wrapped and stowed. We'd dishonor Brady's memory if we didn't complete his mission!"

"Okay, back up for me, please. You have the rights of salvage? Didn't you need to find the ship first?" Will asked.

Amanda flushed. "Our paperwork is all on file. We

have a maritime attorney on hand who has us all ready to go with recovery."

"But if another person or enterprise had found her first…."

"Well, I suppose someone else could have filed for the rights, as well," Amanda said. "But no one else had Brady—or studied the effect of storms on the lake like he did."

Will doubted that a competing group would care how someone had determined the location of a treasure. They would just want the bottom line. "Who else has been searching for the *Jerry McGuen?*" he asked.

"Through the decades?" Jon shrugged. "Anyone with a ship, sonar or a dive suit."

Will smiled. "Recently. Do you know of anyone or any other enterprise searching for her?"

"A year ago there was an article about a company called Landry Salvage that was interested. Their CEO was quoted in a local TV piece on the wreck," Amanda said.

Jon was thoughtful, drumming his fingers on the conference table for a moment before speaking. "There's also a company called Simonton's Sea Search that was interviewed briefly for the same piece. It was one of those little five-minute news segments, you know?"

"It never occurred to you that since the treasure on the ship is worth a fortune, someone else might be eager to acquire that fortune?" Will asked.

"It's not like anyone could just *keep* everything, or

that a salvage effort on the lake wouldn't be spotted!" Amanda insisted.

"Yes, but whether the treasures were returned to Egypt or turned over to our government," Will said, "the finder's fee or percentages could be staggering. Though I'm not seeing a legitimate bid as something that's likely to supersede yours. The black market is where the real money would be."

Amanda shook her head. "That's why *we* needed to find it. Stop the black market activity. And we still need to get down there fast, although…thanks to Brady, our papers have been filed."

Will lowered his head, hiding his expression. The world did go on. They'd found Brady's body in the ship—and they'd made sure their legal work was done, probably as soon as Brady Laurie was on his way to the morgue.

"The mission won't be stopped—will it? I mean, I know there's competition out there, but Brady drowned. I saw him." Amanda's eyes were anxious as she looked at Will. "Poor Brady—but he must have died happy. He did find the *Jerry McGuen*."

Will doubted that Brady had died happy. Drowning was a horrendous death.

"The salvage is not being stopped," Will said. "And, so far, the medical examiner's conclusions are that Brady Laurie died as a result of forgetting his deep-water time because of his excitement."

"So…why the FBI?" Amanda asked, obviously still puzzled.

"The director of the documentary is an old friend of Sean Cameron's—Sean's an agent in one of our special units—and the producer, Mr. King, is anxious about what's happened. Not to mention all these rumors about the curse. Because of their association with us and their concern that the salvage and the documentary go well, they came to the agency. And because our most senior officer, Adam Harrison, has great relationships with state governments, we were invited in. We're not sensationalists. We're here to disprove a curse, as much as anything else and, hopefully, make sure there are no more accidents."

"Oh!" Amanda said, blinking away tears again. "Well, as long as our work isn't stopped. Brady—oh, God, I miss him, I loved him, but he was acting like a cowboy. He just *had* to get down there before we were really ready. He knew not to dive alone. I mean, come on, an experienced diver knows never to dive alone. Anywhere. Not even in shallow reefs in the Keys, much less here. He just thought he was better than anyone and… We *are* diving the wreck tomorrow? An exploratory dive before we start with the salvage?" she asked anxiously.

"Yes," Will assured her. "Everything will go ahead as planned. Just one change," he told her pleasantly. "I'll be joining you, and so will another member of my unit."

"What?" Amanda was obviously dismayed. "More

people down there? You don't understand how careful you have to be with artifacts. You don't—"

"I'll do my best, Dr. Channel," he said. "My colleague and I will meet you at the dock tomorrow morning." He rose to signal that he was leaving—and that he'd be back.

"Yes, but…" Amanda started her protest and then frowned. "I could probably answer any other questions you might have right now. Where are you going?"

"I'm afraid I have another meeting," he informed her, "but I'll see you tomorrow."

He smiled politely and exited the room, and then the Preservation Center.

It was situated near the aquarium, on South Lake Shore Drive, and when he stepped out the front door, he saw Lake Michigan. The water glittered in the sun, and he wished he could get out on a boat in a dive suit right away, but he had a meeting with a member of Logan Raintree's crew.

And with a dead man.

He turned away from the lake and headed for his rental car.

2

More than eighteen thousand deaths were reported to the Cook County office of the medical examiner yearly. Of those, some six thousand received an autopsy.

The office handled investigations for a large part of the state; in January 2011, there'd been such a backup due to the number of bodies and the holidays, they were stacked one on top of the other. The morgue had been overcrowded due to what the press had dubbed "the killing season," when gang violence had erupted on the South Side.

Kat knew these things because she'd done nothing but read since she'd boarded her plane for Chicago's O'Hare International Airport.

Cook County wasn't different from any other large metropolitan area. People died. Thankfully most of them died naturally.

But some did not. Some died because of gang violence, and sometimes they died in police custody or in jail. Some died because of domestic violence, and some were simply and pathetically in the wrong place at the wrong time—victims of random crime. Some died "suspiciously" or without apparent explanation.

Despite the fact that she wasn't in Chicago because she *wanted* to be, she wasn't disturbed by her particular assignment here. While many people feared a medical examiner's office as a frightening and gruesome place, Kat had always found that an autopsy—though invasive—was a service that man had come to do for man. It was an effort to let the dead speak for themselves, to seek justice, find a killer or, conversely, prove accidental death when no other human was at fault. Autopsy helped the living, too; some medical advances would have never come about without autopsies determining the cause of death. In medical school, she hadn't started out feeling that she'd rather work with the dead than the living. It had been during her residency that she'd discovered she had a penchant for unspoken truths... and that, even when silent, the dead could sometimes tell their tales.

The Texas Krewe—her unit of their section within the FBI—was supposed to investigate whatever couldn't be answered by the evidence. Usually it wasn't because of incompetence or because leads weren't followed by the local police. They were called in when the leads themselves were *unusual*. Some people described those leads as paranormal.

But in this instance...

A diver had jumped the gun. He'd jumped the gun on an incredible discovery mainly because he was the scientist who'd been determined to find the wreck of the *Jerry McGuen*. He'd been looking for ancient Egyptian treasures lost along with the ship.

And those treasures included a mummy.

It just had to be a mummy! she thought, wincing as she conjured up an image of Brendan Fraser and his hit movie. And of course there was the mummy in *The Unholy*—the recent Hollywood remake of a 1940s film noir—had been that of an evil Egyptian priest who'd turned out to be real.

"Sad beginning to this whole thing, huh?"

Startled, Katya looked over at Dr. Alex McFarland, the M.E. who walked her down the corridors and past offices, vaults and autopsy rooms. He seemed a decent enough sort, cordial and receptive. Bald as a billiard ball and wearing spectacles, he reminded her of Dr. Bunsen Honeydew of Jim Henson's Muppets fame, the epitome of what the general public expected a doctor or scientist to look like.

"Very sad," she agreed. The victim had been in his thirties, an expert on Egyptology and an expert diver. A young man with his life stretching out before him.

And now that life was cut short.

McFarland rolled his eyes. "Tragic...and almost no one's talking about the boy's death. Of course, the disappearance of the *Jerry McGuen* has been one of the great mysteries of Lake Michigan since she went down in the late-nineteenth century. There's more coverage given to the discovery than to the poor boy's death. And

God help us all—the curse! But, then again, although Chicago is hardly considered to be one of the world's great dive spots, the lakes hold a lot of wrecks where divers frequently go. I don't dive myself, but we have many professional *and* recreational divers in the area. Many of them say he was being careless, that he took chances in his excitement and shouldn't have been diving at seventy-five, eighty feet on his own."

"You should *always* dive with a buddy," Kat said. "Sadly it's often the divers—even expert divers—who go out on their own who wind up in autopsy. There are no guarantees in the deep."

"You dive?"

"Yes," she told him.

"Well, then, I'm sure you'll enjoy this. Like I said, the Great Lakes are filled with shipwrecks. I find the lakes and wrecks fascinating. I've studied them all my life—to the point of obsession, I'm afraid. Many are known, but many are not. Lake Michigan has a surface area of 22,400 square miles and its average depth is 279 feet with its greatest depth being about 923 feet," McFarland said. "It's the largest lake completely contained in one country in the world, and ranked fifth largest on the globe."

McFarland obviously loved Chicago. He sounded very proud of the lake.

But then he sighed. "Lots and lots of room for tragedy over the years, and lots of room for ships to disappear. Sure, finding wrecks in the deep, frigid waters of the North Atlantic is a challenge, but if you've ever looked out at the lake, you might as well be staring at an ocean, it's so immense."

She glanced over at him; McFarland knew the power of water, and he seemed well up on his history of the area. He was as fascinated as everyone else by the discovery of the sunken ship.

"The exploration is still going on," she said.

"So I understand. The world doesn't stop spinning because one person has died." McFarland shrugged. "You *have* heard that everyone's talking about a curse, right?"

"Yes," she said. *That's why I'm here.*

Normally, of course, they would never have been called in because of an accidental death that occurred while a man was scuba diving. Such deaths would be handled by the medical examiner's office, but there usually wasn't any hint of paranormal activity, so no reason for their unit to be brought in.

"You can't stop the wheels of progress when there's been a great discovery, I guess," McFarland said.

"Every day is money," she murmured. "Someone's livelihood. In this case, many livelihoods."

That was true. Kat didn't know nearly as much about film as Sean Cameron or a few of the others who belonged to one of the "Krewe" teams, but from their time in California she'd learned how much money could be involved. In the file Logan had given her she'd read that production prep had already begun; crew and talent had been hired. Of course, Alan King was, according to *Forbes,* a billionaire, so if he lost money on the enterprise, he'd probably be just fine. But making the documentary meant much more to the struggling historians running a nonprofit organization dedicated to preserving the past.

Sean would arrive soon. He'd taken a short holiday with Madison Darvil after their last case. When they got back from Hawaii, Madison would resume her work in California, and Sean would come here.

She smiled just thinking about it. She loved Sean; they were old Texas friends. She felt sure that he and Madison would be able to keep up with their demanding jobs—he with the unit, she with her work at a special effects company—and maintain a relationship.

Kat returned her attention to Dr. McFarland and the situation. At the moment, however, that didn't seem to help. Whatever had happened to Brady Laurie was still confusing.

But in every case, someone needed to speak for the dead....

"Well, from what I understand, Alan King doesn't care if he loses money on a film as long as he produces a documentary that makes him proud," Kat said to McFarland. "King already has his director and shipboard cameraman—who are two men my team and I actually know. They're from San Antonio. I understand that King also has underwater videographers on-site, ready to detail every single step of the ship's recovery...

and that they were there when members of the Preservation Center found Mr. Laurie."

"That's the information I have, too," McFarland said. "I wasn't at the site. The body was brought here. And I swear that man hadn't been out of the water for more than two seconds before the curse hysteria started."

She didn't believe in curses; she did believe in the way a curse could be used to prey on people's minds. She'd seen people die because of what they were convinced was true, hearts that had stopped beating because of fear.

"I don't think there's an Egyptian tomb that *doesn't* come with a curse—or at least a rumored curse," Kat said.

McFarland grinned. "I see you've read up on all this. The man who discovered Amun Mopat's tomb, Gregory Hudson, was aboard the *Jerry McGuen* when she sank, which, of course, gave rise to the belief that the curse is real. To tell you the truth, the only curse I see is the wicked Chicago weather. But you've probably heard our old saying. 'If it weren't for the weather, everyone would want to live here!'"

"The *Jerry McGuen* carried the mortal remains and effects of the New Kingdom, nineteenth dynasty priest—or sorcerer—Amun Mopat, beloved of Ramses II," Kat said. "He had his own burial crypt and chamber built before his death. He'd filled it with treasures and—in his own hand, the story goes—chiseled a curse into his tombstone, damning anyone who disturbed his eternal life. Or disturbed the place where his body rested while he joined with the pharaohs and gods. He was apparently quite taken with himself. He wanted to be a god like the pharaohs." She smiled. "According to some of the research a colleague pulled for me, he had blood ties to Ramses II. He felt he should have been seen as a god all his life."

"Yes, very good. You seem very well informed." McFarland shrugged. "But I don't understand why they've called the FBI in on this, except that…curses and ghosts are your specialty, right?"

"I assure you, I'm qualified to be here, Dr. McFarland," Kat told him. "I received my doctorates in medicine and forensic pathology from Johns Hopkins."

"Yes, I heard you were well qualified, Dr. Sokolov—and I'm sure you'll understand what we're dealing with better than the fellow who's already here."

"Agent Chan is here now?" she asked. She wished she'd had a chance to meet with him earlier. Introductions over a corpse were always a bit awkward, even if she *was* a medical examiner and far too familiar with morgues.

"Yes, he arrived about ten minutes ago. He said you were informed that you'd be meeting him. He's *not* a doctor," McFarland said, his tone irritated and more than a little condescending.

"But he is an agent," Kat reminded him.

McFarland opened the door to the autopsy room; they were both gowned and gloved.

Kat usually noted the corpse first.

But this time she noted the man who belonged to the original Krewe.

He greeted her as she entered, with words rather than a gloved hand. "Hello, Dr. Sokolov, I'm Will Chan. I believe you were expecting to meet me here?"

"Yes, of course. Logan told me you were already in the city," Kat said.

She didn't mean to stare at him in obvious assessment.

But she did. She probably would've been tempted to stare at him anywhere. He wasn't just an appealing, attractive or handsome man, *he was different*, and not merely because of his striking appearance. There was an aura about him, an energy that immediately caught and held her attention.

She had to look up at him, but she was only five-four, so it seemed that she looked up at most of the world. Somehow, with him, it was...disconcerting. Or maybe it was the circumstances that were disconcerting. *We don't know each other, except for what we know* about *each other. And yet...*

She'd been given so many files to read on the plane, she had to mentally put what she knew about Will in order. He'd become an agent with the original Krewe of Hunters when they'd solved a case at a historic mansion in New Orleans. Before that, he'd performed as a magician and an illusionist. He was also astute with video, film and discerning what was really just smoke and mirrors, recognizing what lay beneath the surface. Will had gone through the academy and passed with flying colors. He was a talented agent.

And, of course, he'd happened to be in the city.

She cleared her throat, not wanting to seem gauche. "Logan gave me an extensive file," she said. "You're a film expert, as well?"

"I know a few things about it," he said, lowering his head with a quick smile. "I come from a long line of illusionists."

He was tall with intriguing features. His background was Trinidadian and he'd spoken with a slight accent that made her think of the Caribbean island. His hair was dark. His eyes, just as dark, were slightly almond-shaped. His features suggested Asian and perhaps Indian antecedents, and then again, there was something classic about them. His face seemed to be sculpted in the mold of a Roman statue, but with the rugged chin of an American cowboy. She found herself studying him—and almost forgetting that he was standing beside a corpse.

"Yes, and I'm one of Jackson Crow's team, and most important, I was in Chicago when this happened," he said.

"Right." Kat nodded. "And so…what have you learned?"

"He hasn't learned anything yet," McFarland said. "I haven't gone over the autopsy report with him," he added. "We knew you were on your way."

Kat nodded again, but looked at Will Chan.

McFarland had no idea just what this man—a Krewe member who could speak with the dead—might have learned.

She glanced away from Will Chan with determination, unable to still the curiosity stirring within her. As part of Jackson Crow's team, he'd been specifically chosen for his position.

Because of a special talent.

McFarland drew out his report and frowned as he studied it. "As we all know, Mr. Laurie was a white adult male, thirty-six years old. No alcohol in the system, no drugs. His body was found drifting in the hold of the *Jerry McGuen,* at a depth of eighty feet in Lake Michigan, Chicago jurisdiction. Autopsy revealed no sign of violence and showed that Mr. Laurie was in perfect health at the time of his death. The lungs were filled with salt water, so I'm planning to officially sign off on this report as death by drowning, accidental."

Kat gazed at the corpse. When it came to their *unofficial* role with the Krewe of Hunters, she was always glad of her medical degree and her specialization in pathology.

People didn't think she was crazy when she touched the dead.

She moved forward, inspecting the dead man and then touching his arm.

She waited, hoping for something. A sense that he

was still there, and that she could communicate with the remnants of his life, spirit or soul.

But she heard nothing in her mind, saw nothing at all in the part of her own soul that was different from other people's. Her skill, or gift, or whatever one chose to call it, was out of the ordinary—but shared by some. Like Will Chan…

She glanced up at him again. He was watching her, and his striking dark eyes divulged none of his thoughts.

Stepping back, she gave her full attention to the visual aspect of the corpse.

Drowning. She hadn't done the autopsy herself. She saw that Dr. McFarland's Y incision was neatly cut and just as neatly sewn with small, competent stitches. It didn't take a brilliant doctor to detect when the lungs were filled with water, and she didn't doubt his conclusion on that.

She turned from the body to the report. The man had definitely drowned.

But she didn't like the coloration of the corpse. Blue lips—natural, given what had happened. However, the lips were also puffy, and one side of his mouth seemed more swollen than the other. And there were curious bruises on the arms.

"You're aware of the bruising?" she asked McFarland.

"Of course." He was obviously indignant at her question. "I make painstaking notes. Every bruise is listed in the report, and you will have a copy of it for your files."

She forced herself to ignore McFarland and Chan, studying the body once again. She was certain that McFarland was adept at his work—and from what she'd seen thus far, his notes *were* painstaking, just as he'd said. But the medical examiner needed to note the condition of a corpse *and* assess possible causes for that condition. McFarland's Y incision on the dead man had been nothing short of artistic, and she was sure he'd inspected the man's vital organs and taken all necessary samples for the pathology lab.

Brady Laurie showed no postmortem lividity in his lower extremities, which led her to believe that he'd floated, probably upright, after death.

But the bruising on his face still bothered her. So did the bruises on his arms. Those were smaller—the size of fingertips.

"What do you make of these?" she asked McFarland.

"Bruises. As I mentioned, they're noted in the report," McFarland said curtly.

Chan cleared his throat as he eased around the gurney. "What would've caused bruises on both arms?" he murmured. Kat had the same question. They weren't as conspicuous, perhaps, as the contusions around his mouth, but unmistakable nonetheless.

"The man was a diver. He was dealing with a lot of equipment. He knocked around in one of the ship's holds until he was found by other divers from the Preservation Center," McFarland said. "He could have gotten them from an air tank or from some of the equipment he had piled on him. He was carrying a camera, and he was wearing one of those headlights divers use during night dives or cave dives. There was a dive knife strapped to his ankle. He had a huge light on the camera, as well— and, like I said, he bounced around the hold."

"Still…I don't think we should discount these bruises," Kat said.

Chan seemed to agree. He moved around the corpse again, studying the bruises on Brady Laurie's arms. Then he angled forward. "They look like fingerprints," Chan said. "See? If I were to reach out and grab him…"

He demonstrated, putting his fingers just above where the bruises showed on the flesh.

"You think he was held down?" McFarland sounded skeptical.

"I think it's possible," Chan said, and he turned to Kat.

"More than possible." She stepped forward, gently touching Brady's lips with her gloved fingers. "And there's some injury around the mouth…."

McFarland seemed troubled now, staring at the corpse and then referring to his notes. Finally, he shook his head. "Mr. Laurie was down in that hold alone. *All* alone. I don't know anything about him as a man. Perhaps he had a temper. Maybe he got into an argument with someone before he went down. Maybe someone grabbed him roughly. I imagine he had a few bouts with his fellows at the Preservation Center. He could have gotten these bruises in a scuffle with a friend—even roughhousing for fun."

Kat looked at him incredulously.

"This isn't the body of a man who engaged in any kind of serious fight!" McFarland said firmly. "The bruises are small. There's no injury to any of his bones. There are no real cuts, just some chafing around the mouth. He came in here having drowned. He definitely did drown."

"But you *assumed* he might have been in a scuffle?" Will asked. "Do you often hear of fistfights among historians who don't agree with each other?"

"There's no real violence to the body. And historians are human like everyone else," McFarland said.

"That's true, but I spent the morning with this man's coworkers—and there was no difference of opinion. They all wanted the same thing," Will told McFarland. He sighed. "Doctor, please look at these bruises. Look at the way they match my hands. Think about a regulator. If it was ripped out of a man's mouth…"

"You would have exactly that kind of trauma," Kat finished.

"And exactly that kind of bruising," Will said impatiently.

His tone made McFarland bristle, and Kat frowned at Will.

He ignored her.

Despite the tension in the room, Kat kept her hand lightly on the icy-cold arm of the corpse. She knew that Will was right; she had noted the particular patterns of the bruises on Brady's arms almost immediately. And combined with the marks around his mouth, they suggested certain conclusions. But then, she was a diver. McFarland was not. And the man who'd been brought to him had been floating alone in the hold of a sunken ship.

At this rate, however, they weren't going to be welcome back at the morgue.

She wished she could get some feel for the man who'd been Brady Laurie.

Nothing. She was getting nothing from the body. If only Brady Laurie was still somehow here...but his body was cold. Empty.

"This is ridiculous. It's...it's not like he has massive bruising anywhere," McFarland sputtered.

"The bruises may darken, giving us a better idea," Kat said. "He hasn't been dead that long," she reminded him.

"He might not have gone ten rounds at the WWE SmackDown," Will put in, "but it looks to me as if he was held in a firm grip shortly before his death."

"It doesn't make sense that one of his coworkers could have gotten angry enough to have killed him. It's not like they're out to claim the treasures for themselves," Kat said.

"So?" McFarland's voice was strained. "What? A mummy crawled out of an inner sarcophagus *and* an outer sarcophagus—not to mention careful waterproofing—to rip his regulator out of his mouth?"

"Of course not," Kat said.

"This man was the one who discovered the ship! He was *alone* down there," McFarland emphasized.

"Maybe—and maybe not," Will said. "Others had to have known. Brady Laurie had done careful charting before the preservation group sent out requests for financial help, trying to sell their research as a documentary. This is the age of computer hackers, so plenty of people could've found out. And Lake Michigan hasn't been closed, has it?"

Kat wanted to kick him for his sarcasm.

"Agent Chan, I have been at this job for over twenty years," McFarland began.

Kat stepped in quickly. "Of course, Doctor, and your autopsy and notations are commendable. But there are factors involved that weren't included in the information you were given. You had no reason to suspect foul play. But with the possibilities out there—"

"*What* possibilities? A curse! A *swimming* mummy?"

Will shrugged and replied casually, "No, I'm sure the mummy would have deteriorated if it had somehow come to life," he said. "Money, Doctor. A treasure of inestimable worth. We don't *know* if any other party discovered the wreck due to Brady's research. It *might* have been a simple drowning. And then again, maybe not. At this point in the investigation, we have no idea who else might have been out on the lake."

"He died by drowning," McFarland insisted.

Will raised his eyebrows. "Yes, he died by drowning. But whether it was accidental or not—that's a completely different question, isn't it?"

"You're really suggesting he was murdered?"

"I'm more than suggesting, I'm saying it's quite likely," Will said. "Your findings were absolutely correct, Dr. McFarland, except that…they weren't. Brady Laurie was grabbed and he was held in the water. He drowned not because he ran out of time, but because his regulator was ripped from him. *That's* why he has injuries on his lips."

"Young man, what you're suggesting is a remote possibility!" McFarland said.

"Remote? I don't think so."

"Dr. McFarland, the point is…there *is* a possibility," Kat said.

"And not so remote," Will added.

He looked over at Kat. He was challenging her to step up to the plate. She wasn't in the least worried about doing that; she just wished she didn't have to.

She looked back at Will, who watched her steadily. And then, her heart sinking because she'd so badly wanted this to be *nothing,* she turned to McFarland. "Doctor, this is your morgue and your call. But…under the circumstances, I'd change that report if I were you. At the very least, hold on to it for a couple of days and let us do some more investigating. There's a good possibility that this was willful death caused by person or persons unknown."

3

"Could you have *been* any ruder?" Kat demanded of Chan.

"Could he have *been* any more incompetent?" he fired back.

They were out on the street. Car horns blared now and then, and the whir of fast-moving traffic seemed to be all around them.

Kat shook her head. "There's still nothing to actually prove him wrong, Agent Chan. The bruise could conceivably have been caused by jostling around."

"I never went to medical school, Agent Sokolov, but I don't think you need a degree to recognize bruises on postmortem flesh. My fingers fit perfectly into those bruises, so I'd say whoever killed him had nice large hands. Brady Laurie wasn't any kind of a hulk, although he was certainly strong enough to defend himself to some degree. But you dive, so surely you're aware that a lack of oxygen can quickly deprive you of energy and skill, leaving only the instinct to survive—and fight against whatever is keeping you from breathing.

An actor in a James Bond movie may be able to hold his breath forever while waging a heroic battle, but in most instances, you expend what air you have in trying to fight, and then…" He broke off, his implication grim. "And you agreed with my findings. Otherwise, you wouldn't have said what you did."

"I believe your findings suggest further investigation."

"Beyond a doubt."

"But that would usually suggest *not* insulting the medical examiner to the point that he doesn't want you back in the morgue! In any city, we need to be on the best terms with local authorities," Kat told him.

Will Chan stared back at her for a moment, then shrugged. "All right, fine. I should have tiptoed around his feelings. We should have pleasantly gone along with him—and then he would've released the body and we'd be left with nothing. Well, excuse me. You can go back in and ask the good doctor out for coffee or drinks, but I'm headed to the police station."

He turned and started walking. Kat glared at him, her temper soaring. She decided to go after him and practically had to run to keep up with his long strides. She caught him by the arm and was surprised by her own strength when she spun him around to face her.

"Look, *my* team was the one called in. You just happened to be here. This is my investigation, and I need you to stop your high-handed behavior before you offend every cop in the city of Chicago, as well."

"Why would I offend a cop who's dealt with a situation competently?" he asked. "And I'm sure you've been informed that I've already begun the investigation. I did so right after Logan Raintree got the request and called Jackson Crow and Adam Harrison with the information."

"Great. Except that you offended the medical examiner. Did you offend the film people, too? Or any of the others we'll have to depend on for access and information?"

"I haven't offended *anyone,* Agent Sokolov. What I did was conduct a very professional meeting with the film crew and then speak to the two researchers who worked with and found Mr. Laurie. I've *politely* informed them that we'll be diving with them tomorrow. Unless, of course, you prefer to maintain your investigation here on the surface. I will certainly understand."

She wondered what would happen if she simply combusted with anger on the street.

"Agent Chan, it was my understanding that *I* was to examine the corpse at the request of the producer, Alan King, and that if I found anything I didn't believe to be completely straightforward, *then* an investigation would begin."

"Well, Agent Sokolov, I was told last night to step right up and get things going since I was in the city. That's what I did. When a body pops up, the first hours can be the most important—as you know—so time was of the essence. Would you like me to share what I've learned? Or would you rather let someone else die while you start your own investigation?" he asked.

I'm a professional, but I cannot work with this man!

She took a deep breath. "You do realize, Agent Chan, that we didn't just go in and *prove* that Brady Laurie was murdered. Yes, it's *possible* that he was held in some way while his regulator was ripped from him, but it's not a foregone conclusion. There are other reasons such bruising might have occurred."

"Evidence locker," he said.

"Pardon?"

"Laurie's dive gear is in an evidence locker down at the police station, since the police were with the rescue units when he was brought in. I'm going down there to meet up with the local investigator and see exactly how much air was left in Laurie's tank." He paused. "I was a day ahead of you—although, yes, it's *your* case. I've seen the footage that was taken when the body was discovered. Laurie was dead when they found him, which wasn't long after he'd gone down himself. I still can't accept that it was a simple drowning."

"Wait—whoa! I didn't know there was footage!"

"Yes, there's footage. And you can call Bernie right now, or you can take my word for it. I haven't been to look at the evidence yet, but I intend to. You can get together with King Productions now or come with me and see the footage later. Your call."

She really wished it would be professional just to slap his determined and impatient face.

Another deep breath. "It's my call, yes," she said. "But I will come with you. As you pointed out, I can see the footage later."

He stood his ground but seemed slightly taken aback, something of a smile almost curving his lips.

"We're not on opposing sides," she said. "It doesn't matter who makes what call. We're here to find out if a murder has occurred, and if an investigation is necessary. I'm here for Brady Laurie, Agent Chan, not for a pissing contest with you."

Now his lips did curve into a full smile. "Sorry. But the M.E.'s findings were just too easy."

"Look, if there was no reason to suspect foul play, his findings really weren't negligent."

"You're defending him because he's an M.E."

"I'm only saying what's true, especially in a big city where you can have days when the bodies just pile up," Kat said.

"All right. I'll apologize when I see him again—*if* I see him again—and let's pray I don't. As to the rest, time can mean everything in this kind of investigation."

"I know. But I'm not sure whether we can answer all the questions we need answered or if those answers will lead to more questions. If we find air in the tank…"

"Then there's a good chance he was murdered."

He'd turned already. She suddenly hated the fact that he was as tall as he was. Keeping up with him was an effort.

"Even if the air is gone, we can't be certain of what

happened. The air might have bled out after he died," she said, catching up with Will. "And if there *is* air in the tank, it still doesn't prove that the regulator was ripped from his mouth."

He stopped so abruptly that she plowed into him. He reached out one hand to prevent her from falling.

"No, we won't prove anything one way or another, not without additional evidence. But it *will* be interesting to find out if there is or isn't air in his tank and to take a look at the regulator."

"You have a car?" she asked him.

"You don't?"

"I got into my room around midnight. I took a cab from the airport."

"I'm in the garage."

He started walking again. This time, she kept a certain distance.

He'd rented a Honda. When Kat climbed in, he indicated a folder thrust between the seats. "Notes from my meeting with Amanda Channel and Jon Hunt at the Chicago Ancient History Preservation Center—and what I've dug up from recent newspaper clippings."

Kat quickly leafed through the folder while he maneuvered the car out of the parking garage. The center sounded like a truly commendable enterprise. Nonprofit, it was dedicated to preservation. The staff was small and included three researchers, a receptionist and a general assistant. Grad students came and went. Of course, now with Brady Laurie gone, it was down to two researchers.

"Landry Salvage and Simonton's Sea Search," she murmured, skimming various articles written about the elusive *Jerry McGuen*. "These can't be the only two parties interested in finding the ship."

"I'm assuming that over the last century, countless individuals and companies have tried. Think about discoveries in the past. Both the *Titanic* and the *Atocha* took years and years of fruitless searches before finally being discovered." He glanced over at her. "Laurie must have been a brilliant historian and scientist."

"But not as brilliant a diver," Kat said. "He shouldn't have gone down alone."

Will shrugged. "Maybe it wouldn't have mattered."

"What do you mean?"

"Maybe the first person to come across the treasure was supposed to die," he said cryptically. "Or maybe his coworkers weren't supposed to be so close behind him, who knows? But I believe we'll find out."

"You have a lot of confidence," Kat told him.

He flashed her a smile that was surprisingly charming. "That's what we do—find things out. So far, my team hasn't stopped until we've gotten the answers. Don't tell me *your* team gives up so easily."

"We haven't given up yet!" Kat said indignantly.

His smile remained in place as he drove.

At the station, they were led first to one desk and then to another, and finally to the officer in charge of the accidental death investigation, Sergeant Riley. His supervisor had advised him to expect fed agents, and while he was pleasant and seemed to have no problem offering them assistance, he was confused about why they were there. "Sad, but the way the papers tell it," Riley said, "Laurie went down on his own and drowned. You would've thought he'd know better. Every year, every damned year, there's a diver lost somewhere in the lake, some fool so convinced of his own ability that he just goes down—and comes up dead." Riley was in his early thirties, tops. He was medium in height and size, and wore a white tailored shirt with the sleeves rolled up. "At the moment, the personal effects found on the corpse are in the evidence room. We'll go sign them out and you can study them all you want."

"Were you there when Brady Laurie was brought up?" Kat asked him.

"They were on the lake. Our marine unit went out to the site. He was declared dead at the hospital, but there'd been attempts at resuscitation before that. I took over the investigation when his wet suit and dive tanks were sent to us, and I've been awaiting the medical examiner's report, but…I have to admit, I wasn't expecting anything to come of it," Riley said.

He walked them back to the evidence cage, where they were introduced to the officer in charge and signed in. "Was the equipment tested for leaks?" Will asked.

"Immediately. No problems."

"Fingerprints?"

"Um, no."

"Ah," Chan said.

Riley frowned. "Is that a problem? I doubt we'd have gotten anything, anyway, since divers in the lake wear gloves. And then, of course, our technicians worked with the equipment to find out if it was faulty in any way."

"But it wasn't?"

"No."

In the evidence area where the tank, regulator and buoyancy control belt had been stowed, along with Laurie's weight belt, Will looked back at Kat. "May I?"

"Go right ahead." Laurie's equipment had not been disassembled; the "octopus" with the regulator, secondary system and computer console was still connected to the air tank.

Will examined the computer at the end of one of the hoses. He grimaced and beckoned to Kat. She came over and stood next to him, staring down at the dials. Brady Laurie had died with five minutes of air still available.

"There was air in his tank," Will explained to Riley. "*After* it was checked out for leaks."

"Well, so there is," Riley said. "Then he must have panicked and spit the thing out."

"Experienced divers don't panic when they have a regulator and air. He had a secondary system, too," Kat said thoughtfully. "Properly attached to his BCV." Riley was looking at her blankly. "This," she said, indicating the buoyancy control vest. "He could easily have reached for it if he'd had difficulty with his main regulator," she said, pointing to the mouthpiece. "It allows for the flow of air."

Riley shook his head. "We really think it was just a tragic accident."

Kat stepped in front of Will. "I'm sorry, Sergeant Riley. We don't."

"You're taking over the investigation?" he asked. To Kat's astonishment, he sounded hopeful.

He must have read her mind. "Hey, big city here, folks. I have my hands full, so…the chief already sent down orders to set you up in one of the conference rooms."

"Good," Will said. "Thank you." He pulled a sheet of paper from his pocket. "Can you see that we have access to this equipment, and a technical officer if need be?"

"Whatever you want that we've got," Riley assured them.

"Can you also connect us with the officer in charge of the marine patrol unit?"

Riley was happy to do so. He was happy, perhaps, to do anything that would make them someone else's responsibility.

Outside the station, Kat took out her phone. "I've got to tell Logan I can't say for sure that Laurie died by accident," she explained to Will. "Do you need to call in, as well? Now might be a good time."

He shrugged. "I don't have anything to report yet. Jackson Crow knew I'd be staying on for a while."

"Oh?"

"Hey, I happen to love Egyptian history," he told her.

"You seem delighted that there might have been a murder," she said sarcastically.

"Death never delights me." His voice had grown serious. "You came into this expecting an accidental drowning—which is also what the police believed. But whenever there's big money involved and a massive black market, I expect trouble. We need to put a stop to it or it's going to continue." He studied her for a moment. "Hey, this is what we do," he said. "You shouldn't be in this if you can't hack it."

"I can hack it just fine," she snapped. "You forget I'm a doctor—a certified medical examiner and forensic pathologist. I've studied all manner of deaths."

"No, I didn't forget," he said. "I couldn't possibly—you constantly remind me."

He walked away so she could make her call.

Kat looked after him, frustrated, her temper soaring again. Then she flushed and turned away. Was she afraid she didn't have control of the situation? Mental note: *quit reminding people that I'm an M.E.*

Wincing, she made her call.

She told Logan that yes, it appeared that they should investigate, although she had nothing solid as yet. He promised that more team members would be there within twenty-four hours. "I'm assuming that you've met Agent Chan?" Logan asked.

"Oh, yes."

"And he's capable and professional?"

"All that," Kat said drily.

"And what else?"

"He's an ass," Kat said. "He stomped all over the Chicago M.E. I try to speak first now to protect us from the wrath of local authorities."

Logan chuckled softly. "I know Chan. I met him at our special units base in Arlington. He's, shall we say, irreverent, but apparently excellent at what he does. He's familiar with film, video and computer alteration, so he'll be great with the film crew. And he dives, which is a major asset on this case. Are you going to see the *Jerry McGuen* soon?"

"If I know Chan, very soon," Kat said, glancing over at her new colleague.

"Keep me posted on any developments," Logan told her. "I should be there by midafternoon tomorrow." Then he rang off and Kat returned the phone to her purse, signaling that the call was finished.

Chan approached her seconds later. "Ready?" he asked.

She nodded.

Their next stop was the harbor, where the police search and rescue boat that had brought in the body was docked.

The harbor and the lake were beautiful that day. Summer was still with them but would begin to fade in the next few weeks. Today, though, the water glistened under a benign sun.

They were able to see all four officers who'd been on the search and rescue boat. Officer Aldo Reynald had been in charge, and he seemed sincerely interested in their queries.

"When we got there, the woman was crying her eyes out…Amanda. Yeah, Amanda Channel. She was kneeling over the dead man. She said she'd done CPR, but she didn't think it helped. She said we had to save her friend. The other guy, Jon Hunt, was walking around the dock, rubbing his chin, scratching his head. I tried CPR as we got him to shore. No luck. We have a state-of-the-art truck to deal with emergencies like this. You get a lot of divers who think they know their stuff and don't, or divers who are used to the tropics and get into trouble in the lake. And naturally we have boating accidents, so…we're prepared. We used every possible method of resuscitation on the way to the hospital, but…then we got there and they called it." He shook his head glumly. "I'm assuming we're going to have to be vigilant as this whole thing proceeds because diving a wreck is inherently dangerous, and a newly discovered one even more so."

Reynald was lean and fit; he was obviously experienced, practical—and compassionate.

"But you believe he was dead when you arrived?" Kat asked.

He nodded grimly. "Dead as a cold mackerel, I'm afraid."

"How long?" Will asked next.

"He couldn't have been dead more than half an hour or so," Reynald told them. "I'm not sure what I'm basing that on, other than that I've pulled more than a few bodies out of the lake. Like I said, he was declared DOA at the hospital."

"Were there other boats near the dive spot?" Will asked.

"Boating on a good day on Lake Michigan? You bet."

"Close to the dive site?" Kat continued for Will.

Reynald drew in a deep breath. "Yeah, near enough, I think. The other Preservation Center boat was there—as well as the one the dead man had been on. Oh, and the film crew has a snazzy research boat, too. There was a sailboat maybe two hundred feet away and others farther out...."

One of his fellow officers chimed in. "There were two motorboats nearby. One was a Cigarette—nice speedboat. I noticed that because I always wanted one. The other...a little cabin cruiser. Looked like the people aboard were fishing."

"Fishing," Kat echoed dubiously.

The officer grinned. "Not that long ago, Lake Michigan was so polluted you could die from eating fish you caught out there. But it's cleaned up. You'll find lots of people fishing in the lake now."

"Did you notice anything else about the boat?" she asked.

He shook his head. "I'm afraid I didn't."

"Either have a dive flag up?" Will asked.

"Neither," the second officer replied.

"We were called in on an accident, and rescue was our main objective," Reynald told them. "I feel like a fool because we're also law enforcement officers. Do you suspect it was more than an accident?"

Kat answered carefully. "We're not sure yet. We're just investigating at this point."

"Well, we're here anytime you need us," Reynald said.

They thanked him. As they headed back to the car, Will seemed thoughtful. He glanced over at her. "You tired? You want to call it quits for the day?"

She scowled back at him. If she'd been falling off her feet, she'd never have admitted it to this man. "I'm fine. What do you have in mind?"

"Two quick stops—Landry Salvage and Simonton's Sea Search. Neither may really help. Salvage companies don't usually drive around in Cigarette speedboats, but…"

"And if someone else is searching for treasure, that person may not be involved with a salvage company at all," Kat added.

He paused at the car door, looking over it. "True. But you have to know something about diving to get down there. You'd have to follow the research to find the ship—and you'd have to follow Brady Laurie out to the site…and gone after him right away."

"Maybe it's someone who works for a salvage company," Kat suggested. "Not the company itself."

"That would be my bet." Will grinned as she joined him in the front seat. "Your choice—Landry or Simonton's Sea Search first?"

"Simonton's. I like the alliteration," she said.

Simonton's was just north of the pier. There was a massive vessel with all kinds of cranes and netting at the dock. The office itself was small and looked more like a sea shanty than a professional building. Inside, Kat was surprised to see that it was nicely outfitted with modern office furniture and file cabinets that occupied most of the wall space. The walls were decorated with old anchors, flags and other boating paraphernalia. A receptionist who introduced herself as Gina led them to a back room, where the walls were decorated with sea charts and maps, and the rear wall held the figurehead of a beautiful siren.

The man standing behind the desk was in a windbreaker, deck shoes and jeans. His desk was strewn with papers, despite the computer that took up at least half of it. "Hi. I'm Andy Simonton," he greeted them. "What can I do for you?"

He was young, maybe thirty, with slightly shaggy blond hair and bright blue eyes. He swept out a hand to indicate the chairs in front of his messy desk. They sat.

"You're with the FBI?" he asked curiously. He didn't seem afraid or threatened in any way, but rather intrigued.

"We're looking into the death of Brady Laurie," Will said.

"Sad affair, that drowning," Simonton murmured.

"This is your company?" Kat asked him.

Simonton nodded. "My father's company, really. He wants to retire. I've been handling the business for about a year."

"And what is your business, exactly?" Will asked.

Simonton looked confused. "Um, salvage."

Will had the grace to laugh. "No, I'm sorry, what type of salvage? What are you working on now?"

"Oh!" Simonton said. "We're conducting two recovery missions. A Florida boater underestimated the power of the lake and sank a sixty-foot sailboat, and we're also working on recovering the cargo from the hold of the *Mystic Susan*—she's a merchant vessel that went down with crates of high-fashion clothing," Simonton explained.

"That does sound like work. Not terribly exciting," Kat said sympathetically.

Simonton gave a nonchalant shrug. "It pays the bills, and quite nicely, too. Oh, and Mrs. Ciskel—she's the wife of the Florida boater—is furious because she had a lot of jewelry aboard when their boat went down. I'd like to find that cache myself. To return to her, of course. She's promised a massive bonus if we get back all her jewels." He frowned. "Now, what's this all about?"

"We were wondering if you'd ever had any plans to explore and salvage the *Jerry McGuen*," Will said.

"We were invited to the reception put on by the Egyptian Sand Diggers."

Kat glanced at Will. "The Egyptian Sand Diggers?" he repeated. "Who are they?"

Simonton waved one hand in the air. "They're a local service club—and they're just a little nutty, you know? In love with all things ancient Egyptian. Some of them are true scholars, while the rest are more what you'd call armchair historians. They held a reception about six months ago, and they shared all sorts of current information on expeditions into the Valley of the Kings, the closing of the Great Pyramids for maintenance, stuff like that. And they had an exhibit on Gregory Hudson—he's the guy who discovered the Amun Mopat tomb way back—and the *Jerry McGuen*. They were trying to encourage local salvage companies to search for her. Unfortunately, I don't have the time or money to go on a wild-goose chase, although I wish I *had* gone on that goose chase. I suppose the location is pretty well-known by now and anyone might have found her after she shifted on the seabed. See, it was wide open. The State of Illinois gets everything recovered in this area of Lake Michigan, but the salvage company that finds it does get certain rights. The original company went bust soon after the sinking of the *Jerry McGuen* and the passengers' families were paid off with what was left, so any descendants aren't really a factor. Now, as far as the salvage goes, the State of Illinois would probably return most of it to the Egyptians."

"Do you know of anyone else who was planning to go after the ship?" Kat asked.

"Landry," he said. "He and my dad were always competitive. Maybe he wanted to find it just to rub in my dad's face—or my face now. He was at the reception, by the way."

"How many boats do you have, Mr. Simonton?" Will asked.

"I have a little Mako for my own pleasure," Simonton said. "You can go see her if you want. She's sitting right outside."

"This looks like a good operation." Kat smiled. "And obviously a successful one."

"I'm all about paying the bills," Simonton said. He tapped a pencil on his desk. "Can I do anything else for you? I'm sorry, but I'm kind of busy and…well, honestly, I'm not really sure what you're after."

"We think someone helped Brady Laurie drown," Will said bluntly.

Simonton gaped at him. "Wow. Well, I can't see how that could have happened. I mean, his own people were right behind him and they're the ones who found him." He sat back, staring at them, still not threatened, just surprised. "Um, you're welcome to search anything we own or, uh, whatever."

"Thanks. If we need to search, we'll get back to you," Kat said. "What we *could* use is information on the Egyptian Sand Diggers."

"Oh, sure!" He started rummaging through his desk. "That invitation is in here somewhere…. They used nice stationery and calligraphy on it."

He gave up with a sigh and stood, heading out to the receptionist's desk. "Gina, can you find me that invitation from the Egyptian Sand Diggers?"

Simonton stood by the door as Gina searched for the invitation. Kat leaned over and whispered to Will. "Why don't you just call the *Tribune* and announce that we're looking for a murderer? We're not even sure of it ourselves!"

He shrugged. "What? You think people will believe the FBI is involved because we want to dive a wreck?"

She gritted her teeth again, but before she could respond, Simonton returned with the invitation. "Here you go. Their address is right there, where it says RSVP."

"Thank you," Kat said, accepting it. She smiled. "You were really helpful. I hope we can count on you in the future, if we need to."

He gave her a warm smile in return. "Oh, you bet!"

"You did a lovely job. Maybe I should let you do *all* the talking," Will muttered as they left the office.

"What?"

He turned to her. "Mr. Simonton was quite…taken with you. That's good. He'll help us."

"Agent Chan, that is hardly—"

"Professional? Sorry. But you were being all nicey-nice, and in this case, it seemed to work. I say we go with it."

"I say it's better than you offending M.E.s and cops!"

"McFarland needed to know that he'd make a fool of himself if he crossed Laurie off as an accidental death.

Now he knows, and he won't do it. And I was perfectly polite with the cops. I don't blame them. This is a tough town, and when they can close the books on a situation, they have to do it. I honestly don't think it occurred to most people working the drowning that it *might* have been an *assisted* drowning—or murder. Now, they'll think about."

"Are we going out to talk to Landry or the Egyptian Sand Diggers?" Kat asked. She decided to let his previous remarks—a backhanded compliment if ever there was one—slide.

"Let's check out Landry first," Will said.

Kat agreed, getting out her phone.

Will glanced over at her. "Are you getting someone to look up the Sand Diggers?"

She nodded.

"Good idea."

After a brief conversation, Logan promised that he'd learn whatever he could about the avid amateur Egyptologists. By the time she'd finished, they were pulling into a lot by the glass-and-chrome offices of Landry Salvage.

"They seem to be doing a bit better here, don't you think?" he asked Kat.

"Either that, or they're more impressed with appearances."

Where the offices of Simonton's Sea Search had seemed like an old-fashioned sea shanty, Landry's was almost sterile. The floors were bare, the white walls adorned with single black strokes of paint. The reception desk was sparse, and the woman who greeted them was young, very pretty and very blank. It seemed to take her several minutes to figure out who they were, and then several more to understand what they wanted. The little sign on her desk identified her as Sherry Bertelli.

"Oh, oh, oh!" she said at last. "Oh! You're here about the professor or the Egyptologist or the...whatever he was who died so tragically!" She pushed a button on the single piece of office equipment before her. "Mr. Landry, the FBI is here to see you."

They heard an impatient reply. "The FBI? Whatever for?"

Kat leaned over the desk. "Agents Katya Sokolov and Will Chan, Mr. Landry. We'd like to speak with you. We're hoping you can help us."

There was a moment of dead silence, and then Landry said, "Of course. Come on in. Ms. Bertelli will escort you."

Sherry Bertelli rose quickly. "This way, please."

It was hard to tell where glass walls and doors met. They went down a long hallway. Eventually Sherry Bertelli pushed on a glass panel, and they were ushered into another state-of-the-art ultramodern office where Landry was standing behind a black chrome desk.

"How do you do, how do you do?" he asked, stepping around to shake their hands. "I'm Stewart Landry.

Have a seat, please, have a seat. Would you like coffee or anything?"

"No, no, thank you, we're fine," Kat assured him. Will held one of the chairs for her, then took his own. Stewart Landry sat back at his desk. Sherry Bertelli just stood there.

"That's all, Sherry, thank you," Landry said.

Without a word she turned and marched out of the office. Landry cleared his throat. "Sherry's, uh, very popular with our clientele," he said, as if excusing his receptionist's undeniable limitations.

Landry was somewhere between fifty and sixty years old. His suit was designer label, his nails were clean and buffed and his silver hair was well groomed. Kat had to wonder if there wasn't something more intimate going on between him and Sherry than the typical employee-boss relationship.

"Now, how can I help you?" Landry asked.

"Frankly," Will said, "we're trying to find out if you'd considered diving the site of the *Jerry McGuen*. We understand that a group called the Egyptian Sand Diggers was encouraging local interest and, as I'm sure you've read or seen on the news, a diver died at the site."

Landry frowned. "Yes, I saw the news, and I knew Brady Laurie. He was quite angry at that reception and behaved rather badly. He wasn't a member of the group, made very clear that kind of thing was beneath a *true* historian such as himself. He argued with the members that he was already on the case, and that he and his colleagues needed to find the treasure, not any of us 'money-grubbing bastards.' Don't get me wrong—the death of any young person is lamentable. But Dr. Laurie was out of line. The Egyptian Sand Diggers invited us *all* to that soiree, and I think it was because they didn't believe Laurie was right in his calculations. He was, of course. That's obvious *now*."

"Did you plan to dive the site at all?" Kat asked, returning to the original question.

He shrugged. "Honestly? It was an intriguing thought. But as to planning any operation—no. Our big ship is out in Lake Huron working on a ferry that went down. We have some smaller vessels working more shallow waters, but as to the *Jerry McGuen*… If Laurie *hadn't* found her, we might've made an attempt to see what our sonar could identify in the area. Thing is, no one really knew exactly where she went down, other than that she was supposedly near Chicago. You might not realize it, but the lake is huge. Searching it is almost like searching the North Atlantic. When you're just looking at the lake, it seems to stretch out forever. And when you're boating on it alone, you can feel as if you're the last man on earth."

"But the treasure in the *Jerry McGuen* is of inestimable worth," Will commented.

Landry nodded. He smiled suddenly. "But searching for that kind of treasure—needle in a haystack. I can tell you that Brady Laurie was obsessed with it. I wasn't shocked when I heard about his death. He was threatened by all of us—no, no, that came out wrong. No one ever *threatened* him, but…check with the Egyptian Sand Diggers. They were pointing out the historic value of the find, which *we* already knew, and he got furious. Their president is a fellow named Dirk Manning, and what they call their 'guardian'—an old fellow who's been involved in it since he was twenty-one—is a man named Austin Miller. Talk to one of them about Brady Laurie. In my opinion, he had no real interest in joining the group, but he probably spoke to those gentlemen more than anyone else. Me? I believe Laurie was so obsessed with the ship that he signed his own death warrant."

Will stood up and shook hands with Landry. Kat stood, too. "If there's anything I can do, please let me know," Landry said.

"Thank you." Kat smiled—then remembered Will's earlier remark about her niceness.

"I'll have Ms. Bertelli show you out," Landry offered.

"We can find our way," Will told him, "but thanks."

When they passed Sherry Bertelli, she was sitting behind her desk, flipping through the pages of a fashion magazine. She looked up long enough to smile vaguely at them and wave. "Ta-ta!"

"Yep, ta-ta," Kat responded.

She didn't realize Will was laughing until they were in the car again. *"Ta-ta?"*

"I simply returned the courtesy," she said primly.

"I get the feeling they didn't hire her for her math skills."

Kat shook her head and turned to him. "This is just about impossible," she said. "No one, not even the first responders, really knows if anyone else was near the site when Brady died—or was killed. It sounds like he could be extremely hostile about anything concerning the *Jerry McGuen*. He did dive alone—and went down almost a hundred feet in cold water. This wasn't a pleasure dive to a warm-water reef."

Will glanced at her, then looked at the road again. "But you saw his body."

"Yes. I saw his body. And seeing his body made me believe this is worth investigating. But what we saw doesn't guarantee that Brady Laurie was murdered. There are other explanations for the bruises. It's possible that he might have gotten into an altercation with someone. He was furious with the Egyptian Sand Diggers and apparently everyone knew it."

"So you think one of the Sand Diggers was out on a boat, slipped into the water while pretending to fish and killed Laurie?" Will asked. "Why? The Sand Diggers supposedly *wanted* someone to find the treasure."

"I don't know," Kat said. "We'll have to ask them. Logan should be getting back to me with some information pretty soon. We can check them out tomorrow."

"Tomorrow afternoon. Tomorrow morning we dive the site."

Kat turned to him. "You sound excited about it."

"I am. A shipwreck like the *Jerry McGuen?* Come on, you have to be somewhat excited!"

"Thrilled to pieces," she muttered. Maybe one day, she'd tell him about the experiences she'd already enjoyed because of Amun Mopat!

"You don't believe in a curse, do you?" he asked, grinning.

"No. I do, however, believe that people can go a little crazy because of them."

"I agree," he said. "I spent a lot of time in the Caribbean. Islanders can be very superstitious. I've seen men who felt convinced they were possessed, and women who managed incredible feats of contortion in a ceremonial dance. The mind is a powerful influence on the body."

Kat nodded.

"You think someone would sabotage the mission to keep Amun Mopat from being brought back to the surface?" he asked. "That's an idea."

"Crazy people can latch onto anything, but…at this point, I don't know *what* I think or feel," Kat told him. "Except that it's been a really, really long day!"

"And it'll be an early morning," he said.

She was glad he'd said that; his stamina seemed to be on a par with the Energizer Bunny's. She hoped he was taking her back to her hotel. "I'm at a place called the Edwardian off Michigan Avenue."

"Yep."

"You know that, of course," she said.

"Of course."

He didn't just drop her off; he brought the car in front to the valet. She sighed as she saw him get out and walk around to her. "You're staying here, too."

"Government dollar." He shrugged. "We go where they get their deals," he said. "I'll meet you in the lobby at eight."

"We're diving at 8:00 a.m.?"

He hesitated. "You're not required to go down."

"I wouldn't miss it. Remember? We're excited about this."

"Would you like to get some dinner?"

"I think I'll just go upstairs and order in," she said.

"Good night, then."

There was a small restaurant in the hotel. He walked toward it, a folder and an iPad in his hands. He was going to keep working, she realized.

And she *was* starving....

He stopped suddenly, a curious frown tightening his brow. She was startled to notice again what a striking and unusual man he was.

He walked back to her. "All day I forgot to ask... Well, I suppose you would've said, but...did you get anything from the corpse?"

Kat studied his eyes. She was surprised, after the day they'd spent together, to feel strangely close to him. But then, when you were one of the lucky or the cursed who'd always assumed they were ever so slightly crazy, there was an instant bond with others who shared that luck or that curse. She shook her head. "No, and I was hopeful. We're always hopeful," she said quietly. "You?"

"Nothing at all. And I just think that in this situation, with the money involved in salvage, what seems to stink *does* stink. I really believe he was murdered. I grew up in the islands. I've been diving since I was a kid. No, he should never have gone down alone, but from what I've learned and seen, there was nothing that should have caused him to lose control. His equipment was in perfect working order. Even after being tested for leaks, his tank had air." He paused. "It's strange. We still can't explain why some souls stay around, and some don't."

"Maybe some people who die by violence aren't compelled to stay on earth to see that justice is done," she said. "Some may find peace—who knows? There's an incredible amount that we haven't begun to understand."

"Ain't that the truth," he said. "Well, get some rest."

He started to walk again. *He was a workaholic,* she thought. Usually so was she. But she really *was* tired.

Still, they were supposed to be working this case together. She sighed.

A mummy. Great. It just had to be a mummy. The mummy of Amun Mopat.

"Wait," she called. "I'll join you. We can discuss what direction we'll take after the dive."

Yes, she was going to dive. And the idea gave her the creeps.

She suddenly wished the *Jerry McGuen* had remained lost to the world forever.

4

Will passed his iPad over to Kat as soon as they'd ordered. "Just click Go. You'll see the footage that was taken when they found Brady Laurie," Will told her.

Startled, Kat looked at him. "You had this all along?"

"Yes. But the cops who were on duty when Brady was brought up, not to mention the salvage companies, are easier to visit by day—not at night."

She didn't respond, thinking he might have told her he had the film footage. Sure, he *said* he was giving her the lead in their investigation, since *her* Krewe had been called in. Somehow, he was taking the lead, anyway. She felt like getting up and going to her room, but reminded herself that she was the one who'd said they weren't in a pissing contest.

Kat touched the icon, and the footage leaped onto the screen. She lowered the volume, not wanting anyone nearby to hear, but there really wasn't any sound, other than the videographer's breathing, and then, of course, the muted screams when Amanda and Jon came upon the body of Brady Laurie.

As she'd heard, Brady could be seen floating in the hold. Jon had come upon him first; he'd tried to get the regulator back in Brady's mouth. Amanda had been at his side soon after. For a few minutes, there was nothing but shots of the inside of the hull and the flooring, covered with plankton and other growth, and strewn with holes. The videographer had momentarily forgotten his task in the horror of their discovery. When he regained control, Kat was glad to see that once they'd found Brady, they had left behind all curiosity and interest in treasure; they started back to the surface immediately. In the course of doing that, they had to make a few safety stops. At the surface, the footage ended.

"I met with Alan King, Bernie Firestone and Earl Candy last evening, as soon as Jackson reached me," Will explained, studying her across the table. "Earl wanted to destroy his film—he doesn't want gawkers watching the discovery of a man's death. I promised him that when the investigation's over, I'll destroy this copy."

"Of course," Kat murmured. She pushed the iPad toward him, frowning. "I just don't see how anyone could have gotten to Brady between the time he went down and when his coworkers and the film crew arrived."

"Easy enough, I suppose. Down in Lake Michigan, it's damned dark. If someone was already down there, knew the lake and was a good diver, he—or she—could have found Brady's coordinates just before Brady did… and waited for him. Remember, Brady had made a big thing of his belief that he could find the *Jerry McGuen*.

would've taken you for a steak eater—in Chicago, anyway," she told Will.

"Ah, but we're going down nearly a hundred feet tomorrow," he said. "I'm going to keep it light."

"But you do eat steak?"

"Yes. You're a vegetarian?"

"I'm a wannabe. I like cows. They do no ill, not to my life, at any rate."

"Russian?" he asked her.

He changed focus quickly, she thought. "My dad," she said. "My mom is a good old American mix of English, Irish and Scandinavian. You?"

"I was born in the States. My parents are Trinidadian. A mix of English, Chinese and Indian," he said. "Your first time?"

She sat back at the question, stunned at his audacity.

He laughed. "I meant your first time with a ghost."

She wished she wasn't so pale and that a flush didn't instantly cover her from head to toe. "A ghost. Of course," she said, looking down. She raised her eyes again. "I was at a Civil War reenactment with my parents. I was about ten. I talked with a soldier. Everyone assumed I'd talked to a reenactor, and I believed them. Years later...I was at my grandfather's funeral. He was desperate that my grandmother find his financial records. He died suddenly, you see, and had barely written a will, much less made sure that his affairs were in order. She was old school and hadn't paid bills or known anything about finance. He told me where to look for

If someone hacked into his computer ⌐
blogs, they could follow his reasonin⸋
where the ship might have ended up. That's on⸋
perhaps, someone could've been surprised by Brady. If
you know the area, you keep to the depth, follow your
compass and then come up at a distant point."

"True," Kat said. "But still, the timing…"

"How much diving experience have you had?" he
asked her.

She tensed inwardly. "A fair amount in the
Caribbean—around a number of the islands. I've dived
cold-water springs in Florida and caves in Mexico. I
haven't done a lot of cold-water diving, so I admit I'm
grateful it's still summer."

"I don't see the temperature as much of an issue.
Think about how much time—at that depth, with safety
stops—it took Amanda and Jon to get down there. And
then to go back up—and call a search and rescue boat.
The depth isn't that great, but we're talking time and
water pressure."

She nodded. "So you think it could be Landry? Or
Simonton?"

"Maybe neither," he said with a grimace. "And I
don't know whether Brady Laurie died because he surprised someone down there, or if the intent was to start
killing people so the search would end."

"Let's hope it's the first."

Their meals arrived; they'd both ordered fish. "I

his papers." She hesitated. "I think my grandmother had something of whatever this…ability is, too. She seemed to understand right away how I knew things—and she warned me to be careful. People would make fun of me, or worse, she said. They'd see that I was locked up. And then…when I was in residency after med school, I was present at the death of a child. There's nothing worse. But she'd written a letter to her parents, filled with love. She'd had a severe case of cystic fibrosis and wanted them to know she was at peace, and that she loved them and her sister. She told them that her time with them had been happy. After that…an old M.E. I knew talked me into changing course. Who knows? Maybe he had a bit of it, too. So I went to work as an M.E., and I wound up working with the San Antonio police a lot—and with Logan Raintree, who was with the Rangers' office then. Eventually, we all met Jackson Crow and worked a San Antonio case before becoming, unofficially, the Texas Krewe. And you?"

"I was born in the States but I spent a lot of time in Trinidad and the other islands. Conversing with the dead is far more accepted in some of those places. I think I was five. I was in Jamaica. A fisherman had been murdered." He shrugged. "The corpse told me who did it. If only it was always that simple." His grin was engaging. "Actually, of course, it *wasn't* that simple. I told my father, who told the cops, who almost arrested my father. But when they investigated, they found out that what I'd said was true. Then, of course, they wanted to arrest my father for being an accomplice. So I learned to keep quiet. I didn't go into law enforcement at all. I went into magic—I'm a really good magician, should you ever need one—and from there, I segued into film. And then I was called in to work with Jackson Crow, and wound up taking the training at Quantico…and here I am."

"Strange how we were all found," Kat said.

"Maybe. Maybe not. Adam Harrison worked quietly with the FBI for years before his units were formed. And for him, it came from *not* having the gift, while his son, who died young, had been blessed with it. After that he began to seek out those who did."

"I guess if you know it exists, you can find it," Kat said.

Will glanced at his watch. "We should get some sleep. We'll be at the dock early in the morning. I'll meet you in the restaurant at seven. We should have something to eat before we head out."

Kat felt her teeth grind. He was taking control again. She decided that was a childish reaction, telling herself he was right; they were going diving.

But for some reason, that made her grab the bill the moment it came to the table. He didn't protest. Apparently, he had no hang-ups about a woman paying. She tried to take a deep breath; she really *was* acting childish. It was just that this was the first time she'd been on an investigation without Logan and the others, and she couldn't help remembering that the whole thing had begun because *her* unit knew the filmmakers who'd requested that they step in. So she felt a little proprietary....

They left the dining room and headed for the elevator. She hit the button for the fifth floor. He didn't hit a button at all. She should have known. Their rooms were next to each other.

The accommodations had been booked from their central office in Virginia. Tomorrow, Kat was certain, she'd discover that Logan and the rest of her unit were booked into the surrounding rooms. Logan's would be a suite with a big round table where they could work on their computers and discuss their findings.

"Good night," Will said.

She wished him a brusque good-night as well and entered her room.

She shouldn't have been tired; she should still have been on L.A. time. But, as she'd said earlier, it had been a long day.

A very long day, she thought.

Just last night she'd been in a comfortable bed in L.A., dreaming about being on a ship.

She flinched, unsure why it bothered her so much that she'd dreamed about the ship—and then been sent out to investigate a death in a shipwreck.

She really wanted to sleep. She didn't want to dream.

Before climbing into bed, she pulled out her octopus, dive boots, mask and flippers. It had seemed prudent to bring her own equipment. With those objects packed in a rolling dive bag, she was ready for morning.

When she did fall asleep, her dream wasn't the same.

This time, it was about mummies.

She was somewhere…somewhere in a green darkness. There were wall sconces that burned bright blue here and there along the walls. She didn't seem to be walking, but floating.

Suddenly, ahead of her—a plethora of mummies. They all had their arms outstretched and moved with the slow, staccato movement she'd seen in classic mummy movies.

Even in her dream she paused to think that such an image was ridiculous. Mummies were bound with their arms crossed over the body. In any case, a mummy couldn't just reach out an arm—it would break off!

But these mummies were coming toward her. And behind them, she saw a man. It was, of course, none other than the evil, robe-wearing high priest Amun Mopat. The priest who had wanted to be a pharaoh, a god.

He was laughing. In old movies, all villains had a maniacal laugh.

They were coming closer and closer and she kept floating toward them. Now that, too, was totally idiotic. She never understood why people in films just stood there and screamed. The mummies moved so slowly. If she turned and ran—or floated more quickly—she could easily escape them. In movies, the heroines usually tripped, and then lay on the ground screaming as the mummy or monster closed in on them. Scenes like that made for great movie posters!

In her dream, she reminded herself that she was a medical examiner and that she understood the human body. She understood the nature of human remains in any condition, even mummified. If she met the mummies, she could fight them—break them into a million pieces—and she'd be fine. But there were so many....

She floated into the fray. As she'd expected, the mummies were brittle, dry and fragile. They weren't much for fighting.

But behind them was Amun Mopat, watching her from beneath his hooded cape.

They stared at each other, and she wanted to run but couldn't and then—

Then she woke, startled by a sound. Glancing at the clock radio, she noted the time—4:31 a.m.

For a moment, she lay in bed, vividly remembering her dream and puzzled by the sound that had awakened her.

It came again and her eyes flashed to the door. Someone had tried to enter her room. The sound had been that of an electronic key card.

She rolled over and reached into the bedside table for her FBI-issue firearm and jumped to her feet, instantly alert. There was no sound now. She walked to the door and looked through the peephole. She saw nothing. Thinking quickly, she grabbed her key card from the side table and dropped it in the little pocket of her nightshirt and walked back to the door, looking out again.

She waited, then slid the top bolt, cringing when she heard the noise it made. Gun at the ready, she threw open the door.

There was no one out there, but Will Chan's door had opened, too. She knew he was standing much as she was—his firearm leveled.

"Will?" She whispered his name.

He stepped out of his room, wearing floor-length pajama pants and nothing else, and his hair, while dead straight, was disheveled, as well. He gave her a nod, which she knew to mean *cover me,* and walked out into the hall, turning from one direction to another, striding away from the elevator bank, and then back toward it.

There was definitely no one in the hall.

"The elevator," he said softly. He was standing by it.

She nodded. "I'll take the stairs."

As she went down the stairs in her long T-shirt of a nightgown and bare feet, stopping to look out at every floor, she thought she should have opted for the elevator.

Will was waiting for her when she got to the bottom.

One lone clerk was on duty at the reception desk across the lobby. Kat arched a brow at Will. "Did he see anyone?"

"Nope. What did you hear?" he asked her. "What woke you?"

"It sounded as if someone was trying to get into my

room with a key card. What did you hear? Did they try your room, too? Maybe it was just a drunk on the wrong floor," Kat said.

"Maybe. Or maybe someone *was* trying to get into our rooms. And maybe that someone has a room at the hotel."

She shook her head. "That's rather stupid, isn't it? Trying to break in on agents in their rooms? Obviously we're armed. And even more obvious—we're going to have the doors bolted."

"Maybe the intent wasn't to hurt us, just to throw us off," Will said.

"The clerk says no one's gone through the lobby?"

"Not since about 1:30 a.m. And he assured me he would've noticed. The last customers left the restaurant at about 11:00 p.m., and the last drinker left the bar at one-thirty. He says it's been quiet ever since— quiet as a tomb."

"But there must be back entrances to the hotel," Kat pointed out.

"True. But if someone came or went, that someone is long gone. However, we can go get dressed, come back down and speak to the security guard."

"There's a security guard on duty tonight?"

"It's a legit hotel. Yes, there's a security guard."

"And I guess he didn't see anything alarming?"

"He's watching the cameras—except that all the cameras are watching the entrances. They aren't installed in the hallways yet."

"What about the elevators?"

He shook his head. "The cameras in the elevators inexplicably went down sometime this afternoon. They have a call in to their service center for tomorrow."

"Coincidence?"

"Ah, what do you think?"

"I don't put a lot of faith in such convenient coincidences," she replied.

"The guard makes a sweep every thirty minutes and watches the screens in between."

"So he'll know if anyone went in or out of the building."

"No one went in or out. I already asked," Will said. "You were slow coming down those stairs."

"I was not!" Kat protested. "I checked out each landing."

"Naturally. But it gave me time to talk to the clerk and have him call security. I don't think the guard's bad at his job—I'm sure he'd handle rowdy young drunks or a bar fight just fine—but I doubt that he's ready for a major espionage job. I'll go over the tapes tomorrow, but whoever got in was, I'm afraid, one up on the guard."

"But we didn't imagine someone in the hallway," Kat said stubbornly.

"No, we didn't," he agreed. "Okay, let's go back up. We're not going to get anywhere now. I'll ask for the tapes and inspect the machinery when I've showered and dressed. It's almost 5:00 a.m., and we have to be up and out in a few hours. I know cameras and security systems. I can check it all out and you can grab an hour's sleep."

"Right. Like I'll be able to go back to sleep now," Kat muttered.

"Later on, you're going to wish you got more sleep," Will warned. Kat noted that the clerk was staring over at them. She was barefoot, and her T-shirt only made it halfway down to her knees. She smiled and waved at him.

"You guys okay?" he called over to them. He had to be in his early twenties. Crew cut, wearing a suit, he still had the voice of a young man. "You want me to call the police or anything?" he asked worriedly.

"No, no, we're fine," Kat assured him. She held her Glock behind her back and realized that Will had already moved his from sight. She wondered how he'd managed to hide it while talking to the clerk—a half-naked man with a gun approaching him at five in the morning would surely have upset the young man.

Will bent down and scooped something from a large ornamental planter. Ah, that explained it.

He hit the elevator button. Waving to the clerk, they both backed in.

"Maybe we *should* have contacted the local police," Kat said. "They could have done a more thorough search."

"No. Whoever it was is gone or back in a room somewhere in the hotel. I'll make sure the elevator cameras are working by tomorrow night. I don't like to bring the police in unless we really need them. If they don't find anything, we become the boy who cried wolf and I don't want to create that impression."

He was right, Kat decided. Again.

"But it's your call, of course," Will said.

"Quit that," she told him.

"Quit…deferring to you?" he asked.

She scowled at him. "You seem to defer to me only when you want to annoy me."

"That's not my intent."

"Then quit it!"

"What? You *are* the lead investigator. You've stated as much."

Kat wasn't sure whether to laugh or be angry. She let out a sigh of exasperation. "You hit on it today. We're here to work. And we work as a team," she said. "Logan isn't here, and Jackson isn't here. That makes us the only Krewe members present right now. That means we need to cooperate."

"Makes sense," he said.

"Does the clerk know we're FBI?" she asked him.

"I don't know," Will said, shrugging. "The manager does, since this is Adam Harrison's hangout when he's in Chicago. But as for the night clerk, I have no idea."

Back on their own floor, he was alert as they walked down the hall. "Until tomorrow, we're supposed to be the only people on this floor."

"So someone wasn't just at the wrong room."

"Rooms," Will said. "I heard a key card slide into

my door, too. There are eight rooms on each floor. It's a 'boutique' hotel, remember?"

"But sometimes people do get off on the wrong floor."

"They do—but not after they've slipped invisibly past a night clerk."

"What if the clerk had earphones on and was listening to AC/DC?" she asked.

"What about the security guard?"

"Maybe he was listening to another heavy-metal band," Kat said.

He grinned, then paused, staring at the wall by her room, frowning.

"What…" she began to ask.

"The wall. There's something on the wall."

She stood close to him, examining the wall, which looked as if someone had stuck a yellowed and dirty old bandage against it.

"This looks like…"

"Mummy wrapping," Kat said. Her dream rushed back to her. "Except it's not. Mummies are treated after they're wrapped, and this just seems like someone's idea of a Halloween prank." Her tone was harsh. Despite her training, common sense and logic, it was unnerving to see that someone had been outside both of their rooms, either out to do actual harm or trying to…unnerve them.

"Mummies aren't always treated," Will said quietly. "There are a number at various museums around the world that haven't been soaked in any kind of resin.

The reign of the pharaohs went on for thousands of years, and I don't know about all their interment rites, but I've seen mummies that were buried only in wrapping. I agree with you, though. I don't think this is real. I think it's something bought from a Halloween shop. But I'm going to get an evidence bag and see what we can find out."

She waited, her fingers tight around the grip of her Glock, while he went to his room for an evidence bag. He returned in a matter of seconds. He'd relinquished his gun—because he felt there was no more danger or because he had faith in her, she didn't know—and had brought a knife and the bag. She noticed then that his chest and arms were lean, sleek and well-muscled, and that he could move with the silence and agility of a cat, despite his height and build.

He scraped the fragment of slimy gauze from the light gray wall into the bag.

"What now?" she asked.

"You're not going back to sleep?"

"I had my alarm set for six-thirty. Not much point now, even if I felt I could fall asleep."

He shrugged. "Then we'll be good and early. I'm going to shower and dress. I'll meet you downstairs at six. That's when they have the coffee ready so we should get the first cups."

She nodded, wondering if she should say what was on her mind—that she didn't like the idea of people crawling around the hall.

He seemed to read her thoughts. "You know what? I'm going to do a setup. It won't take long and it'll help put you at ease."

"I *have* been trained. I'm not a coward," Kat said.

"There's a major difference between being wary and being a coward," he said. "Give me a minute, and you'll see what I'm up to."

The man seemed to be prepared for anything. He disappeared into his room and reappeared with a small camera, a thick wad of duct tape and a desk chair. He used the chair to stand on while he attached the camera just above her door. It was wireless and she thought it was small enough to go unnoticed, especially with the ornate trim over the lintel.

"You've got a laptop, right?" he asked her.

"Of course."

"The camera works on a frequency. It'll come in on a screen in my room, but I can have it zapped on to your computer. Then you can see what's going on in the hall, and so will I. Any problems with that?"

"Not at all. In fact, I really like it," Kat said.

"I have to grab a bit of software." He disappeared into his own room again, then followed Kat into hers. She showed him where she'd set up her computer on the desk and he went to work. As he did, she noticed the door to the adjoining room—his.

He'd been concentrating on the task at hand, and when he finished, he turned to her. "There's your icon. Hit it, and you'll see whatever is going on in the hall."

"Thanks. I wonder if we should unbolt the connecting doors, too."

He grinned. "Not a bad idea. Hey, knowing someone might be in the hallway is creepy, no matter how well-armed you are," he said. "And it's hard to take your gun in the shower, especially when you're washing your hair."

She laughed. "Which is exactly what I want to do." She walked over and unbolted her side.

"I'll do the same from my room," he told her. "Though I'm not expecting anything else for now."

"You think it was done to warn us?" Kat asked.

"There's nothing in the local news about us," he said, "but I'm sure that word gets around and those who need to worry about us are aware. But, yeah, I think it was done for effect. Okay, meet you downstairs at six."

He strode to the door and opened it.

"Thanks again," she called after him.

"It's what I do," he said. "See you soon."

A moment later, she heard the bolt slide open on the other side of the connecting door. The sound made her smile. With the camera in place and the connecting door unlocked, she felt safe enough to take a shower.

The first day manager came on at 6:00 a.m. He arrived a little early and was surprised to find that Will was waiting for him the minute he stepped into the lobby. But apparently he'd been informed that he was getting an FBI crew as clientele. He didn't blink an eye when Will asked if he'd allow him to look through their security footage. If the technical crew who handled their video surveillance didn't show up that afternoon, Will went on, would the manager let him check out the elevator cameras that evening?

The manager, Jonah Rumble, didn't mind. Will ran through the tapes from the night before and decided that nothing had been altered. Whoever had come to their door had clearly returned to a room in the hotel. Knowing that, he thanked the security man on duty, and the manager, then discreetly made a call to the office in Virginia.

Afterward, he found Kat waiting for him. She was talking with the manager and had obviously charmed him. But then, it seemed that his diminutive blonde counterpart had a way of charming everyone she met.

Maybe he should leave her to it. He should've been a lot more patient with Dr. McFarland but he *wasn't* a medical examiner; he'd just been around enough corpses now to know a few things. It frustrated him that he could make a few observations and discern that Brady had taken a beating, yet the expert missed what had been apparent to Will. That seemed inexcusable to him. And hiding his feelings was not Will's strong point.

He'd learn.

"Anything?" Kat asked politely as he joined them.

He shook his head.

Jonah, the manager, turned to him to apologize. "I'm

so sorry. I can only imagine that another guest was lost or disoriented, realized the mistake and moved on to his or her own room. In this day and age, we should probably have more security, but…we're a small hotel. We specialize in a business clientele and we seldom have even a minor disturbance. Mr. Harrison's been coming here for years, and truly, he's never had a problem. I understand that his office made your travel arrangements."

"The hotel is just great, and we're sorry to have disturbed you," Will said, glancing at Kat. "We truly enjoy it here."

"Well, thank you," Jonah said. "I assure you that we'll be vigilant as to the elevator cameras. Still, no harm was done."

"No harm at all," Will agreed pleasantly.

"Then, please, coffee is available in the lobby. And if you want to reach me, the reception staff can find me at any time, day or night."

Will thanked him, took Kat's elbow and led them toward the coffee.

"How'd I do?" he asked her.

"Suck up to a pathologist or a cop like that, and we'll have it made," she told him. "But shouldn't we get a list of hotel guests?"

He grinned. "Of course. I've called the higher-ups to see that we're given the list. If Adam makes the call, we won't have to hear about privacy laws and all that."

"Good thinking," she said.

Complimentary coffee was served out of a silver urn

on a marble counter by the restaurant. He poured them both a cup of coffee and offered her cream and sugar.

"I take it black," she said.

"We all do, I guess, with the places we go and the hours we keep," he murmured.

"You're right. I used to add cream," she said, heading toward the dining room.

He followed her. She was a strange choice for one of the Krewes, he thought. She was tiny—maybe five-four, and a hundred and five pounds. She was a blue-eyed blonde and looked like a little Russian fairy princess. Katya Sokolov was also a certified medical examiner. He'd always known that. It was her appearance and her manner that surprised him. She was just so…tiny and perfect.

Each Krewe member had a talent beyond that of communication with the dead. His was film and cameras—and determining what was illusion, what was reality. He knew that in the Texas Krewe, Sean Cameron was the video/film man, and of course, Sean's association with the documentary crew hired to film the salvage of the *Jerry McGuen* was why they were involved.

"I got a nice long email from Logan Raintree this morning. Research on the Egyptian Sand Diggers," she told him as they chose a table in the dining room.

"And?"

She drew out her phone and pulled up the email, not reading but checking it now and then as she spoke to him.

"The society was actually formed back in 1932. There've been many times that Egyptology was the rage, and even as we plunged into the Great Depression, this group raised money to find the ship. Through the years, many of the members have been high-ranking politicians, respected scientists, you name it. It's a private society—like the Masonic Order or the Shriners or Elks—that does community service. Their dinners and dances and events support major children's hospitals. Right now, they're busy supporting exploration in the pyramid of Cheops—or Khufu—one of the 'great' pyramids at Giza, built over four thousand years ago for the pharaoh. But they've also financed various expeditions and the preservation of Egyptian antiquities from the different kingdoms."

He nodded eagerly. "The Old Kingdom, which would be roughly the third millennium, leading up to the New Kingdom, the Greek and Roman periods, and then invasion by what we consider more or less modern Europeans. Ramses II, or Ramses the Great, was a nineteenth dynasty king and ruled from 1279 to 1213 BC."

"Yeah, he was a warrior king, and very nicely played by Yul Brynner in the old movie," Kat said. "He was considered a magnificent general and a good ruler, whether he did or didn't lose half his men when the Red Sea fell back after Moses. So Amun Mopat, as his high priest, is of tremendous interest to scholars." She grinned. "Those poor people in the Sand Diggers must have been cringing when the movie *Sam Stone and the*

Curious Case of the Egyptian Museum was originally made. A number of liberties were taken."

"Maybe they were upset, maybe not. Maybe they were happy to see some interest—any interest—in ancient Egypt. And maybe they enjoyed sharing their information. Just as they were probably happy to correct everyone when the press got it all wrong reporting on your last case in California."

"You know about that?"

He laughed. "I read the papers. Usually online, which means the New York, L.A., Chicago and London papers. I know the FBI is downplaying our part in the Hollywood case as much as possible, but if you're with a Krewe...well, you read between the lines. And I guess it must be somewhat disconcerting to go from Amun Mopat to...Amun Mopat."

"It's what we do, right?" She smiled, aware that she was paraphrasing an earlier remark of his.

"Yeah, it's what we do. And I love Egyptology," he said. "I'm looking forward to seeing the artifacts on that ship. *Especially* the mummy."

"I'm used to the dead. But I've never been asked to examine the remains of a mummy, although I know pathologists who have. I believe in speaking for the dead, but...I think my sympathies are with the people who died on the ship, rather than a priest who apparently lived well and had many convinced that he was all-powerful."

"And Brady Laurie?" he asked quietly.

"I know we're learning more about him. That he was determined to follow through on his discovery and that he might have had a temper and—in short—been human." She paused. "I really wanted his death to be an accident."

"But you don't buy that any more than I do," he said.

"No," she admitted.

"Okay, we'll figure out what went on," Will said solemnly. "And I'm intrigued by this group. Neither Amanda Channel nor Jon Hunt at the Preservation Center mentioned them to me. Then again, maybe they just dismiss them as amateurs."

"Yes, but the Sand Diggers are also avid—and scholarly," Kat said. "And apparently they do good works."

"Do we know where to find them?"

"Their meeting house is on Michigan Avenue," she told him. "We can start there, and if we don't find the two men Landry mentioned—Austin Miller and Dirk Manning—we can get information on their schedules. I'm sure Logan sent me their home addresses. I'll go through the notes again."

"Then I say we head over there after a lovely morning of diving!" Will said. "Hey, come on. How often will you see a freshly discovered shipwreck and treasure so far untouched?"

Only in my dreams, Kat thought. *Only in my... dreams.*

She realized that she dreaded seeing the *Jerry McGuen*.

No.

She dreaded discovering that she'd already seen it.

5

Kat remembered meeting Alan King, Bernie Firestone and Earl Candy in Texas, when she was involved in the case at the Longhorn Saloon. They'd been helpful, and they were interesting people—and friends of Sean Cameron's. She'd seen more of Bernie and Earl, but when the case came to its conclusion, she, Logan and the others had dinner with the group, and she'd enjoyed their company.

They all met at the docks. It was decided that Kat and Will would go out on the film crew's boat and meet up with the Preservation Center's boat at the dive site. Today's dive would be on video, from beginning to end.

Kat was glad. That meant lots of people in the water.

And it meant that *everything* would be on video.

Bernie Firestone was a man of about forty, pleasant, with graying hair and warm brown eyes. He greeted Kat with a crushing hug and called out to his main cameraman, "Earl! Dr. Sokolov is here. Agent Sokolov these days, right?"

"Yes, Bernie. Hey, Earl!"

She received an equally warm hug from Earl. He was stocky and shaggy-haired and reminded her of a teddy bear.

She'd only met Alan King, the billionaire producer, once, but he, too, was friendly when they greeted each other. Alan didn't look or behave like her idea of such a wealthy man. At the moment, he was in swim trunks and a worn T-shirt and his cap of white hair was unruly in the breeze.

He shook hands with her and Will, and thanked them for being there.

"Happy to," she murmured, feeling somewhat guilty. She didn't tell him that it hadn't been her choice.

"Amanda and Jon haven't arrived yet. You want to come into the cabin and have some coffee?" he asked.

"Sure, more coffee sounds great," Will said.

Kat wondered about the wisdom of that, considering they'd be spending time in dive suits, but she supposed one more cup couldn't hurt, and they'd have a chance to talk with the filmmakers for a few minutes.

The filmmakers had hired a charter out of Chicago, and the cabin wasn't luxurious but comfortable and well-appointed. The charter came with Captain Bob Green, who looked like he could've been whaling in New England a century earlier, and first mate Jimmy Green, his nephew, an eager young man in his early twenties. They went about their business on the boat, apparently unfazed by any rumors of a curse.

"You've had private security watching the site since

Brady Laurie was brought up, right?" Will asked as they sat at the galley table and Bernie got them coffee.

Alan King nodded.

"And?"

"Nothing. Well, boats on the lake, but nothing at the dive site," Alan said. "Thing is—it's a dive site. We can't station people 24/7 down at the wreck. And we can't stop other boats from being out on the lake. My people have reported curious boaters going by, but they just see them looking over, then moving on. Someone with the right equipment could anchor at another spot and go beneath the surface."

"That's true, but not so easy. You have to know how to dive, and you have to allow for air consumption," Will pointed out.

"It's not *that* deep," Earl Candy said, sitting next to Kat. "I was worried about this project, but you don't have to go below a hundred feet. When you think about it, it could have been a lot worse."

Alan turned to Kat. "You're a pathologist, Kat. You saw Brady Laurie. Are we being alarmists? *Did* he die by accident? We were down there, you know, when his body was discovered."

She hesitated. "Mr. King, I can't say for sure. There were some suspicious marks on the body that mean an investigation is in order."

"I heard a talk-radio show today." Alan sniffed impatiently. "The host had on half a dozen people who were convinced the 'curse' is real—that Amun Mopat hadn't wanted his tomb raided way back when, and that he doesn't want his watery grave disturbed. Half the guests on the show were convinced that Brady Laurie was killed by Amun Mopat."

"If there's one thing I'll say *didn't* happen—it's that a mummy came out of a sealed container and killed a guy!" Bernie said. Then he sighed. "But it doesn't mean that evil isn't alive. We all know it is. Evil exists in psychopaths the world over."

"Bernie, could you show me what kind of equipment you're working with?" Will asked. "Were you able to get the remotes I suggested?"

Bernie nodded. "Anything I film will show up on the screen over there," Bernie said, pointing at the console.

"We can rig up a remote camera, too, for when no one's down there?"

"I got the little remote casing yesterday afternoon," Bernie said. "Yeah, we can watch whatever goes on," he assured Will.

"And we have a videographer coming in from the Keys. He's done underwater work all over the world, so we'll be in good shape," Alan King told them.

Jimmy Green came halfway down the ladder to the cabin. "Your scientists are here, and they're getting ready to head out."

"Then we're ready to follow," Alan said.

Forty-five minutes later, they were at the dive site. They linked up with Alan King's security boat, a little cabin cruiser. The two men aboard looked more like surfers than security; they were both young and muscular, wearing swim trunks and Ts.

"All is well?" Alan called to them. The taller of the two gave him a thumbs-up.

To the east of them, the Preservation Center's boat drifted close, then anchored.

Kat realized that Will was standing next to her. He'd begun crawling into his wet suit and squeezed his arms and torso inside as he spoke softly to her. "The woman is Amanda Channel and her partner is Jon Hunt. They're the two main Egyptologists at the center."

"The two who found Brady Laurie," she whispered.

"Yes."

"Yoo-hoo!" Amanda sang out across the water. "We're going to do an assessment dive. We've got some netting and collection bags, and we'll probably pick up a few small pieces if we find any. Tomorrow, we'll bring the cranes and wrenches and go for the crates."

"All right, we're ready," Alan shouted. "But Jimmy Green is going down with us as dive master. We've had one death down there. Jimmy will be along for safety. When he says it's time to come up, it's time to come up. We can make a second dive this afternoon for more logistics and cataloging."

Amanda said something to Jon; she clearly wasn't happy about being told how to dive a wreck, even if her coworker had just died.

Kat started to gather her equipment. Earl was already suited up; Captain Bob was helping him with his tank, a distraction that didn't seem to bother Earl as he was busy rolling video. She hurriedly got into her booties, suit and slippers, added her weight belt, then checked her tank, opening the air gauge.

She'd tested it as recently as this morning.

Sitting, she slid into her BCV, which was attached to the tank. Jimmy came by to give her a hand up. The last thing she saw before she dived backward into the lake was Earl—filming her as she held her mask and light in place and went in.

Even wearing a full neoprene wet suit, gloves and booties beneath her flippers, Kat felt the shock of Lake Michigan's water the moment she hit the surface.

Because other divers were descending with her, she could see a strange array of colors as beams from the flashlights they wore strapped around their heads were darting in a number of directions. It seemed that a stream of dust motes—tiny bits of lake growth and remnants of anything left behind—danced in the shades of blue and green.

At thirty-three feet they made their first safety stop. Then again, at sixty-six.

Kat swallowed hard, clearing her ears.

They followed the anchor rope down. There were eight of them in all—dive master Jimmy Green, the three men working on the documentary, Amanda Channel and Jon Hunt, and Will and Kat. She tried to sort out who was who by the colors of their dive suits. It wasn't difficult to find Will; she could see his dark hair streaming like a strange halo around his head.

She released more air from her BCV, and her weight belt kicked in, helping to carry her ever deeper.

And then…

They were there.

When the massive hull of the *Jerry McGuen* first appeared, she had to admit it was an impressive sight. Long sea grass undulated around the ship's rusting hulk, along with denizens of the lake.

Despite storm damage and years of resting at the bottom, covered by silt, sand and muck, the *Jerry McGuen* still retained a majesty, a splendor. The hull was broken or rusted in many places. It was almost like looking at a stage or film set, Kat decided, because she could see into the grand salon and into what had once been elegant staterooms.

Amanda was in the lead, moving toward the cargo hold.

Kat found herself pausing by the grand salon. For a moment, she felt a sense of déjà vu that was almost overwhelming.

The massive staircase could still be seen. Pieces of glass from the wrecked chandelier were strewn about, picking up the divers' lights and glinting strangely on the shipwreck. Kat began mentally restoring the salon to its former grandeur—and thought she could see men and women in elegant bygone dress, sashaying along the floor.

Surely, she saw the couple who'd walked by her in the dream!

The room was at an angle in the thick muck of the lake bed, but her imaginary people floated along....

She felt and heard a tap on her tank and turned around. Will was studying her, his eyes piercing behind the glass of his mask. She gave a thumbs-up and followed him toward the others, who hovered around the hold.

The people she'd seen in her dream were long gone, if they had ever existed; predators, small and large, at the bottom of the lake effectively made sure of that.

Crates in some kind of tarps, astonishingly intact after all the years and the brutal effects of the cold water, were wedged here and there. Earl Candy watched as the divers made their way through the broken-out hull to view the contents.

The hold was massive; some watertight doors to other compartments stood ajar, while others remained closed. Bags of ballast sand had split apart in places, and smaller boxes and crates had shattered.

Something sparkled in the lake silt that now covered the floor of the hull. Kat was beside Will and touched his arm lightly before diving down to see what it was.

He followed her. Whatever glimmered was covered with growth, but Kat began to carefully dust away the sand, silt and zebra mussels. Will helped her, pausing for a moment to gesture at a metal box nearby that had opened. He moved to collect the box and returned, pointing at the lid. She realized it was thick, heavy wood and had withstood pressure, cold and water to survive. Of course, the lake, being freshwater, didn't have the bore worms that ate away at wooden artifacts that went down in the oceans and salt seas.

There were hieroglyphics still faintly discernible on the box. Will slid it into the netted bag he'd carried down, attached to his weight belt. She continued to work at the object that seemed imbedded in the ground. At last, still covered with grit and slime, it came free.

It was a dagger. And it would have fit perfectly into the box Will had retrieved.

She handed it to him, and he added it to the bag. Earl Candy turned the camera on the two of them. Will waved to the camera; she did the same.

Then Earl tapped his dive watch, pointing across the hold. Kat saw that Jimmy had tapped on his tank, informing them that they were to surface.

Will nodded. Earl gave a kick and went over to Amanda and Jon, who were working with waterproof charts, cataloging everything they saw. Amanda looked stubbornly at her own watch, but Jon sent her a fierce frown.

None of them could—or should—forget Brady Laurie.

They made the appropriate stops, using the anchor chain as their guide. As they surfaced, they all returned to Captain Bob's boat.

Jimmy came up first and was soon ready to help the other divers shed their gear.

For a while, the conversation was excited and coming from everyone at once.

"Oh, my God! It's spectacular!" Amanda was saying.

"There's so much left!" Jon agreed.

"Definitely a historic moment," Alan said.

"I got really great film. My God, when it just suddenly appears there in the green darkness, it's *awesome!*" Earl was already filming them on deck as they talked about the discovery.

"Look what I brought up!" Amanda said, walking toward him. She had a box of specially treated cloths and she took one, using it to lift one of the little objects she'd found. "Thank God stone preserves so well! These are what they call *shabti* statues. Some tombs had over four hundred of them. They represent slaves or workers who would do menial tasks for kings and priests who passed into new lives. They're very hard to see clearly now, because they have to be cleaned. We're setting them in water again until we get them to the center for proper preservation."

"We found a box and a dagger," Will volunteered, taking one of the specially treated cloths Amanda had used before reaching into his net bag. "I can't read hieroglyphics, but whatever dye they used to stain the box is still visible. And the dagger appears to be jewel-encrusted. There's shell attached, but I assume the center will know what to do."

"You found *that?*" Amanda asked.

"I found the box. Kat found the dagger," Will said.

"And you *touched* them?" Amanda asked incredulously. She spun around, telling Earl, "Get that camera off now!" She pushed him when he didn't move quickly enough. She whirled to face Will and Kat. "This is an historic expedition. What's the matter with you? You are not trained or equipped to handle treasure!"

Will's face didn't betray an ounce of emotion. "Dr. Channel," he said, "I may not have your training, but I've dived many a wreck. We were gloved down there, just as you were. If you're disappointed that the value of the dagger outweighs that of the three *shabti* pieces, I'm sorry. But you will not be able to do this on your own, and if I understand correctly, you barely have permission from the State of Illinois to control this dive site. Only Alan King's promise of a complete record of the event has allowed you to rush it through. And Mr. King has asked us to work along with you. I'm sorry if this disturbs any of your proprietary feelings about the search, but we are here, we will remain here, and if we're able to find any artifacts—which will go into the same cache as those you bring up yourself—we will continue to do so."

"Agent Chan! I am a highly trained historian and scientist!" Amanda snapped.

Jon was behind her by then, but Amanda kept spewing her venom. "You are nothing but a government lackey, here for a ridiculous purpose. And pseudo-

Egyptologist though you might be, you're endangering treasure! You will not pick anything up!"

Alan walked over to Amanda. "What did either of the agents do that could be perceived as any different from what you've done?"

"Why, why—they're trying to pocket treasure!"

"If we were trying to pocket treasure, Dr. Channel," Kat said indignantly, "why would we produce it for a camera?"

"Hey, everyone!" Jon Hunt cried. "Amanda, they didn't do anything at all. As long as items are treated tenderly the minute they reach the surface—and only extracted when they can be easily picked up—there's absolutely no harm done. Come on, let's be honest. That dagger's a beauty. I wish I'd found it."

"Dr. Channel, there are dozens of organizations and companies I could finance on this dig," King said politely.

Kat thought that Amanda was about to stomp her feet.

She smiled at the woman. "Will may be an amateur Egyptologist, but if so, I imagine he has the knowledge to rival many a person who's doing it for a living. As for me, I despise mummies, so I will certainly never be stealing anyone's treasure—or thunder, for that matter."

"Please!" Jon said. "You—"

"Fine!" Amanda broke in. "Will you at least let us return the objects to cold water until we're back in the lab?"

Will handed over the dagger and its box. Carefully. Jon was still staring at Amanda; she caught his stare and flushed. "Look, I'm sorry. You just can't imagine what this means to us. Forgive me, all of you. Mr. King, I'm really grateful. But…what happened to Brady—it was an accident. I feel horrible, but…"

Her voice trailed off. Kat wondered just how bad the woman really felt. Her coworker hadn't been dead for even forty-eight hours.

But then, maybe Brady Laurie would've acted the same way. Maybe to him the discovery had been everything, as well.

"Let's take an hour or so to eat, relax, chill out," Bernie Firestone suggested.

"I had Jimmy stock us a galley full of good sandwich stuff," Captain Bob said. "I say let's relax so we can get into the second set of tanks this afternoon and take another dive!"

"Turn the camera back on," Bernie told Earl.

The others were starting down to the galley. Earl paused in front of Kat. "I never turned it off!" he whispered. "Great shots of a diva!" Winking, he walked on.

Only Will was left topside. He grinned at her. "Thanks."

She shrugged. "Can't have a team member attacked," she said.

An hour later they were back in the water on their second dive. This time, Alan King had said everyone was to see what he or she could bring up safely and easily. He'd mollified Amanda by letting her give them a lesson in the collection and care of artifacts. It was mostly common sense, but Kat listened to her drone on.

"Some of the pieces we were able to pick up today," she said, "were accessible because of the storm and the shifting sands that more or less righted the *Jerry McGuen*. When something that size shifts through the power of wind and water, things are going to crash around and get broken. So there may be a lot of little treasures we can find. In fact, we probably need a few more days with handheld vacuum sifters to make sure we don't wreck anything small and precious while we're going for the big stuff. Also, according to federal law, the ship and its cargo belong to the State of Illinois until it goes through all the courts, so we don't want to do anything that will bother state officials."

Like kill a man, Kat couldn't help thinking.

She stayed silent and apparently attentive, as did Will.

Soon they were heading back down.

Divers always checked their tanks before donning them. She saw Will looking at her as she checked hers, arching a brow.

She smiled, and arched a brow in return.

In truth, it wasn't that she didn't appreciate the fact that they were bringing up treasure from millennia ago. What a marvel that such artistic objects could have survived time and the deep cold waters of Lake Michigan.

But once again she was drawn to the broken-out part of the hull that seemed to be a window into the grand salon. She could see where the deck had been, and where a large gash had been ripped in it. Staring into the salon, seeing the ghostly wreckage that remained and remembering what she'd seen in a dream, she found herself thinking of the cold that had suddenly come to her. The ridiculously low temperature of her hotel bedroom had surely brought on that vision! But in her dream the couple had passed her, and then she'd turned to look out at the sea again.

There had been a nebulous shape, huge against the ice storm that was coming and the strange light and darkness created by the full moon.

She realized that while the other divers had moved on, toward the hold, Will was waiting for her. Again, she noticed his striking eyes behind his mask. He was watching—and wondering what she saw.

He sensed she was seeing something, and that made her oddly uneasy.

She turned away from the salon and smiled around her regulator. She let out a little more air from her BCV and kicked her fins slightly, passing him. He followed.

Amanda had her waterproof chart and marker dangling from her belt; she hadn't forgotten the observations she wanted to make.

But she seemed more obsessed with finding little treasures that had, most probably, fallen from various containers when the *Jerry McGuen* shifted. She was studiously examining the silted flooring of the ship.

This time, Kat took a good look at the cargo hold. The ship had been built with the customary precautions, bulkhead doors to prevent flooding from one compartment to another. Some were closed tight, Kat saw, and she assumed that what lay behind those doors would be well preserved. Some were just ajar.

The real work of salvage would take months. Maybe even years. But the others were busy picking up whatever fragments they could find in the sand, and she went to work with them until Will nudged her, pointing to Jimmy, who was tapping his watch. She checked her air gauge and knew he was enforcing a safety time with a few extra minutes. She had no urge to argue.

Once again, they began their ascent.

When they surfaced, Amanda was ecstatic at the amount they'd brought up. She talked to the camera, describing their findings, talking about what might still remain and what had probably been lost. But they were walking into a time machine, recovering treasures from the days of Ramses II that had been lost during the Victorian era.

As far as any threat of danger went, the day had been entirely calm.

The only upset was caused by Amanda, who wanted to dive again. She was argued down by Alan King; he warned her that they were looking at months of work, and that while she might have the stamina, he didn't.

"But we need to work quickly. There's so much that could be stolen by other divers!" Amanda protested.

"We have a boat guarding the area. I have men continually coming and going from the boat so they're alert and ready. They're all licensed divers and licensed security," Alan said. "We've been given this chance, and others haven't. Let's take it slowly and carefully," he advised her.

"But—"

"We're in it for the long haul," Alan said firmly.

Will sat next to Kat. He was quiet, his expression solemn. She imagined that he was inwardly smirking.

"Amanda, look at the many treasures you'll have to study every night," Kat said.

To her surprise, the woman cast her an angry glare. "It's the integrity of the situation!"

"Something I mean to maintain." Alan didn't raise his voice but his determination was unmistakable.

Kat glanced over at Earl. He wasn't aiming the camera at Amanda. Kat was certain Amanda had no idea she was being filmed, but she could see the little red light; Earl hadn't let a minute of her argumentative behavior slip by unrecorded.

Jon spoke up quietly. "Amanda, we're lucky to be where we are. This whole thing's in court—to decide exactly what our percentage will be and how the salvage will be handled. In the meantime, we're here at all because of who we are—and because we're documenting everything so carefully. Let's enjoy the process, huh?"

"I thought it was a great dive!" Jimmy Green said cheerfully.

Kat watched the Chicago shore and its renowned skyline as they motored back in. She could see the various harbors and, to her right, the peninsula with the Shedd Aquarium and, beyond that, the magnificent skyscrapers. *The city was beautiful,* she thought. "City of the big shoulders"—she remembered from an American lit course that this was how the poet Carl Sandburg had described it.

And the lake, so beautiful, too, was part of the history and grandeur of the city. It had been treacherous throughout history. Ships caught in storms had gone down since the days of earliest discovery.

Because of weather. Or collisions. Or...

She recalled her dream. Night on almost any body of water could be dangerous. Storms could be killers. And yet...

What was it that she'd seen in the dream? The large black thing that had loomed up suddenly from the depths? Did it mean anything?

No, it had been a dream. Just a dream.

They arrived back at the wharf late afternoon. Will was impatient to leave, wanting to visit the office of the Egyptian Sand Diggers, and they set off as soon as they'd divested themselves of their diving equipment. They returned to the hotel briefly to shower and change, then made their way to Michigan Avenue.

He found parking nearby and they walked down the

street until they reached the address—a building that had a historical marker. They paused together to read it. The Shelby-Turner House. This Colonial Greek manor was built for the fur-trader Angus Turner in 1859. Purchased by the Shelby family in 1880, it was donated to the Society of Egyptian Sand Diggers in 1932.

They walked up the steps to the door. Will lifted the heavy brass knocker, and Kat almost jumped when a little peep-door above her head slid open and a pair of bright blue eyes surrounded by wrinkles stared out at her.

"Password!"

Surprised, Kat turned to Will.

"Um, Ramses?" Will asked.

The door started to close.

"How about FBI?"

"FBI!" the voice repeated.

The door opened. The man with the bright blue eyes was short and wizened but had the kindly, bearded face of a Santa Claus. "You're with the FBI? And you need to speak with *us?*" Before they could answer, he hurried on. "Welcome, FBI. Which one of you is *F* and which is *B* and where is *I?*" He chuckled at his own humor. "Sorry, couldn't resist. I'm Dirk Manning. President of the society, or Grand Vizier as we call it here in old Cairo!"

"May we speak with you?" Kat said. "I'm Agent Kat Sokolov and this is Agent Will Chan."

"Come in, Agents. I'm alone here right now. We can

talk in the parlor. Can I get you something to drink? You're on duty, of course—coffee? I always have a pot brewing."

Kat started to say no, but Will said, "We'd love some coffee. Can we help you?"

"I may be old, but I can pour coffee," Manning told them, grinning. "But come along, follow me. You can see a bit of the place."

The house had beautiful columns, a grand entry and a staircase that led to a balcony above. There were Egyptian pieces *everywhere,* covering the walls, in display cases here and there, standing sarcophagi, statues, death masks. Manning led them through the entry to an elegantly appointed parlor and, beyond that, a dining room that could easily fit thirty people and finally into a large kitchen. Even there, the wallpaper featured a series of hieroglyphics.

"This is…quite a place," Kat commented.

"Yes, I daresay. Some of the pieces—the ones we've locked up—are real. Most of the others are copies of famous artifacts like the Tutankhamun death mask." Manning winked at her. "We have some pieces of old Chicago history, too. Did you know that the city was originally called Chigagou, which means 'wild garlic place'? Father Jacques Marquette and Louis Jolliet were the first to meet with the Illinois Indians and map the area. They weren't the first to *see* it, but it was thanks to Jolliet's foresight that the canals were dug. That's what made Chicago—to my biased mind, anyway—the greatest city in the Midwest. At first, there were twenty miles of swamp and slush surrounding the lake. That had to be drained. Oh, and once upon a time that—" he gestured vaguely in the direction of the lake "—was known as Lake Chicago. Then Michigan won out. Oh, well, Michigan's a beautiful state!"

There was a large old butcher-block table in the center of the kitchen with chairs around it. Will pulled one out for Kat, then sat beside her. The kitchen did seem a cozy place to talk, but she doubted they'd have to do much talking to get information from Dirk Manning.

"So. I guess you didn't come to hear about Chicago's history," Manning said, growing serious as he sat across from them.

"Mr. Manning, we understand you had a party during which the society tried to encourage salvagers and divers to look for the *Jerry McGuen*," Kat began.

"We did, we did! We invited archaeologists, salvage companies, film companies, divers we knew, charter captains…. Brady Laurie wasn't the only one to suspect that our last massive storm might have shifted things in the lake," Manning said. He shook his grizzled head slowly. "Brady was already working on that principle. A brilliant young man! We were trying to recruit him into our ranks." He made a face. "He wasn't like that skinny little witch, Amanda. He *wanted* to be a member. He told us that all history and investigation demanded scrutiny, and he believed that we loved the subject almost as much as he did. Sure, it's not our vocation or our job—more like an avocation. Actually, keeping up this place is my job right now, but then I'm retired. Ah, I'm so sorry about that boy." He shook his head. "Brady drowned. What does the FBI have to do with it? Ah! Black market!"

"Things haven't gotten that far yet, Mr. Manning," Will was saying. "We're trying to find out if anyone else was going for the treasure."

"What makes you think that?"

Some of Manning's statements, like his insistence that Brady was practically one of them, contradicted what Landry had said, but Kat decided not to deflect the old man from his train of thought. Besides, Landry might well have his own agenda.

"We think someone might have helped Brady drown," Kat said.

Manning shuddered visibly. "Oh, dear God! That's horrible."

"Yes, but we'd like to eliminate the possibility if we can—make sure no one out there is killing for the treasure…or the history," Will said. "That's why we need your assistance."

"Well, we tried to get everyone interested in the shipwreck," Manning told them. "Hmm. I was doing a lot of interviews with the press that night. If you want to know who really talked to our guests, it's my dear friend Austin Miller."

"We'd love to talk to him," Kat said.

"I'll give him a call."

To her astonishment, the Santa-looking man whipped out the newest smartphone on the market and hit speed dial. A moment later he frowned.

"What's wrong?" Will asked.

"I've been trying to reach Austin for the past few days. He hasn't returned my calls."

"Maybe we should just drop by," Kat suggested.

Manning nodded distractedly. "I'll go with you."

"Sir, we didn't mean—"

"If he doesn't open the door, I can let you in," Manning said. "I have a key. I feed his cat when he's off on a jaunt." He smiled, then grew somber again. "I guess I'm a little worried. He's an old codger like me. At any rate, the house isn't far."

Manning was, for whatever his age might be, surprisingly agile and quick. He ushered them out, setting the alarm and locking the door, then marched purposefully down the street. Austin Miller's house, a few blocks from the society's headquarters, was similar—historic, beautiful, well-preserved. Situated on a corner lot, it was surrounded by a stone wall. Lovingly tended gardens and patios were visible through the wrought-iron gate.

"Austin, Austin, you old coot! It's me, Dirk!" Manning said, talking into the speaker at the gate.

There was no reply.

"Humph!" Manning pulled out his key chain, sorted through several keys until he found the one he was looking for and opened the gate. They followed him up a long walk to a porch and then a massive front door. There, Dirk Manning rang the bell and pounded on the door. His expression became more and more concerned.

"I heard something," Kat said.

They were still for a minute. She heard the noise again and realized it was a cat's meow.

"Bastet," Manning murmured. "His cat. She sounds...hungry!"

He opened the front door, and they stood in the entry, gazing around them. The house was exceptionally handsome, designed when molding was an art. There were numerous pieces of Egyptology as decoration, but the house also stood as homage to the Victorian era, rich with dark woods, a grand chandelier, an elegant staircase. They saw no sign of the cat.

The air conditioner was running, and Kat thought she detected a faint odor. She immediately felt a sense of dread.

"Austin! Hey, old man!"

No answer.

"Where's his bedroom?" Will asked.

"Upstairs. But his gentleman's den is just through that door to our left," Manning said.

Kat and Will strode to the door. Will opened it.

The odor Kat knew all too well became intense.

At first, nothing seemed to be in disarray. Then she saw that the desk chair had fallen backward, and although she knew they were too late, she rushed around the desk.

They'd found Austin Miller.

6

Dirk Manning hadn't just led them to Austin Miller's house, he'd insisted on coming. That could have made him an instant suspect.

But Will had to hold Manning back when they found the corpse of Austin Miller. To all appearances, he'd had a heart attack while sitting at his desk. The massive explosion of pain had, it seemed, sent Miller falling backward in his chair. A pill vial lay on the floor near his right hand with tiny white capsules of what was probably digitalis scattered around it.

Kat glanced at Will and left him to deal with Manning as she carefully made her way to the body. She went down on her knees by Austin Miller's side. Looking at her and then the corpse, Will saw that Miller's eyes remained wide open.

"Dial 9-1-1," she said quietly.

"He can be helped!" Manning cried.

"No, Mr. Manning, I'm so sorry," Kat said. "He's… gone. I'd say he's been dead a few days, but I don't have any equipment with me to figure out a more precise time. And, of course, the authorities must be alerted."

"Austin!" Manning wailed.

There were tears not just in his bright blue eyes but streaming down his face. Will placed an arm around his shoulders, trying to turn him so he could lead him from the room. "Mr. Manning, you don't need to be in here right now."

"Wait!"

"What is it?" Will asked him gently.

"Horus!"

"Pardon?"

"Horus—there was a statue of Horus that always sat on Austin's desk. It's not there!"

"I'll look for it," Will said.

"You don't understand. That old codger and I knew each other since we were kids. He was like my big brother. The statue was his father's and his grandfather's before that—he said that it would sit there for all of eternity. He wouldn't have moved it," Manning insisted. "He wouldn't have moved it. He wouldn't have moved it."

Will exchanged a glance with Kat. Then he urged Manning out of the room, steering him to a large upholstered chair tucked against the wall beneath the stairway. "Mr. Manning, sit tight. I'll look for the statue. First thing, though, we've got to get the authorities out here." He'd pulled his phone from his pockct and, while he kept an eye on Manning, started to dial 9-1-1 but then stopped. Instead, he called the police station they'd visited and asked to speak to Sergeant Riley.

When Riley came on, he explained where they were and what they'd found.

"I've seen the old guy written up in newspaper articles and on local broadcasts now and then," Riley said. "I'm sorry to hear about his death—but why are you calling me about an elderly man dying of a heart attack?"

"I want you to come out and investigate it."

"I'll come, but we don't really investigate heart attacks when they happen to a man his age," Riley said.

"What if it was caused?"

"A drowning was *caused* and a heart attack is *caused*?" Riley asked skeptically.

"What better way to commit murder?" Will asked in return. "Sergeant, please. I'm afraid these deaths may be the start of something even more sinister. I'd like it if you could pull some rank on this. We're here on behalf of a friend, but I'll get my superiors to see that the governor asks us in. Until then…help us out, will you?"

Riley agreed, promising that he'd send a medical examiner's van and ensure that the scene wasn't trashed. Patting the still-crying Manning on the knee, Will stood and moved away, calling his own boss, Jackson Crow. Jack would talk to Adam Harrison, who'd get them the authority to take over the investigation, which would include *any* mysterious deaths surrounding the discovery of the *Jerry McGuen*. "You want to stay on this?"

Jackson asked. "Logan and part of his crew should be arriving soon."

"I started with it, so yeah, I'd like to see it through."

"Fine. How is working with a new agent?"

Will hesitated, slightly amused. "Okay. At first I felt like I was working with Tinker Bell. Now…she's all right."

By the time he hung up, he could hear a siren. The sound seemed to make Manning, if anything, more miserable.

"They'll be coming for me soon," he muttered. "My oldest, dearest friend is gone. I guess I'm going to be next."

"Mr. Manning, you're in great shape and you have a lot of wit and knowledge to continue offering the world. Plan on many more years with old friends—and not-so-old friends," Will said.

They'd left the gate unlocked. Will was gratified to see that Riley had sent two officers to secure the scene. They didn't go into the den but one stood by the door and the other came over and asked Manning if he needed any assistance.

Will was free to return to the den. He paused in the doorway, trying to absorb everything in the room.

The French doors that led out to the patio were open; a breeze was rustling the curtains. Someone could have come in through the patio. Will had noticed a security system control pad near the front entrance, but it hadn't been set. Maybe Austin Miller typically set it just before he went to bed.

The cat, a slender animal with spotted fur, suddenly jumped over Will's foot and stalked into the center of the room, meowing loudly.

If only she could talk! Will thought.

"Was it a heart attack?" he asked.

Kat looked up at him. "It appears so, but…this is Chicago jurisdiction," she said.

"I have Jackson Crow getting Adam to arrange an official invitation for us," he told her. "That'll give you leave to do the autopsy."

Kat stood with a shrug. "We don't have authority yet. When an M.E. gets here, it's going to be his or her responsibility."

"But you can be at the autopsy?"

She nodded. "The thing is, I suspect we'll find out that it *was* a heart attack. Another 'accidental' death."

"So you don't think it was accidental?"

"No. It looks to me as if something terrified him. He knew his heart would give out and reached for his pills, but…I think they were knocked out of his hand. And then whoever, or whatever, watched him die."

The cat meowed again.

"She—Bastet—must be hungry," Kat said.

"And she must be something of a guardian cat, too," Will noted. "She could've left anytime, because the French doors over there are open. But she stayed inside screaming, wanting someone to come and take care of her master."

"I know." Kat's eyes were sad.

"Have you seen any other disturbance in the room?" Will asked.

She shook her head, and Will moved across the room, exiting onto the stone patio with its wrought-iron chairs and a table with a colorful umbrella. Beyond it was lawn and then the walls and the walkway, all bordered by trees and bushes. The wall wasn't particularly high, maybe five feet or so. It would've been easy for anyone to slip over. But to have come straight to the open doors of Austin Miller's den, the intruder would've needed to know not only the garden but the house. Whoever it was had escaped without being seen. Will walked through the yard, looking for any kind of evidence that anyone had been there—impressions in the soil, broken twigs, fibers caught on the stones. He heard himself hailed as he walked along the wall.

Sergeant Riley had arrived, and a medical examiner's van and a hearse had driven up outside the gate. Will hurried over to greet Riley.

"I'll make an initial report," Riley said, "but we've got a man from the Chicago morgue to see to the body."

"Is it McFarland?" Will asked, hoping not.

"No, one of our most senior men, and he knows you want your pathologist on it. So if the call comes in from the governor that the feds can have the case, Dr.

Randall won't care. You really think it was more than a heart attack?"

"I think it was a heart attack—I just think something led up to it," Will said. "Can we tape off the house?"

"The whole house?"

"I believe someone was in there with him."

"Sure. Tape is cheap." Riley shrugged. "I'll go in and get things started. You're lucky I happen to be the one on this," he said wryly. "Since it looks like a natural death."

"I am lucky. Thanks," Will told him. Because of Kat, he was trying to be courteous, to show his appreciation. He knew very well that courtesy was the way to deal with other authority figures, witnesses or anyone else they might need, and he usually treated them politely. McFarland had just gotten to him, wanting to close the case so quickly.

He resumed his inspection of the wall, confident that Kat could handle whatever was happening inside.

The yard was large, at least an acre, and the wall encompassed the whole area. He finished walking around it once. He'd noticed nothing unusual and was frustrated, thinking he must have missed something.

He started again.

And then he found it.

He was about five feet from the corner, to the side of the main entry and the walkway to the front door. A car parked on the side street, he noted, would not be seen from the front, and the street would be dark at night.

There were also a number of large oaks along the pathway, and they would have provided shelter and shadows.

What he'd found told him he was right.

There was a bit of musty old gauze wrapping on the outside of the wall, caught on a snag. It resembled the mummy wrappings of many an old horror flick.

It was the same as the one he'd discovered in the corridor at the hotel.

And near it, something lay shattered by the wall. The statue of Horus.

Looked like the mummy had done it.

Kat wanted to be alone with the body.

But they were still in Chicago, they were guests here, and she was fortunate that Dr. Randall was inviting her to perform the autopsy with him.

She was at the morgue in a white jacket, her hair pinned into a cap, mask covering her nose and mouth. Austin Miller's body temperature and lack of rigor led her to the conclusion that he'd died two days earlier, sometime between 8:00 p.m. and 5:00 a.m.—just hours before Brady Laurie had met his end. The stomach contents of the deceased might tell them more if they considered the time of his last meal, along with his known eating habits.

She had expected more resistance from those working with her; after all, Austin Miller had been elderly and he'd been on heart medications. But it seemed that buzz about the "curse" was circulating and everyone, especially Dr. Cranston Randall, seemed ready to help her. It wasn't that anyone *believed* in the curse, but it was titillating to think about.

To her relief, she hadn't seen McFarland since she'd come back. Dr. Randall was attending with her, and assistants came and went. Other corpses were due for autopsy as well, despite the late hour.

So far Austin Miller had been disrobed, bathed and photographed. The call had gone to all the proper authorities, allowing her and Will to take over the investigation. No one seemed disturbed by that—but then no one was convinced that any crimes had been committed.

"To see for oneself," Dr. Randall murmured.

"Autopsy? The word's from the Greek *autopsia* and means 'the act of seeing with one's own eyes,'" she said. "Is that what you're referring to?" She was never sure if it was because she was a woman, or because she was small and blonde and fair that people always seemed to doubt her credentials.

"I wasn't testing you," Randall said. "I was just wondering *what* we might see for ourselves, what truth lies below the surface."

They'd just finished the external examination of the body. She paused before going any further. "There's a bruise rising on his right arm."

"So there is," Randall agreed. He picked up the camera again, taking several shots of the area. "Almost like a defensive wound, as if he lifted that arm to ward someone off."

"That's what I was thinking."

"But there are no other external marks on the body. Poor fellow, his feet weren't in great shape, but he wasn't overweight."

Kat had his medical records on her chart so she knew he hadn't suffered from diabetes. Other than his heart medications, not surprising for a man his age, he'd been in excellent health.

"He was fit—until he was dead," Dr. Randall said drily.

"Shall we open him up now?" Kat asked.

"Be my guest."

She took her own scalpel and began the classic Y incision, beginning at the upper left chest and bringing the angle down to the tip of the sternum, then repeating the action from the right, intersecting at the xiphoid process. Her incision extended downward to the symphysis pubis, just above the genital region, curving around the navel. She was always careful; a cut that went too deep could compromise the organs. Just as carefully, she lifted the flaps of skin and subcutaneous fat.

"Beautiful incisions," Randall said.

Soon, the musculoskeletal structure was visible.

"No past fractures apparent in any of the ribs," she noted.

She went on to make notations regarding the organs.

Randall came forward with the rib cutters and freed the sternum and ribs and removed them.

It was usual procedure for the heart to be the first organ examined, which answered their questions immediately. Kat inspected and cut the pericardium. The damage there was acute.

"Heart failure," Randall said.

She looked across at him and nodded.

The removal of the heart showed further sudden and massive damage, but not the kind of fluid accumulation that would indicate he'd been shoved in the chest or struck with a blunt object. Kat hadn't expected anything else, nor did she expect to find injury—other than the wear and tear of age—to any of the other organs. The stomach interested her the most. She and Randall studied the contents together. "Looks like fish and greens, probably consumed about five hours prior to death," he said.

"According to his good friend Dirk Manning, he was punctual with his evening meal. He ate at precisely seven every evening, so that puts his death right around midnight," Kat told him.

"I agree with you, Dr. Sokolov." Randall turned to her. "We found what you were expecting. I can finish up for you if you wish, and I promise I'll be thorough and take every possible sample for analysis." He smiled. "You look as if you're going to drop."

"That bad?"

"Ah, my dear, youth is beautiful—you could never look bad. But you do look exhausted."

She *was* exhausted. And she liked Randall's comfort with his profession, his unassuming competence, his ease with those around him.

"I'll take you up on that offer," she said, adding, "My colleagues may want to see him tomorrow."

"No problem."

Kat left him, shedding her scrubs and washing up. She'd accompanied the body, and Will Chan had stayed at the house. Some of her own Krewe might have arrived by now, but when she went to Randall's office to get her purse, she hesitated only a minute before dialing Will Chan's number.

"Hey. You done already? I thought an autopsy took longer," he said.

"Randall is finishing up. I pretty much found what I was looking for. There were no evident poisons in the stomach, but it'll take a while to get the labs back. I believe he was frightened to death."

"Someone was definitely here," Will told her.

"How do you know?"

"I'll show you. You ready for a ride?"

"Yeah, thanks."

Fifteen minutes later, he drove by the morgue. "You look like hell," he said as she slid into the front seat.

Did people have to keep telling her this?

"That's not a pickup line of yours, is it? If so, it's not a good one."

He laughed. "Sorry. Exhausted, is that better?"

"I am tired. But what did you find?"

He motioned to the glove compartment. She opened it and drew out a plastic bag, then looked at him with a gasp. "It's more of the...mummy stuff!"

"Yep."

"Where did you—"

"On the outside of the stone wall. I believe someone dressed up as a mummy and went after Austin Miller. It had to be someone who knew his habits—where to go and what time. And that he didn't put on the alarm until he went to bed."

"It should actually be easy to figure out who this person is. Someone who dives, knows all about Egyptology, knew Austin Miller and has a boat, or an accomplice with a boat." She paused. "Of course, we're still going on our assumptions."

He turned the corner to reach their hotel before speaking again. "Educated assumptions. Or theories or guesses, whatever. We need to spend more time in the house. I think we may find clues among Austin Miller's papers. Thankfully he wasn't as up-to-date on technology as his good friend Dirk Manning. He didn't even have a computer that I could see. He did have dozens of ledgers, and pages and pages of notes. Also, one of those bookcases was filled with journals written by his father and grandfather."

Something touched Kat's shoulder. Something furry. She let out a startled scream.

"Oh! Sorry," Will said.

"What the—" As she spoke, the furry thing leaped into her lap. It was Bastet, Austin Miller's cat.

She stared at Will.

He shrugged. "What was I supposed to do? The place is locked up tight and I've had them cordon off the whole house, all around the wall, because I don't want visitors—like whoever did the old fellow in."

The cat purred and sat calmly on her lap.

"What are we going to do with a cat?" she asked.

"Hey, I brought the litter box."

"She's your responsibility. I'm a dog person. I mean, if I had a pet, it would be a dog," Kat told him.

"That's an Egyptian Mau—an expensive cat, I'll have you know."

The animal was still happily purring.

"I keep feeling she wants to tell us something," Will said. He gazed straight ahead. "Did you feel that…Austin Miller might be of any help?"

"Not tonight." She hesitated, stroking the cat's sleek head. "I've rarely had anyone speak in the middle of an autopsy. Maybe the soul gets stronger—and stays away from that agony."

"I want to get back in that house," he said. "And I want to go to a meeting of the Egyptian Sand Diggers."

"Did Austin Miller remain there?" she asked. "In his house?"

"I don't know. There were too many people. Riley is a really good guy. He kept everyone away from the death scene—except, of course, the pathology team that was with you when the body was removed. But there were officers inspecting the alarm system and generally milling around. We can find out tomorrow."

"But you want to dive in the morning," she said.

"Yes. I think it's important we be there for the next few days." He suddenly pulled the car to the curb. They were close to the hotel, and she had no idea why he'd stopped.

Bastet curled up on her lap, still purring.

"What?" she asked him.

"Every time we go down to the ship, you stare at the grand salon. Why?"

"The ship's impressive."

He smiled. "You don't lie well, you know."

"What do you mean? The ship *isn't* impressive?"

His smile deepened and he leaned back in the seat. "There's a reason."

"It may be nothing."

He leaned toward her, touching her hand where it lay on the cat's soft fur. "In our world, nothing is rarely nothing. Please, tell me."

"It just seems kind of…well, ridiculous. And maybe it shouldn't." She closed her eyes for a moment. "I feel like I've always seen the dead—which of course doesn't mean that I see *every* dead person. Or that I can pull out a cell phone and dial a ghost. I'm accustomed to seeking them out or having them come to me when we can help them, but I've never had precognitive dreams or visions of the past."

"But now you did?"

"At first, none of it connected. At first all I could think of was how horrified I felt. In L.A. we nearly lost a young woman because of a movie made in the forties—about a murderous high priest named Amun Mopat. You're aware of all this, right? Well, what I *didn't* know was that the author of the screenplay had used a real entity. So, all I could think was, Oh, Lord, you have to be kidding me, not the mummy of that creep! But the night before Logan talked to me, I dreamed I was on a ship and people in Victorian dress were dancing and music was playing, and then...a storm came up."

"A storm destroyed the *Jerry McGuen,*" Will said.

"But in my dream, a couple moved past me, and they were talking about the *curse.* And when we went down to the wreck, I wasn't dreaming, and it wasn't real, but in my mind's eye, I could almost see the ship as I'd seen it in my dream."

"What you see in your subconscious can be important. I know that you're thinking, *Ugh, mummy. Extra ugh, mummy of Amun Mopat.* But maybe we should be looking more at the ship. I don't believe the ship went down because it was cursed or because it carried an Egyptian mummy. I'm not saying that. But maybe there was more to the ship herself. Do you remember anything else about the dream?"

"Yes, actually," she said, petting the cat absently. "I

dreamed that something massive seemed to be coming out of the night and out of the storm. That it was coming toward the ship. Amun Mopat's 'curse,' maybe, except I don't believe in curses, either. I'm a big proponent of the free will concept. But I *do* believe we can fulfill expectations and, for some people, a curse might be an expectation."

"Also known as self-fulfilling prophecies," he murmured. "I'm with you on that. Have you dreamed about this?"

She laughed. "No, although I did have another dream. A typical *The Mummy* dream. I was walking or floating somewhere and suddenly an army of mummies was coming at me. I became pathologist Katya Sokolov in the dream, telling myself I was in no danger because a mummy was brittle and would break when I punched it. But Amun Mopat was behind the mummies, and the mummies didn't break. And then I woke up."

He was silent for a minute.

"I told you—silly dream," she said.

"It's not silly. I think our dreams may be part of how we communicate with ghosts—or souls that still have to depart the earth or this plane or whatever. They talk to us and show us things while we're in a state of unconsciousness, or a different consciousness if you prefer. If you dream again, write it all down as soon as you wake up."

"You're probably right," she said. "I know that in Texas, one of my team members, Kelsey, kept having strange dreams and visions of events that had gone on years before—and they did lead her to the truth. It's just that dreams like this aren't…well, conducive to good sleep!"

He laughed and reached over, ruffling her hair. It began as a friendly gesture, but his hand lingered and his eyes were on hers for a moment. She suddenly remembered how he'd looked in his pajama bottoms and was shocked by the intense urge for closeness that seemed to overwhelm her. She'd recognized him as an intriguing and handsome man the first time she'd set eyes on him; she had, almost without being aware of it, labeled him *sexy* and *sensual* when they'd run around the hotel in their nightwear. But she was surrounded by striking men who were made even more so by their ethics, determination and strength. She wasn't sure why Will Chan suddenly seemed more seductive to her than any other man.

Maybe he returned that thought. He quickly withdrew his hand, setting it on the steering wheel. "I'm not leaving, you know, until this is over."

"I didn't think you were going to drop me off and head for the airport."

"No, I mean when more agents show up. I gather Logan's already here. But I've checked in with Jackson Crow, and I'm staying on this. I guess because I was here when it started and I feel I have to see it through."

"I understand that feeling."

"I'm just saying that…well, we're in this together. Don't keep things from me."

"I'll say ditto to you."

"Look, I know you weren't fond of working with me. I can tell that you think I can be rude and blunt."

"I think you *can* be a total jerk."

Grinning, he turned to her. "Okay, I promise I'll try not to be."

"So what annoys you about me?" she asked.

He was thoughtful for a minute. "Nothing. Absolutely nothing." ·

He put the car back in gear, and they drove the last few blocks to the hotel.

7

It was late when they finally returned to the hotel. Will was tired, too—and he hadn't performed any autopsies.

When they arrived, the desk clerk told them that five more of their "company" had checked in—Logan Raintree, Kelsey O'Brien, Tyler Montague, Jane Everett and Sean Cameron. He was also quick to assure Will that the cameras in the elevators were now functioning, although, he said apologetically, it would be some time before the hotel had cameras in the hallways. Will thanked him as he and Kat walked to the elevators.

"I wonder if I should wake my Krewe," Kat said, "and find out what, if anything, they've found out or have planned."

"Let's get Bastet settled first, huh?" Will suggested. Kat was holding the Mau; Will was lugging a litter box, a bag of litter and the cat food he'd bought. Luckily the hotel was pet-friendly.

"Good idea. And it *is* late. I'm sure everyone will be up early in the morning," Kat said.

Upstairs, while she continued to hold Bastet, he maneuvered his key card while balancing his purchases. But he'd barely opened the door when he heard her name being called.

Logan Raintree stood in the hallway across from them.

"Hi, Logan! Just a second," Kat said.

"You two went out and bought an Egyptian cat?" Logan asked. "Aren't you getting carried away with the subject matter?"

"She's...she's an orphan," Kat said. "Want company in the suite?"

"Love it. Come on over and bring me up to speed," Logan told them. "I can show you the printouts of the research we've done."

"Great!" Will strode into the room, aware that Kat was following him, still carrying a compliant Bastet. He decided the bathroom was the best place to set up a litter box. He'd never had a cat before, but it seemed logical.

"Hey!" Kat called to him.

"Yeah?" With the litter bag half-open, he looked out at her.

"Did you think to buy some dishes?"

"Dishes," he said blankly.

"Pet bowls. For the food. And water. I know a cat can go a while without food, but water's a necessity."

He stared at her, wondering how he'd forgotten such a basic. If he'd thought of it, he could have taken bowls from Austin Miller's house, but the only thing on his mind had been that this animal needed to be cared for.

Kat laughed, and he liked the sound, sweet and un-affected. Her lips curved upward and her eyes seemed even bluer, even brighter. He cleared his throat, looking away.

"Mmm-hmm," he managed.

"It's okay. The restaurant's closed, but there's a soap dish in my room I can wash out. We'll use that for water. You can rinse yours out for food," she said. "Somewhere—in between diving, researching and trying to communicate with the spirit world tomorrow—we can find a pet shop."

"Or just grab the bowls from Miller's house."

"That, too," Kat agreed.

In another few minutes, they had Bastet set up. They left her happily ensconced on Will's bed, regally cleaning her paws.

"Wasn't Bastet a goddess?" Kat asked him as they crossed the hall.

"Yes. The ancient Egyptian cat goddess."

Logan opened the door as they knocked. He was alone.

Will had only met him a few times, when they'd all been back at their special-units offices in Virginia. He was lean and fit, with a controlled, wiry strength; he was also calm and levelheaded, a man who thought before he spoke. Logan reminded him of his own team leader, Jackson Crow. While they were the authority figures in their groups, they knew how to work in ensemble situations, and both had an uncanny sense of who to send where and under what circumstances.

"The others are all in bed?" Kat asked him.

Logan nodded. "But we're good to go in the morning. Kelsey is going to investigate the members of the Egyptian Sand Diggers and find out who else was at that party. I've got Tyler checking on the people at Landry Salvage and I'll take Simonton's Sea Search. Jane will stay at the police station and be available to you—or whoever needs her. Did you learn anything at the autopsy, Kat?"

"I learned that he died of sudden and massive heart failure, which was not really unexpected. The doctor on duty was wonderful. I told him my colleagues might want to see the body. He's an experienced old-timer, and a team player to the nth degree. An excellent connection," Kat said. She nudged Will. "Show Logan what you found."

He reached into his pocket and took out the two evidence bags. "The first I scraped off the wall right here on this floor when Kat and I thought we were being followed. The second came from the wall surrounding Austin Miller's estate."

Logan stared at the bags and then at Will. "It looks like the wrapping from what we perceive as the stereotypical mummy," he said.

"Exactly."

"I'll get these to our lab first thing in the morning," Logan told him.

"Thanks," Will said. "I'll be interested to see what they come back with."

"Me, too." He turned to Kat. "You want to keep up with the diving expedition?"

"Yes. I think it's important."

"I noticed the camera in the hallway. Is that yours?" Logan asked Will.

He nodded. "I'll look at the footage before I go to bed."

"Great. We'll meet for breakfast in the morning," Logan said. "Now, get some sleep. We'll see you down-stairs around seven."

They bade him good-night. Will was glad Logan had come, and glad that Kat's team was there to handle the strenuous and exhaustive work of investigating the many people who might have been involved.

Across the hall, he opened the door to his room and Kat opened the door to hers. "Well…good night," he said.

"Good night."

They both went into their rooms. For a moment, Will hesitated, wondering if he should knock on the connect-ing door and ask if she wanted it locked again, now that others were here. Then he wondered why it had even occurred to him—except that, after today, he felt he knew her.…

And knew that he was incredibly attracted to her.

He shook off the thought and decided just to check out the hallway video on his computer.

He sat down and studied the video feed. He saw Logan and the rest of Kat's Krewe arrive, and he saw the maids come and go. Nothing else. He had a feeling, though, that they wouldn't have a visitor again. Not when there were so many agents on the floor.

He drummed his fingers on the desk. *Someone wants something.*

Yes, of course, the vast treasures of the *Jerry McGuen.*

But his intuition said it went deeper than that. Why kill Austin Miller? The elderly gentleman wouldn't have been anywhere near the ship or the water.

He was pretty sure that whatever was taking place wasn't a one-person operation. The person who'd gone down to the ship just minutes before Brady Laurie couldn't have been alone. He'd have needed help, someone nearby on a boat. To the best of Will's knowledge, there was no scuba gear that would enable anyone to go to that depth—and make it back to the Chicago shoreline.

He scribbled a note on a pad.

Timing. Who had access to a small craft—and no alibi for the morning of Brady Laurie's death?

He yawned, glanced at the connecting door and almost jumped when he heard the cat meow. He rose, rubbed Bastet's head, stripped down to his briefs. He put the cat on the floor and crawled into bed.

He started to doze off; he was so tired that sleep

came quickly. But he was startled awake by the sound of a plaintive cry.

He blinked in the darkness of his room, then turned on his bedside light. The cat was scratching at the connecting door.

He stood and walked over to the cat, picking her up. "Hey, people have to sleep around here, you know? I volunteered to take you. You have to be happy with me."

The cat meowed pitifully again.

And then Will heard the sounds from next door. Muffled cries of distress.

He instantly set the cat down and opened his door, then the door to Kat's room.

She was tossing and turning on the bed, arguing softly—and pushing at something. He couldn't make out the words.

He hurried to her bedside, sitting next to her and clasping her shoulders. It occurred to him that he should let her sleep, but she seemed to be fighting some real demon in her dream. And losing.

"Kat! Kat!" He shook her gently, trying to awaken her from the depths of her dream.

She fought him, striking out violently. He caught her arm to keep her from giving him a good right hook to the jaw or a black eye, and shook her with a little more force.

"Kat!"

She bolted up, eyes suddenly wide open, and stared at him.

"Will."

"Are you okay?"

"I—I— Yes, yes, of course," she said. In the light streaming from his room, he could see her clearly. Her eyes were the brightest, clearest, most beautiful blue he'd ever seen...or could ever imagine. And she might possess the greatest strength and will in the world, but at that moment, she seemed fragile to him.

"You were dreaming again."

She nodded.

"The ship—or the mummy?" he asked.

"The ship. I was on the ship. I could see everyone, so elegant and beautiful and having a wonderful time. The sky was gorgeous—and then everything changed. The storm came in. I kept hearing people screaming about the curse. And then, when I turned, there was something coming at the ship. Something huge and ominous... You can't have a tsunami on a lake, can you?"

"Well, no, but in a storm... You've seen the lake. It's huge and, in bad weather, the water can be an extreme power."

She shook her head. "I just didn't feel it was part of the storm."

He could feel her trembling beneath the thin fabric of the oversize T-shirt she wore to bed. He wanted to pull her to him and stroke the softness of her hair, hold her close, feel the beating of her heart, of his own heart....

He started to stand. She reached out to stop him, her movement impulsive. "Will—"

"I'll stay here and work for a while if you want."

"I, um, that's silly. You need to get some sleep. I need sleep. Like *real* sleep. Badly."

"Oh, I'm not that much of a sleeper."

"No. You have to go back to bed. You have to. Just leave the doors between the two rooms open." She hesitated. "Did I scream?"

As if on cue, Bastet leaped up onto the bed beside her.

Will laughed. "There's your answer. The cat was scratching at the door to get into this room. And when I went to stop her, I heard you crying out."

She smiled, shaking her head. "Okay, Bastet, we'll keep the doors open. Then you can come and go as you like." She flushed, looking at Will. "Do you mind? I'm not a coward. I wasn't best in my class on the firing range, but I did score in the ninetieth percentile. It's just that…you can't shoot a dream."

"I don't mind at all," he assured her. "I'll hang around in here if you want."

She shook her head again firmly. "We have to dive tomorrow. I want you to be well rested."

"Okay," he said. "But if you need me, holler!"

"I'll send the guard cat," she promised. "Oh, would you turn on the small desk light?"

"You've got it." He went over and turned the light on, said good-night and left her. She lay back as he did, and he was stricken by the sight of them, Kat and the cat, curled comfortably together in the blankets. At the moment, though, he saw only one of them. The woman. He was gratified that she seemed so comforted by his nearness. Her eyes were closing and she let out a sigh, arms curled around her pillow and blond hair a radiant halo.

He returned to his own bed. He was afraid to dream, even though he wouldn't dream of the ship or the mummy.

He would dream about Kat Sokolov, her blue eyes intense as sapphires, her hair teasing his skin, and his hands…all over her.

He lay down.

And prayed for morning.

Kat was delighted to see Kelsey, Tyler, Jane and Sean in the dining room with Logan when she stepped inside. Her Krewe had become like family to her. She wanted to ask Tyler about his recent vacation and ask Sean about Madison, but they were already deeply involved in the case at hand. Sean rose first to give her a welcoming hug. "Amun Mopat. Can't get away from the guy," he said with a grimace.

"If we're lucky, the salvage crew will find the *real* Amun Mopat's sarcophagi and mummy," she said.

Will came in behind her; he'd stopped at the coffee stand before joining them. She felt a twinge of guilt, certain that it was her fault he needed the coffee. But he looked alert and well rested. Actually, he seemed more impressive than the first day she'd met him, standing behind the autopsy table that held Brady Laurie's remains. She suddenly found herself thinking they could be an article in a women's magazine: *Can this relationship work? No, they didn't meet in a bar or online—they met over the body of a dead man.*

She quickly looked away from him. They were working, and today promised to be as long as the day before.

And yet…

True, she'd initially thought he was a total jerk. Brash, abrasive, out of line. But now it seemed that he'd merely been indignant about work that wasn't up to par. He could be more than decent, respect her skills and talent, become gentle and empathetic.

Tyler stood to shake hands with Will, and then, as they all sat down again, Sean and Will immediately got involved in conversation. That was natural, since they were both technical whizzes when it came to computers and cameras. They all ordered; Kat decided she'd just share with Jane because she didn't want to eat heavily. There was a fair amount of chatter around the table until Logan cleared his throat.

He passed out a stack of folders. "Everything we've discovered so far. Will, make sure you have all our numbers on speed dial. Tonight you and Sean will meet up with the film crew when you've finished with everything else, so until then… Will and Kat, get going. We'll be in contact after the dive. Whoever's most caught up with their research will meet you at Austin Miller's house."

Will nodded. He rose, and Kat rose beside him.

"Have fun, you two," Tyler said, rising. Despite his respect for his female colleagues, Tyler stood whenever a woman did, and whenever she entered a room. Sean Cameron was like that, too. It made Kat smile. Sean always said it was a Texas thing. Or maybe they just couldn't let an old courtesy die.

"It'll be a blast," Kat said.

Jane shivered. "I don't envy you in the least. That water is cold!"

"Ain't it the truth." Kat smiled at Jane. Her coworker was a trim, attractive woman and a brilliant artist. She could have been doing just about anything. She had an uncanny ability to draw a face from someone else's description—or to build a recognizable face from the skull of a dead man.

"I think I'll be diving with you tomorrow," Sean said. He rolled his eyes at Kat. "I guess we're in this one because of Bernie, Alan and Earl, so..."

"Yeah, you're right. You get your just-vacationed butt down there!" Kat teased him.

"We'll be in touch as soon as we're up and out," Will said.

They left, pulling their equipment. Although it would've been easier to leave it on the boat yesterday, Will had decided they should keep their hands on their personal dive gear; he didn't intend to take any chances. *And he was right,* she thought.

In the car she asked him, "Did you get some sleep?"

"Oh, yeah. I slept well." He glanced her way. "Any more dreams?"

She shook her head. "No." She looked out the window and then asked, "The cat's going to be all right in your room, isn't she?"

He nodded. "I left a note for the maid."

"She slept at my feet all night," Kat said.

"I'm sorry. Was she a pain?"

"No, I guess I'm growing to like her."

Somehow, something had changed. She was aware of his scent, the sleek darkness of his hair and the strength of his hands and long fingers on the wheel.

It wasn't a good idea. Really. It wasn't.

She gazed straight ahead. "So, you think you'll be fine working with my team?"

"Sure. Why not? They seem great, and God knows, we don't have to hide anything about ourselves—and no one in either group is ever going to talk to anyone else about us. It's like an instant fusion, you know?"

Instant fusion. Yes, well, that wasn't exactly true. It had taken her more that an instant to feel this way.

Amanda and Jon were already at the lake. Bernie, Alan, Earl, Captain Bob and Jimmy Green were there as well, setting up for the day and planning to leave within fifteen minutes.

Alan King stood before them on the boat, hands on his hips. "So Austin Miller died of a heart attack?"

"Yes," Will said, nodding gravely.

"Massive heart failure, actually," Kat said.

Bernie joined them on the dock, Earl filming all the while. "Does that seem a little odd to you?" he asked.

"Odd!" Amanda came walking over. "Odd! The man was eighty-three or eighty-five or something like that, and he had a heart condition. What could be odd about heart failure? Oh, I know. You're all thinking about the curse. Well, curses are idle threats. It's just that the great and powerful didn't want their graves robbed. Intelligent people don't believe in curses."

"Still," Jimmy said, rolling a line of rope on his arm, "it's a sad coincidence. A diver—the first diver to reach the ship, an experienced diver—drowned. And now, poor old Mr. Miller, dead of a heart attack. And both of these men were so committed to preserving history and respecting the past."

Amanda looked at Will. "The FBI believes that an elderly man dying of heart failure is worthy of the taxpayer's money?" she asked.

"Hey, we're the FBI," Will said cheerfully. "We think everything's suspicious."

"It's sad," Jon Hunt muttered. "Just sad. Austin Miller was a nice guy. I liked him a lot. He was passionate about the things he loved, and he was generous with local charities." He glanced at Amanda. "You've got a one-track mind, Amanda. I miss Brady, and I'm really sorry about Mr. Miller."

"I miss Brady, too," she said. "But, please! An old man having heart failure? It happens, you know? He led a good life."

"We can finish this argument as we move on out!" Captain Bob called. "Come on, people, time is money!"

Alan didn't seem perturbed by the captain's insistence that they get moving. Kat didn't think it was because it was *his* money; she thought he was simply ready to be on his way.

There was a brief discussion as to whether both boats were necessary, but in the end, Amanda wanted the research vessel because of the equipment on board.

They took off for the dive spot side by side. As they headed out, Kat looked at Will, noting a strange expression on his face.

"What?" she asked him.

"I'm too easy to read, huh?"

"What are you thinking?"

The motor was loud and no one around could hear them.

"I'm thinking there's something suspicious about Amanda," he said. "Maybe that's not fair. I don't like her very much."

"Mmm," Kat said thoughtfully, "but we know she didn't kill Brady Laurie. She was with Jon Hunt and the film crew, going down to the ship right behind him. She was seen by several people."

"Yes. But this hasn't been a one-person job."

"But she was *here*. She couldn't have been diving ahead of Brady because she and Jon were behind him, and she couldn't have been on another boat for the same reason."

"I know. It's frustrating. But there's something about her I just don't like."

"She's abrasive," Kat said, then inhaled a deep breath. "We could still be crazy—looking for something that isn't there."

He shook his head. "Get serious. You would never have supported me with McFarland when we saw Brady Laurie's corpse if you didn't know I was right."

She turned away; Bernie had taken a seat on the other side of her.

"So, are we going to make it through this?" he asked. "I don't believe in curses. Okay, so I *say* I don't believe in curses. But this is starting to look more like the 'Tut' curse every day. A young diver—dead. An old Egyptologist who encouraged the search for the ship—dead."

"There's no curse, Bernie," Will said. "Bad things happen sometimes. But no man has the power to invoke a curse, unless others let him do it. Unless they *give* him the power. Remember that, Bernie."

"I'm remembering," Bernie said. "I just hope we get through this," he repeated.

"You know we will, Bernie," Kat told him.

"If not, I'm looking for another line of work!" Bernie muttered. He got to his feet, calling out to Earl. "Hey, we're coming up on the spot. Get some footage of the research vessel coming in."

Once again, they suited up. The usual care was taken in descending. Jimmy Green watched over them like a watchdog while the security boat team and Captain Bob were on the lookout from above.

This time when she went down, Kat was determined to hover by the grand salon. She felt able to do so, knowing that Will would stay with her and that he believed in her—more than she believed in herself.

And so, while the others dove the next seven or eight feet downward and toward the aft, Kat held her ground, staring into the grand salon.

She began to see it all again.

She could almost hear the music.

And then it seemed that she was there. She was standing on the deck looking out at the beauty of the night, but she was watching it anxiously. One of the crew members had been talking about the feel of the air, saying that the wind didn't seem to bode well. Someone else said they were nearly home, nearly at Chicago. She listened to the people as they walked past her. One man told the woman who clung to his arm that they were perfectly safe. He laughed at the idea of a curse.

"Could one person possibly reach out from the grave to hurt another?" the woman asked.

"Don't be silly. Only the living hurt the living."

Kat wanted to turn to the woman and tell her that the dead *could* come back, but they had no greater power than anyone alive—all they had was the strength to influence, to insinuate horror into the human mind, something done just as easily by the living. But although she seemed to be part of it all, she wasn't. She couldn't say anything. She was there—and yet she wasn't.

She wanted to scream; she wanted to warn them to man the lifeboats, to get out while they could before the danger struck.

They didn't understand that the danger wasn't going to be the storm.

She turned to the water again, and it was coming. The dark shape that seemed to accompany the icy wind. She lifted her arms, as if she could push it back, as if she could somehow stop it. But the massive dark shadow was bearing down on the ship.

It was coming closer and closer....

A wall of water was washing over her and she was breathing it in. She began to choke.

She realized the frigid water was engulfing her.

She was drowning in it.

8

Kat was suddenly jolted. She felt someone shove something at her face, and her instinct was to fight back. But she realized the thing pushed into her mouth was her regulator. Will was forcing her to take it back; she'd evidently spit it out, forgotten to breathe. She tasted the cold water, felt it on her teeth. She coughed, choked, coughed up water, and then she was able to take in a sweet breath of air. She saw him looking at her, his dark eyes intense and huge behind his mask, and she felt his hands on her while he watched her, watched her breathe.

It seemed that aeons had passed, that the others must have seen her strange behavior. Seemed that it must be time to go back up.

It wasn't. She saw that the others were busy down in the hold, looking at the doors that were ajar, those that were open and those that were sealed.

She inhaled deeply, and Will used his thumb to indicate that they should go back up; he was worried about her.

She shook her head, trying to smile. He frowned.

She shook her head more firmly and gave him an A-OK sign. She spoke around her mouthpiece, knowing the sound would be distorted. "I'm fine, really. Let's finish."

He didn't look happy, but he didn't stop her when she released more air from her BCV and continued downward to the hold. Earl Candy turned the camera on her and Will, and she went all the way to the bottom, determined to find more of the spilled treasure that was covered in zebra mussels and lake bed silt.

She was able to retrieve a few encrusted objects before Jimmy Green gestured that their time was up. As they moved toward the anchor line, she knew that Will was almost on top of her. He was still worried. She couldn't protest. She might have drowned with seven people surrounding her if Will hadn't been there to snap her from the past to the present.

Back on board, Kat was stunned that no one else had been aware of whatever had happened. With the camera going and Amanda taking center stage, demanding the ancient trinkets others had found to display before the camera, Kat couldn't say anything to Will. He behaved as the others were behaving—happy about a productive dive that had allowed them to better chart and understand the condition and position of the ship, and the treasure that remained within. When everything had been shown, the real treasure of the day seemed to be a necklace. The true beauty of it would be hard to see until it was cleaned, but it was gold chain, Amanda said, with a golden sculpture of the god Horus attached. At last she finished with the camera and walked over to Alan. "That's it. That's all we brought up this time. He can turn the camera off."

Alan stood. "Dr. Channel, we're documenting *everything* that happens."

Bernie stood next to him. "*I* tell my man when to turn off his camera."

Amanda pursed her lips and stalked away.

Will was checking the tanks for the second dive. He glanced up as Kat approached him. "You sure you're okay?" he asked.

"I'm fine, and, um, thank you."

He shrugged. "It's what we do."

That seemed to be his mantra, she thought.

"You have more belief in whatever it is I'm seeing than I do," she said, speaking in a low voice.

He looked around to assure himself that they weren't being watched. She took a step back. He'd stripped off the arms and chest of his suit because the sun was hot. He was bronzed and lean and she wanted to touch him.

"There's something at the end of this…vision that's so horrible you don't want to see it and I'm afraid for you to see it—especially in seventy-five or eighty feet of water. Do you think you should go down again?"

"I'm fine, I swear. And if you're next to me…"

He laughed. "You pack quite a wallop for a little girl," he said.

"I'm not a girl."

"Okay, you pack quite a wallop for a highly educated and brilliant but tiny agent—how's that?" he asked her.

"Better." She paused. "Did I really hit you?"

"You tried. Last night and today. But I'm fairly bright and well-trained myself."

Kat noticed that Earl and Bernie were speaking somewhere near them. It was a private conversation, and she didn't mean to listen, but even on the decent-size boat, they were close.

"Alan should just pull the plug on that bitch!" Earl said.

Jon Hunt heard them and came over.

"No, no, please. I'll speak with Amanda. She's just intense. You have to understand that while you make documentaries on many things, we *live* ancient history. Please, try to understand her, and I promise, I'll talk to her," Jon said.

"She doesn't seem to care that a good friend of yours died on this expedition! All she cares about is her own agenda. She wants the big stuff done immediately, and she wants to call all the shots," Bernie said, folding his arms. "We're here because the center is considered the best of its kind and isn't trying to stow away anything that legally belongs to the State of Illinois. She's pushing the boundaries, and if she isn't careful, she'll bring the curse of politicians and lawyers down on us!"

"I'll talk to her!" Jon said again.

Kat excused herself to go to the hold to get a bottle of water. She wasn't part of this argument.

But as she started down to the galley she paused. Amanda was on the phone; she'd gone there for privacy.

Kat would have left.

But she was here to investigate, to learn what she could.

And even if she hadn't been, she couldn't have left fast enough to avoid hearing Amanda's frantic whisper. "I'll find it! I'm telling you, I'll find it!"

She snapped her phone shut and turned and saw Kat. Her face went red, but she quickly rallied. "Hey, sorry. That was a friend of mine. I lost her Adele CD and I told her that if I couldn't find it I'd buy her another one. I can't believe she called me in the middle of all this about a *CD!*"

"Well, people do love their music," Kat said mildly.

"I guess. But…" With a shrug, Amanda stepped toward the galley's counter. "I'm putting together sandwiches. We'll take another thirty minutes before our next dive."

Just then Jimmy came down the galley steps. "Ready for… Oh! Amanda. You're getting started on lunch. Great. Thanks!"

"Sure. No problem. We all have to eat, right?"

She was extremely pleasant. Kat grabbed her water, and moved to Jimmy's other side. With their assembly line, they had a stack of sandwiches prepared in a matter of minutes.

Topside, she saw Will in conversation with Bernie

and Alan. Earl was filming sailboats that passed in the distance.

She didn't get a chance to talk to Will before they went for their second dive, but she intended to keep a close watch on Amanda—and to make sure that what she put in her bag came out of her bag when they reached the surface.

I'll find it. I'm telling you, I'll find it!

The words flashed through Kat's mind as they descended. When she got to the ship's grand salon, she felt compelled to stop again.

She turned.

Will was there. He touched her arm, and she looked at him and knew he'd be there for her, a safety net.

She looked into the salon—and it began.

At first, the characters were ghostly. She heard her own breathing through the respirator; she felt Will close at her side.

Then the characters became real, and the water seemed to disappear. Once again she was alone on the ship's deck. She heard the laughter, the music. The people talking, the warnings about the curse...

It was coming, and she knew it. The wind that became icy cold. The blue sky turning dark. And then the *thing,* the shadowy, shapeless thing, massive in the night. It was coming toward them and then she could see it...

Huge, tall. It was a man. A man with incredibly large dark eyes, his arms crossed over his chest. He wore a tall, turbanlike hat or cap, and jewels adorned his neck. The eyes looked at her, stygian, blank, as if sightless, and yet all-seeing....

It—he—came closer and as he was nearly upon her, she felt pure terror.

Then...

She heard a garbled voice. "Breathe!"

She was being shaken. She blinked and saw Will. She was trembling in the water, freezing, as if she'd been through an ice storm.

But she was breathing....

She didn't choke.

And as she saw him, she felt safe. She was strong; she had faith in herself. But his faith was even greater, and he would stop whatever demons came for her, stop them before they could reach her.

Yes, Will seemed to have faith in her, and he seemed to know her.

He didn't try to get her to go back up before the others, although he realized she'd seen something more. She wanted to watch Amanda, and although she wasn't sure how to convey that to him, he didn't protest any of her movements.

They joined the rest of the group. It always seemed impossible that no one had noticed their later arrival. What felt like aeons when she was staring into the salon must have been just a minute or two.

She and Will went to work. Amanda and Jon were looking over a crate packed in a tarp, trying to determine size and weight and, no doubt, whether or not they could bring it to the surface.

Jimmy Green noted that their dive time was up, and they made the ascent.

There were more treasures, of course. As usual, Amanda commanded the time before the camera, while Jon did as he was told. Will hung in the background with Kat, and it wasn't until the dive trip had ended and they were in the car, headed to the hotel to shower and change, that he was able to ask her what she'd seen.

"I don't know," she said. "I guess I was expecting a mummy to suddenly appear in the darkness. But it wasn't. It was a… I don't know what it was. A giant Egyptian, maybe. I saw a man, with slicked-back hair, wearing some kind of headpiece. He had deep, dark eyes. The eyes didn't seem to see, and yet the *thing* was coming at the ship. It was the great dark shadow that threatened the ship."

"Interesting," Will said. "Maybe once we've gone through some of the journals at Austin's house, we'll figure it out. A giant Egyptian," he murmured.

Kat was thoughtful. "He seemed like a young man, say early twenties, with dark skin and exceptionally fine features. I'm not familiar with Egyptology the way you are, but I've seen pictures of pharaohs that were similar."

"Maybe it was Amun Mopat. We don't actually know what he looked like," Will said.

Kat made a sound of distaste.

"It wasn't *really* Amun Mopat," Will said. "We know he wasn't a giant, and I still don't believe he came back from the dead to sink a ship. However, that might be who or what you saw in your mind's eye. Which could mean many things."

Kat sighed. "Will, when I went down to the galley before the second dive, I found Amanda talking on her cell phone. She said—and I quote—'I'll find it. I'm telling you, I'll find it.'"

"Did she know you heard her?"

Kat nodded. "She said she'd lost a friend's CD. And then she started making sandwiches."

"She could have lost a CD—or she could be looking for something special associated with the ship. But… that's a long shot. The ship's been at the bottom of that lake for over a hundred years. And it's not like Amanda's ever down there alone."

"No, but we've all been bringing up pieces of pottery and stone statues—and the dagger and the box. There *could* be something special down there," Kat said.

"We have copies of the ship's manifest. I've looked through it, but I'll read it more thoroughly and try to discern if there was one special thing among the treasures." He glanced at her. "Tutankhamun's gold death mask was considered the major find in his tomb. Maybe I missed something like that."

Kat grinned. "His death mask is big. Amanda couldn't have slipped anything of that size out of the water!"

At the hotel, they went to their separate rooms. Kat couldn't help remembering that the doors separating the rooms were ajar, allowing Bastet to come and go between them. She felt much safer than she had the first night; they'd all learned that everyone was in a better position with good backup.

She should have been concentrating on her vision, trying to analyze it and determine what she'd seen with her sixth sense, but…she was human. And she was thinking about Will Chan, about his lean and muscular body and the beautiful warm color of his skin. Even though she was all alone, she blushed. She realized she didn't have to; she was an adult and it was okay to be attracted to a man. It was just that this man was a colleague.

It was a while since she'd been in a relationship. Many men had been turned off by the mere fact of her profession.

Some were too turned on by it, and they scared the hell out of her.

But her last relationship had ended not because of what she did, since she'd been seriously involved with another pathologist.

He'd happened to come in when she was talking to a corpse.

She knew he'd been bothered. The relationship wasn't instantly over. It had ended one morning when she'd awakened to find him staring at the ceiling. He had seemed so anguished, and then he'd told her—he believed she had some strange power, and he'd tried, but he couldn't make the relationship work. He couldn't forget that she talked to corpses. And he was terrified that one day he'd see them talking back.

The breakup had hurt. She'd cared about him, and she knew he'd cared about her, as well.

And she'd wondered if she should keep her affairs few and far between and very casual.

There could be nothing casual about a relationship with Will. But while she found herself fantasizing about him in a sexual way, she was also gratified to realize that he was just like her. He wasn't turned off by her science or what lay beyond science.

But...

That didn't mean *he* was fantasizing about *her!*

After she'd dried and dressed, she gave the cat some attention. "Poor baby. Your master is gone," she said. Bastet purred, looking at her with beautiful cat eyes. She seemed to know.

Animals *did* know many things people couldn't understand.

"I've got to meet Will and we have to get moving, Bastet. The day is almost gone."

The animal meowed pitifully when Kat was about to leave. Stroking Bastet, she placed her on the bed. "I'm so sorry," she murmured. "But you have to stay here."

She met Will in the hall.

"I reported in to Logan," he said. "Tyler is at Austin Miller's. He's keeping an eye on things, plus he did a cursory search of the house and yard. I told Logan about the image you 'saw' at the ship and he's going to send Jane out to the house so she can sketch it for you."

"Good idea," Kat agreed.

She looked around as they drove. Chicago was truly one of the great American cities. The lake, a constant presence, glittered in the bright sun. Heading along South Lake Shore Drive, she could see Grant Park and the Buckingham Fountain, the Shedd Aquarium and the Field Museum ahead of them in the distance.

"I'm just wondering," she said to Will, "do you think we should focus on Austin Miller's house—or on the Egyptian Sand Diggers?"

"I think we'll find more of what we're looking for at Austin's house," Will said. "Your team is investigating the Sand Diggers. But the two people who can help us the most with the ship are Austin Miller—well, not Austin himself but the journals in his home—and Dirk Manning. You heard what Manning said—he and Austin Miller were the rock-solid foundation of the society."

"And if Dirk's pain at losing his old friend was faked, I'm turning in my badge and giving up on this," Kat said. "I don't believe Dirk Manning is guilty of anything. And Austin Miller is dead."

"We're back to the salvage divers, then," Will muttered. "And after what you heard Amanda say on the phone, I think she's somehow involved."

"But how?"

"I don't know."

"Obviously, Agent Chan, I'm just musing aloud," she told him.

When they reached the estate, there weren't any patrol cars in evidence, but Kat reasoned that Tyler Montague must have rented the Honda that sat on the embankment. The house itself—the circumference of the wall—was wrapped in tape with regularly posted warnings not to enter.

Kat hit the buzzer; a minute later, she heard Tyler's voice. "Agent Montague. What's your business here?"

"It's Kat and Will," she said. "We've got Dirk Manning's key. Just letting you know we've arrived."

"Enter into the museum!" Tyler told them grandly.

He met them at the door. Kat had known Tyler a long time; like Logan, he'd been a Texas Ranger before joining the Krewe, and they'd worked a few cases together when she was a pathologist with the city of San Antonio.

She was very fond of him. In appearance, he might be the toughest-looking member of the Texas Krewe. He was tall and well-muscled and his passion was martial arts. He and Logan had been close friends through harrowing times.

"Glad you're here," he said, shaking hands with Will, then hugging Kat. "The house is enormous but I knew you'd be coming after the dive and I figured I'd let the others continue with the research and alibis. But I've been here awhile and, so far, I've only gone through the parlor and the guest rooms. I'm assuming that what we're going to discover is either in Miller's office—

his den—or his bedroom, but this entire place is like a museum." He raised his eyebrows. "If we *are* going to discover anything helpful."

"We'll know when we discover it," Will said. He looked at Kat. "Bedroom or office?"

"Office."

"I'll finish the guest rooms, then," Tyler said.

He and Will headed up the stairs, while Kat went across to the office. She made a point of leaving the door open. Maybe Will should have done this room, since he seemed to love all things Egyptian. But she couldn't forget the way she'd found the elderly man. He had loved his den. If there was something to find, it might well be here.

"Where to start?" she said aloud. She pulled open the desk's bottom left drawer and took out an orderly stack of journals. The top one was the most recent. She began to leaf through it.

Despite herself, she quickly became fascinated. He had a clear, easy way of writing that engaged her in the subject. He'd been writing to enhance his own scholarship—and for his own pleasure. She studied the charts he'd made and understood that each Kingdom or period had a number of dynasties. Strange, but until the past few days, she'd thought of ancient Egypt as one phase of history, not realizing that the pyramids had existed for millennia by the time Ramses II lived and died, and the boy king, Tut, was buried in the Valley of the

Kings. Austin Miller's notes were clear and precise...
and interesting.

The last page of the last journal was about the party
being thrown to entice scientists and divers to search
for the *Jerry McGuen*.

"It's time," he wrote, "truly time, for that the ship to
come to the surface, to disprove the concept that any
talisman could bring about a curse. Or that a priest, any
priest of any religion of any era, could rule the heavens
or the earth. This is so much nonsense. Priests and rul-
ers have always governed through fear. When a master
manipulator can control the human mind by using terror
and make that terror widespread, he must be stopped.
Recovering the ship will allow us to show the world
that fear and terror is all a matter of perception. That
whatever Amun Mopat may have carved on his tomb
is irrelevant. Our problem is that salvage divers know
the gain will be the state's, so we'll let them see what
fortune may come to those who seek!"

She read the words in silence, and wondered what
"talisman" he was talking about.

"Mr. Miller," she murmured softly, "don't you know
that because of the movies, there's no such thing as a
tomb that *doesn't* come with a curse?"

She set the journal down. There was one lower in the
stack that didn't align with the others; it was a different type of journal, far older. She opened it curiously.
The handwriting was different, and she saw that this
journal had been written in 1898.

Holding it, she felt her heart leap. The *Jerry McGuen* had gone down in 1898 with her Egyptian treasures, years before Howard Carter had discovered King Tut's tomb.

The name in the book, however, was also Austin Miller. He had to have been this Austin Miller's grandfather.

The older Miller's writing was as engaging as that of his grandson. He spoke about being in the desert, crawling through sand, finding tomb after tomb that had been raided and looted. He wrote about the day one of their diggers had fallen into a hole. The hole had proven to lead to a shaft, and they'd followed it and found the tomb.

At first, none of the men on the dig had been particularly excited. They'd wanted to find the tomb of a pharaoh, and they'd merely uncovered the tomb of a priest. But as they went through that tomb, the hieroglyphics told of a powerful man who had held others—even the pharaoh—in his grip. He was a magician, who could make mist and rain, force love when there was none and tell a pharaoh of victories to come, or when an enemy might attack.

Once the work of removing the precious treasures began, they'd begun to know what they had. Gregory Hudson, the wealthy fur trader from Chicago who'd financed the dig and loved the country of Egypt, its present and its past, was "well pleased," as Austin said, with their discovery.

Kat sat back, engrossed in the story. She heard the clock tolling the hours, but ignored it. This Austin Miller's journal read like an adventure story.

He went on about the months of exploration, and how Gregory Hudson, with his beautiful young bride, had chartered the *Jerry McGuen* to bring them home, along with some of his men and his treasures.

Austin Miller—grandfather Austin Miller—hadn't traveled with him because he'd had to leave Egypt earlier, before their find could be cataloged and wrapped and crated.

And then, just before her arrival, the *Jerry McGuen* had gone down, and she and sixty souls and the treasure had all been lost.

"It made me remember what we saw on the wall of the tomb. Our interpreter was appalled by what he read when we first saw it. In fact, he left without his pay and did not return. But he did tell us that it warned that death and despair would fall upon those who disrupted Amun Mopat's final rest, for he was a god and wielded the scepter of a god. No matter where his remains might lie and in what condition, he would wield that scepter. I could not help but believe that Gregory, his poor, beautiful bride and all the others suffered and died because we should have let the dead rest."

Startled, Kat heard the clock chime again. She glanced up, an eerie feeling creeping down her spine.

The doors to the patio were no longer open; she was

in the house with two fellow agents and no one else. There was no reason to have such a feeling, except...

She saw an elderly man standing before her. Tall and erect, clean shaven with snow-white hair. His eyes were sad and his cheeks sagged heavily.

She knew that face; she had come to know the face and form of Austin Miller as he'd lain on the autopsy table.

"You see me, my dear?" he whispered, and his words were both hopeful and pained.

No matter how many times she'd seen the dead, it was always a shock.

She had so wanted to see this man. To speak with him...

"Yes," she said, her voice tremulous.

"It was no accident. Please, do not let it go as an accident!"

"No, sir, I will not," she told him.

"You'll see that justice is done?"

"Yes." She stared at him. "But we need your help, sir. We believe that someone came upon you, terrified you—and knocked your arm when you reached for your pills. Can you tell me who did it?"

He nodded solemnly.

"Who?"

"The mummy," he said. "The mummy came to me and killed me."

"Anything?" Will asked, looking up as Tyler came to stand in the bedroom doorway.

Tyler shook his head. "The guest rooms are neat, tidy and dust-free. They're filled with paintings, statues and knickknacks, most of them relating to Egyptology, and some of them to the history of Chicago. There's not a single piece of clothing and there's not a scrap of paper with any notes. I've opened every jar and looked in every vase and…not a thing."

"What did you find when you searched the property?" Will asked.

"Nothing, but I noted the same small disturbance in the grass that you did—near the section of wall where you found the scrap of gauze and the broken statue. I'd definitely agree that someone crawled over the wall and came at Miller from his patio doors. Anything in here?"

"Too much. Notes about doctors' appointments, notes about meetings to be held at the house and a 'note to self: pressure Chicago Ancient History Preservation Center.' Obviously, they didn't need to pressure them a lot. Brady Laurie was so excited that he made the most foolish mistake any diver can make—diving alone. Maybe he and Dr. Channel had the same personality trait—no faith in anyone else. Speaking of Amanda, Kat heard her talking on the phone today, telling someone that she'd 'find it,' or words to that effect. She told Kat she was talking about a CD, but she's an iffy character, to say the least."

"Logan has our Krewe looking up backgrounds on everyone involved, so if there's something we should know about her, we should know it soon," Tyler said. "How can I help you in here?"

"Take the dresser," Will suggested.

As Tyler walked toward it, Will's cell phone rang. He answered it immediately. "Chan."

"Will, it's Logan."

"We're still at Austin Miller's house," Will told him.

"Yes, I figured as much." He paused for a long moment. "I have some strange information for you. That material you found—on the wall at the hotel and then at Miller's house."

"The gauzy stuff that looks like mummy wrapping."

"I sent it to an expert in D.C. early this morning. He got right on it, and called me a few minutes ago."

"What is it? A prop from a movie set?"

"No. It's the real thing."

"What do you mean?"

"According to the carbon dating, that wrapping is Egyptian. He estimates it to have been used in the New Kingdom—and it's possibly from the reign of Ramses II."

"What?"

"It's real, Will. At one time, that wrapping covered a real mummy."

9

Will agreed with Logan, who'd decided he'd have Jane return to the hotel, ready to sketch, and that he'd have Kat bring some of the files and journals back with her.

Will hung up and called Kat on her cell. She sounded strange, which worried him, and he hurried downstairs, Tyler Montague right behind him. Tyler hadn't said a word but looked concerned. Will felt a little stab of envy, but he knew that he had the same sense of closeness with his own Krewe, all wonderful people. It would be easy to become attached to this Texas Krewe, as well.

When they reached the bottom of the stairs, Kat was standing in the entry waiting for them, a stack of journals in her hands. She seemed calm enough, and yet a little shell-shocked.

"What is it?" Will asked

"I saw him," she said softly.

"Him?" Tyler echoed. "Who? You okay, Kat?"

"I'm fine," she assured him. "One of our ghosts showed up. Mr. Miller. He found me in the office. He wants us to help him bring his killer to justice."

"He's…gone?" Will asked.

She nodded. "I guess he's still…finding his way. He was standing in front of me clear as day and he spoke to me, said that a mummy killed him, and then he faded away. But he trusts us," she said softly.

"He trusts us…to track down a killer mummy?" Tyler spoke incredulously.

"We've seen some pretty strange things," Kat said.

Will looked at her sharply. "You don't believe in a killer mummy," he told her. "I'm sure you believe exactly what I believe—that someone with access to historical artifacts, as in a researcher or museum employee, is dressing up like a mummy. Most of the costume probably isn't real, but the culprit has taken wrapping from a real mummy somewhere and, accidentally or on purpose, is leaving those bits around to be discovered. There you go. That explains the continuation of the mummy's curse!"

"Well, a mummy from a shipwreck didn't kill Brady Laurie," Tyler said. "Unless things have changed since I went down in the deep, those wrappings—real *or* fake—would start to disintegrate quickly."

"Yes, but how better to give an elderly man with a heart condition cardiac arrest than by walking in on him as a mummy—and then slapping his digitalis out of his hand?" Will touched Kat's cheek gently. "Let's go. It's time for us to meet back at the hotel," he said.

"What about Jane?"

"She'll wait for us there."

"Aren't you and Sean supposed to meet up with the film crew tonight?"

"We will."

They split up at their cars but drove straight back to the hotel. Logan had ordered food to the suite, and serving dishes, warmed by Sterno burners, were set up along one of the buffets. The table was filled with the team members, surrounded by computers and sheets of work they'd printed during the day.

With all seven of them gathered in the room, Logan started a wipe-clean chart to write down what they'd discovered; this was their usual procedure. Someone had access to mummy wrapping used in ancient Egypt. It had been discovered in two places, so obviously that someone had tried to get into Will's and Kat's rooms when they'd first arrived. Someone—or two some-ones working together—had wanted to scare every-one around them with the possibility of Amun Mopat's curse.

Kat reported on speaking with Austin Miller's ghost at his home, and explained how speaking with him veri-fied that someone had come upon him—the mummy, according to Austin—and the bruise on his arm had come when "the mummy" blocked him from getting to his medication. She told them what she'd heard Amanda say about finding *it* during her phone call, and what she'd seen in her mind's eye during the dive.

"How did it go with you all?" Will asked, looking around the table.

"The active members of the Egyptian Sand Diggers number forty. It *was* forty-one, but now with Austin Miller gone...well, it's down to forty," Logan said. "They come from every walk of life and range from the youngest, who's just turned twenty-one, to the oldest member, Dirk Manning. I was able to speak to about five of them at the club today, and they all seemed genuinely sad that Austin was no longer among them. They believe in art and history— and they all say there is no curse."

"I learned that Andy Simonton of Simonton's Sea Search, has a little Mako—and that it was out on the lake the day Brady Laurie died," Kelsey said. She sat perched on the table near Logan. Will had realized that Logan and Kelsey were a couple, but he also saw that it didn't matter when they were working.

He lowered his head, distracted. In his own Krewe, Jackson Crow and Angela were together and, he thought, planning on marriage in the near future. He knew that with most agencies, teams were usually split up if members became romantically involved, but there was nothing usual about how they worked. Their offices were even separate—an *experimental* section of the FBI.

He gave himself a mental shake and returned his attention to the matter at hand.

"So Andy Simonton was out on the lake?" Kat said.

"There's no certainty that Andy Simonton was the one out on his boat. All we know is that the dock master noted it was gone during the day. Andy keeps his little speedboat at a public dock, but the company's salvage ship stays at their own wharf," Kelsey explained.

"I was at Landry Salvage," Jane said. "And they have two large salvage ships, kept at their own dock, and two smaller motorboats, both of which sleep six. However, they're at a private dock, and the dockmaster there didn't remember either of them being gone."

"Simonton's boat was on the lake," Logan murmured, adding that notation to the board. He looked at Will. "I hear you're something of a master magician," Logan said.

"I'm a magician. Magic is tricks, of course, and sleight of hand," Will responded.

"But you did work as a magician?"

"I have done so."

"In eighty feet of water could you make it look like you were a mummy?" Logan asked.

"You can make anything appear to be whatever you want—the key is that you do something that persuades your audience to suspend disbelief. Then you go in with the trick, which might not be perfect, but because your audience is ready to see what you want them to see, they will. Like this." He reached over to Kat's ear and moved his hand forward, presenting a silver dollar.

"Wow, that was good," Kelsey said. "Unless you've been stowing silver dollars in your ears, Kat?"

"No, and you barely touched it," Kat told Will.

Will smiled at her. "When we were talking, I made

the natural movements I might make during conversation. I had my hand in my pocket, but then I waved it near your ear, so you never saw me with the silver dollar."

She took the dollar from him.

"Hey!"

"I think it's mine—it was my ear, right?" she teased.

"That's not the same as making it look as if a mummy's attacking you in the depths," Jane said, frowning.

"No, it's not. You're talking about a much more complicated illusion, but it *could* be done," Will said. "You get the right dive suit. Then you find out what kind of bandaging would work best in the water—appear the most real—and you come down prepared to shed your tank while you perform the illusion. And you've got just that. An illusion. But I don't think Brady Laurie fell for it so easily. That's why there's bruising around his mouth. His regulator was torn from him. And someone held him. At least, I believe I'm correct about that. Kat, those bruises looked like ones that would appear postmortem if someone had been held, right?"

She nodded.

"So all we need to do is find a mummy dive suit," Kelsey said, rolling her eyes.

"Yeah, that would require a hundred search warrants from judges who have to be convinced that a drowning victim was actually murdered and so was an elderly man who had a heart attack. Or maybe we can get Austin Miller to appear before a judge. And if the judge doesn't have a heart attack, Austin can try to convince him that a mummy did him in."

Will's phone rang, startling him. He excused himself to answer it.

"Hey, it's Bernie. I hear Sean is in—the two of you coming over to see what kind of footage we've got?"

"Yes, of course." Will glanced at his watch. "Bernie," he said, nodding at Sean Cameron. "He's expecting Sean and me to see the film they've taken thus far," he told the others.

Sean rose. "Ready whenever you are."

But Will was surprised to realize that he wasn't ready to go. He had, in a short period of time, become accustomed to working with Kat.

"Go see what there is to see," Logan told them. "We'll be here if you need anything."

Jane said to Kat, "Let's get started on the face in that vision of yours." ·

Kat nodded, but Will was glad to see that she was watching him—watching him as he left. She gave him a smile, and he felt something inside him quiver.

Tinker Bell? Yeah, was what he'd thought.

If so, he sure wanted to be Peter Pan.

That's so sophomoric! he told himself.

But when she watched him go and he saw her eyes, he felt rivulets of heat race through his veins.

And he didn't bother to tell himself that she was his colleague.

That just made her more appealing. No, she *couldn't* be more appealing.

She was everything a ghost-seeking illusionist turned law enforcement agent could ever want—beauty, perfection…and understanding.

And then there were the basic but ravenous feelings he'd begun to experience when he was near her, as primal as the earth and air.

"What do you remember most?" Jane asked Kat.

"The eyes. They were large and dark. And they seemed to be rimmed with a black liner," Kat said. "And the face was lean and cleanly cut. Oval-shaped, I think. Classic."

"The nose?"

"Straight. No twists, bulbs, lifts, curves—very straight."

Jane sketched out the oval and the eyes and began shading, drawing in the nose. Then she asked about the mouth.

"Full. Full lower and upper lip," Kat said.

"How's that?" Jane asked, pointing to the sketch.

"A little thinner in the cheeks."

Tyler had come to stand behind them.

"That's him. He's coming along nicely," Kat said. "Maybe darken the eyes a little."

"He looks like someone," Tyler muttered.

"Who?" Kelsey stood over them then, Logan close beside her.

"I can't put my finger on it," Tyler said, "but...there's something familiar."

"He had on a hat. Not a turban, but it had width and substance and made him taller. Let's see...his chest was bare. And he wore a heavy necklace," Kat recalled.

Jane sketched the headdress and Kat instructed her to broaden it.

"That looks like an Egyptian ceremonial headdress," Kelsey said. "I saw a few that were very similar on the pictures and statues we've been studying."

"Egyptian, and how strange in many ways. The ancient culture lasted almost thirty centuries, and yet, so much remained the same throughout the dynasties," Kat said. "I was in the Sand Diggers' house, I was in Austin Miller's house and—" She broke off and looked up at Kelsey. "You're right. There are all kinds of similar faces...."

Tyler, who now sat across from her, took her hands and squeezed them. "Hey, Kat. You seem worried. An ancient Egyptian did *not* come walking across the water to sink the *Jerry McGuen*."

She smiled. Tyler was the team muscle—but he was also incredibly intelligent and surprisingly sensitive for the tough cowboy he often seemed to be. They'd connected like brother and sister from the first time they'd met, a number of years ago. "I know that, Tyler. And don't worry. I definitely don't believe that an Egyptian priest could create a giant image of himself to sink a ship. But I do think there was more than weather out there."

He nodded. "Okay. All we have to do, then, is figure out what happened that night."

Logan sat at the head of the table, frowning as he looked at Kat. "Interesting. The ship went down over a hundred years ago, and while you were able to get a little more information from Miller this evening, he couldn't give you a name—he gave you a mummy. But what you see when you dream *and* when you're below goes back to the sinking of the ship. I wonder if that has any bearing on what's happening now."

"Especially," Jane added, "if Amanda is searching for something specific."

"Well, finding something specific in a ship that's lain on the bottom of Lake Michigan for more than a century is…worse than looking for a needle in a haystack!" Kat said.

"What about Amanda?" Tyler asked. "Any ideas on how we find out whether she was involved?"

"I'd like Will or Sean to get their hands on her computer," Logan said.

Tyler grinned. "There is that pesky little thing called illegal search and seizure."

"Tomorrow, Tyler and Sean should dive with the film crew. Alan King told me that Amanda and Jon were bringing out their larger ship. It has a small crane and they plan to start pulling up a few of the boxes." Logan drummed his fingers on his desk. "Maybe now we'll find out what Amanda is up to."

"That woman is one skinny little witch!" Earl Candy said.

He was showing the film he'd taken the first day, which included Amanda having a fit on the deck of the film crew's boat. Will watched her, even though he'd been there.

He'd seen the other footage, and he knew she hadn't been down at the *Jerry McGuen* to kill Brady Laurie; there just hadn't been time. But maybe there was something hidden beneath the surface that was of more value than they'd imagined.

"How could there be anything more valuable than what they've discovered so far?" he mused aloud.

"The treasure does, in essence, belong to the state," Alan King said. He shook his head. "That's what I don't understand. I don't know much about the black market, but if there were a major piece—wouldn't everyone know once it went on the market?"

"The black market exists all over the world and most collectors will talk about it if, say, a Rembrandt or Matisse appears on the market somewhere. But finding out who actually has it or where it may be or how money changed hands is a nightmare. Once something disappears into the hands of a private collector, it disappears—sometimes for centuries," Will said. He spoke without looking at Alan. Like Sean, he kept his eyes glued to the film. "Then, suddenly, you'll hear about an auction—perhaps an estate auction—and there it'll be."

"And the family supposedly knew nothing about it," Sean said. "What if—"

Will interrupted him. "Hold on. That's the second dive on the second day, right?" He hadn't been the first to get to the *Jerry McGuen*'s hold. He'd been with Kat, hovering near her in case she stopped breathing as she stared at the salon.

"Yeah, second dive, second day," Earl Candy said.

"What did you see?" Bernie asked Will.

Will nodded at Earl. "Go back to the end of the first dive, please."

Sean glanced over at him, repeating Bernie's question. "What did you see?"

"Maybe nothing. It just seemed that something changed. I wish I had a photographic memory, but I don't. Can you tell whether anything's off?"

Earl Candy set his digital video back to the end of the first dive.

He had an angle of the divers starting to go up and, as he followed, he had a shot of the hold as he went up himself. The blue-green darkness of the water seemed to swallow it up and even the bulk of the *Jerry McGuen* slowly faded away.

He fast-forwarded through the footage he'd taken on deck. Then the divers entered the water again and he followed Amanda and Jon down to the hold of the ship a second time.

"Hold it, Earl," Will said, leaning forward to point at the computer screen. "There—that door. That bulk-head door. It was ajar every time we went down. Now it looks as if it's closed tight."

Earl ran the two different views of the hold again.

"Could be motion in the lake," Sean commented doubtfully. "In the water, the motion one of us makes can become amplified, sending currents that displace it elsewhere."

Will looked at Sean, who was looking back at him.

"Could be," Will said.

"But we both think someone else was down there, don't we?" Sean asked him.

"How? How are they doing it?" Alan was distraught. "We keep a boat there as security. We watch for anyone remotely near us on the lake."

Will sat back, folding his arms over his chest and smiling. "I think I might know," he said. He glanced around. "The answer should have smacked us in the face from the beginning."

The drawing was completed and attached to the board. Logan doled out the various journals Kat had taken from Austin Miller's house so that his writing could be read more thoroughly. Will and Sean were still out, but they all said good-night; morning would come soon.

Kat went to her room but walked through to Will's. She cleaned Bastet's litter box and gave her more food and water, telling her as she did that a cat as regal as an Egyptian Mau should have toilet trained herself. Bastet looked at her balefully, as if to say she disdained such activities.

Kat hovered there, wishing that Will had come back. She really wasn't a coward, and she wasn't afraid of being alone, but she couldn't help feeling some dread about the things she saw in her dreams. She realized she *needed* to see them, but that didn't make it any easier.

She remembered the way Austin Miller had appeared to her that evening, and how convinced he was that he'd been killed by a mummy. She'd tried to tell him the mummy had been a man and hoped he'd believed her in the end. "The curse was written on the tomb wall," Miller had said.

"What respectable Egyptian with power and money would die without a curse on the wall? It was to stop tomb-raiders," Kat had told him.

"But we're tomb-raiders, aren't we? We deserve to be stopped," he'd said, just before fading away. He was such a new ghost; he might find tomorrow or in the days to come that he could maintain his soul's image for those who could see. He was a charming man, and she hoped she'd get to speak with him again.

She wondered if they *were* tomb-raiders. But she knew, perhaps more than most, that the saying *You can't take it with you* was entirely true. Dust to dust and ashes to ashes and all that was organic in life would eventually disappear. The soul was the essence of a person, and no amount of finery could change that.

She realized she wasn't frightened on the physical plane. She was a good shot, and she'd learned how to deal with criminals and psychotics in instances when she wasn't armed and someone had to be "talked down."

Kat didn't like being alone now because she was accustomed to Will's presence. She sat in his hotel room with the cat; it wasn't really *his* place, and yet it reminded her of him. His aftershave was very subtle and pleasant and somehow spoke of breezy tropic nights and the sea. His shirts were neatly hung in the closet, his diving gear ready by the door. Always rinsed and always checked. He wasn't obsessive, she'd learned. He was far more casual than she was, unless it had to do with survival—such as diving equipment—or something that wasn't right, like McFarland's desire to shelve Brady Laurie's death as an accident.

She needed to sleep. She stroked Bastet but left her curled up on Will's bed. It was as if the cat missed him, too.

She walked through to her own room, slowly got ready for bed and finally turned off all but the night-light streaming from the bathroom and lay down to sleep.

She started to think about the major players, at least the ones they knew. The film crew, who'd called them in. But she didn't believe any member of *that* group could be involved. There were the two men from the

Egyptian Sand Diggers, but Dirk Manning was nearing eighty and Austin Miller was dead. At the Preservation Center, Amanda—highly suspicious, but constantly with them or on video or witnessed by others. And there was Jon Hunt, a far more amenable scholar with whom to work. Then there were Landry Salvage and Simonton's Sea Search. Landry was rich and definitely aware of what was going on. She didn't want Andy Simonton to be involved; he had seemed too nice and down-to-earth.

That didn't make him innocent, she reminded herself. Many a serial killer had turned out to be the boy-next-door type.

At last, physical exhaustion seemed to settle her mind, and she drifted into sleep. Even as she did, she tried to fight the fact that she was slipping into another plane where she saw things.

She couldn't *really* see things, of course. There was no magic that let her see the past as it had been. People experienced haunting in two different ways. Residual haunting, in which events and the emotions they generated seemed to remain through the violence or energy of what had happened. It was why people saw Civil War soldiers in the misty fields of Gettysburg, or why some houses were haunted by murder victims.

Then there were "intelligent" or "active" hauntings, such as Austin Miller returning to the place he loved, the place he'd lived all his life. Returning to tell her that justice needed to be done, his killer needed to pay—and his killer had been a mummy.

What filled her dreams? Residual haunting or active ones?

They seemed so very real.

She could feel the night and, at first, everything that touched her senses was lovely. How could the moon ride the sky so beautifully before being obliterated by darkness? The breeze seemed soft, but she knew it would grow to be a bitter and icy cold. She could hear the music, the rustle of silk gowns. The sounds of laughter and pleasant conversation were all around her. But as she stood on the deck, she knew what was coming. The couple brushed by her, the woman fearful, the man quick to reassure her.

It all happened as before. The moon was consumed by darkness in the sky; the breeze turned quickly and viciously into a cold wind. The brutal kiss of ice seemed to touch her skin. She heard laughter change to screams.

And from the darkness, she could see it coming. Massive and dark—part of the darkness that covered the moon? There were cries all around her.

"Cursed!" someone screamed.

And there it was....

She saw the figure—the giant figure of the ancient Egyptian. It seemed to be fifty-feet high. It was coming closer and closer and seemed about to devour them all....

She couldn't breathe.

The water was all around her. She was so cold she couldn't feel her body anymore, but her lungs were burning.

"Kat!"

Distantly, she heard her name being called.

"Kat, breathe, breathe!"

She woke. There was something pressing down on her, something pressing air into her lungs. There was pressure on her mouth, but it was a good pressure, and she was no longer cold. She was warmed by the body heat of the man on top of her.

She inhaled deeply, coughed, inhaled again.

She looked into Will's eyes. He was seated beside her by then, watching her breathe, dark eyes filled with concern and relief in one. She edged herself into a sitting position, still staring at him, afraid of what had happened, yet secure because he was with her again.

"In and out, breathe slowly…. I'll get you some water," he said.

He stood and hurried to the bathroom, returning with a glass of water. "Don't talk. Just breathe and sip."

She nodded and leaned against the headboard. She sipped the water until she felt that her lungs were whole again, that oxygen was filling her system. She wasn't dizzy and she wasn't confused.

"I—I guess I drown in the dream," she said.

He nodded. "I don't think you should keep going down to that ship," he said worriedly.

She set the glass on her side table. "I'm not down

at the ship, Will. I'm safe in bed with a bunch of other agents near me—and you *with* me," she added at the end. "I *have* to keep going to the ship. My subconscious or someone from that ship keeps trying to tell me something, and I have to figure out what it is."

"Not if it's 'Hey, you're drowning!'"

She smiled. His muscles were still taut with tension, and his striking face was almost haggard.

"I'm afraid to leave you at all," he told her.

For a moment, time seemed to freeze.

This was it; this was her chance. Should she be flippant? Honest? Was she seeing something that wasn't really there, something she *wanted* to see? The light in his eyes said that he felt as she felt, not just the closeness because of what they were, but the attraction that happened between certain people.

She inhaled on a ragged breath. "Then don't leave me. Please don't leave me," she whispered.

"I'll stand guard, I swear," he said, his voice husky.

She smiled. "I don't want you standing guard ready to do more CPR," she told him. "Stay with me." One more breath and she could get it out. "Sleep with me."

He looked back her. A smile tugged at his lips. "Kat, you don't have to…"

She wasn't sure if he really understood. It was time to risk all. She could live with humiliation; she couldn't live with herself if she didn't carry through with this right now.

She could still taste his lips on hers.…

She leaned forward, slipping her arms around him and pulling him down with her. Finding his mouth, she pressed her lips to his in a way that had nothing to do with protection or security, and everything to do with need. With hunger.

He returned the kiss.

His touch was everything she'd dreamed. She felt the sweet fire of his tongue sliding over her mouth and delving deep within. The strength of his body seemed to seep into her, and she held him close, melding with him as his mouth made love to hers.

Then he drew away, breathless.

Again he said, "You don't have to…"

"Oh, my God, does this feel like *have to?*"

"Lord, I've wanted—"

"I thought you were gorgeous," she broke in, "but… stupid."

"Stupid?"

"Arrogant, a jerk!" The taste of his mouth was like an aphrodisiac and his body so tightly against hers made her feel…combustible.

"Tinker Bell," he whispered around a kiss.

"Tinker Bell!"

"She's a beautiful little fairy," he said, reaching for the hem of her nightshirt.

As she struggled out of it she looked at him and laughed. He smiled, too, and then his eyes were on her body and she molded herself against his chest. She had no idea what time it was; she didn't care. He'd returned to the hotel a while before he'd awakened her because he was in his night garb as well, men's long pajama pants. His chest was naked and solid against her own. His lips fell to her collarbone and then below. Entangled, they slid back into the bed. Under the soft cotton fabric of his pajama bottoms she could feel the rise of his erection, and that alone seemed to escalate an almost frantic desire in her. Yet she suddenly felt a sense of panic, and she stopped, tugging at the thick sleek darkness of his hair so that he looked up at her. "I'm so thoughtless," she said. "Is this wrong? Is there someone in your life?"

"Not now. Not in a long time," he told her. And the way his mouth curved, almost wistfully, made her wonder if his life had been like hers, if those who had loved him hadn't been able to love him *enough*. Or if a greater tragedy had changed his life. She would ask later, because she had to know, but not now.

"I should ask the same, except I'm guessing that since you—"

"There's no one," she said.

He began to kiss her again, and she writhed beneath his touch, euphoric at the feel of his hair, the rippling muscles in his back. Then, just as he had made her nearly delirious with a series of very liquid kisses along her breasts, he pulled back. "Wait. I wasn't planning... I'm not prepared—"

"I am," she said and laughed softly. "Ever hopeful,"

she murmured, meeting his eyes as she marveled at a lock of his hair.

He smiled and moved back against her. She felt the tip of his tongue graze her nipple and his mouth form around it and she seemed to melt into the softness of the bed.

Nightmares were dispelled in the excitement of being alive.

She remembered the first time she'd seen him, how instantly he had drawn her attention and curiosity. Now she could touch him, explore the length and contours of his body, and she did. She felt his every kiss, his every caress, so keenly. She moved against him in turn, fascinated by the way his body seemed to tremble beneath hers. Her kisses covered his abdomen, teased his sex, and then she rose again to meet his eyes. He held her there, studying her eyes as if in equal wonder. She knew that sex was instinct, and yet she knew equally that this was somehow different. Tonight was like breathing. She found herself laughing, feeling his fingertips on her skin, his kisses growing more demanding and intimate. It seemed as if the world would explode except that he rose, shimmying up her body again, the pressure of his flesh and heat so ecstatic it was nearly agony. Then he lifted himself above her, and she was so eager for him that he seemed part of her, a fit that was custom-made, exquisite. Slowly he sank into her, deeper and deeper, and she felt as though the world itself stood still. They both moved as if there'd never be enough time, as if they had to fulfill the yearning, desperate to reach a climax, desperate to prolong it. Every fantasy she'd ever had about lovemaking occurred. Heaven seemed real, above her and around her, in the touch and feel of him, the beating of his heart....

For long moments they lay panting, damp, their breathing ragged, their pulses still racing. He stroked her hair and drew her against him. He didn't speak, and neither did she.

Eventually, he said, "We should sleep."

"Yes, we should."

But they didn't. Not then. They were a modern wonder of the world to each other, and there was simply no way they could restrain that feeling so easily.

They made love again.

And when Kat finally slept it was deeply, and if she dreamed or was plagued by any nightmares, she didn't know it.

"An underwater propulsion device," Will said. "A diver propulsion device." He was speaking to the group at the breakfast table. "I believe that our mystery diver, the person who killed Brady Laurie and has been looking for something ever since Brady's calculations found the *Jerry McGuen,* has what is basically an underwater motorcycle," he said, looking at each person in turn.

"Like James Bond," Jane murmured.

Will smiled. "I have some friends up on the northeast coast who have them—they're great for going after lobster. Yes, you've seen them in movies, but they *are* real. I think they were developed for the military, but they can be bought easily enough, although not quite as easily as a regulator or a dive tank. Even with that kind of motorized help, you have to watch your pressure, but as long as you take the proper steps descending and ascending, it can get you somewhere quickly *and* allow a fair amount of bottom time." He glanced at them all. "Someone could have a boat anchored a good distance away, and still be able to get to the site, spend time there, then return to the boat."

"Why didn't we think of that before?" Logan asked blankly.

"Because we don't see a lot of people using them," Kat suggested. "Considering the temperature of the water at depth, and the speed, it would be one cold ride. Not all that pleasurable. A lobsterman does it for the lobster. He isn't thinking, 'Oh, boy, let me go freeze my buns off!'"

"In other words, even with that security boat at the site," Logan said, "we have no real idea how many times someone might have been down there."

Will nodded. "What we need is Brady Laurie's computer. The police went through it, but I don't think they'd have known what to look for. And we need to find out who he was communicating with about the *Jerry McGuen.*"

"I'll get hold of his computer," Logan told them.

"I'll start research on motorized diving mechanisms and vehicles—and who might have one," Kelsey said.

"And I'll work with the pictures and reference books," Jane put in.

"Kat and Will, you need to get going for the dive. The big guns are coming out today, right?" Logan asked.

"Some of them, yes. They're bringing the larger research vessel with the crane," Will replied.

When Kat and Will rose to head out to the dive site, Tyler and Sean rose, too.

Sean grinned at them both. "Safety in numbers," he said.

"I'm all for it," Will muttered.

The four of them piled into his rental car, stuffing their scuba gear in the trunk. It was a tight fit, even with Kat, the smallest, in the cramped backseat.

"This is good. One of us needs to keep an eye on Kat while the others are watching Amanda and the salvage efforts," Will said. He felt a pinch; she'd gotten him from the backseat. He was startled and caught her eyes in the rearview mirror.

But Tyler turned to her. "You're daydreaming in the water?" he asked.

"I'm fine," she insisted.

"You'll be fine as long as one of us is with you," Sean told her firmly.

"Hey, I'm not arguing," Kat said. "It's just that…I'm a good diver, so once we're past the salon and down in the hold, don't worry about me."

When they got to the dock, they discovered that they were all going out on the *Glory,* the Preservation Center's main exploration and recovery vessel. It was outfitted with the cranes and wenches and chains they'd need to bring up larger objects.

Again, Amanda was taking the lead. "I can't stress enough how important it is to make sure the crates are properly secured. We're going back more than *three thousand years* to the New Kingdom and the time of Ramses II. One of those crates contains the sarcophagi, inner and outer, of Amun Mopat, and it's possible—just possible—that we could safely bring up the mummy. That would be extraordinary. We'll make news across the entire world. You can't imagine what an amazing feat that will be. So you have to understand that the filming doesn't matter," she said, looking at the crew, "and that protecting us because someone drowned earlier doesn't matter." She paused again and looked at the agents. Then she stared at Captain Bob and Jimmy, who'd been hired on for the day, Captain Bob to watch the boat and Jimmy to keep an eye on the divers.

There were also two interns from the Preservation Center, two twentysomethings, Ted and Carlo. They were gazing at Amanda wide-eyed.

"You are all working for me on this," she announced.

"Actually," Alan King said, "I believe we're all working under the jurisdiction of the State of Illinois and that I'm still financing what's going on. But we appreciate your expertise, Dr. Channel, and we will be excruciatingly careful in all endeavors."

"Yes, that's it. You have to understand the value of what we're doing. And if you don't, we should let it go to someone else!"

When they turned away, Will heard Jon warning Amanda, "Hey, ease up. The film guys could get pissed off and pull out."

"Yeah?" Amanda said. "And go through all the paperwork to get started again—with someone else?"

Jon sighed. "You don't need to come on like the Hulk," he told her.

As they walked away, Will joined the Krewe; the others were carefully checking their air tanks.

Kat sat at his side, staring out at the water as they headed to the site. Sean came over and hunkered down near them. "I'm going to take a few minutes after the first dive to work with Earl on setting up a remote. After what you said last evening, I think we need a camera down there. Someone's coming and going from the site, or at least that's what it looks like."

Will nodded. He indicated Kat with the slightest movement of his head, but she saw him. "Hey, if you need to work on that, too, just do it!" she said. "I only have the vision or whatever it is when we first reach the salon. Once we get to the hold, I'm okay, and coming up I'll be okay, too. If we're connecting chains to big crates, I have a feeling that all hands will be required."

"If I'm needed, I'll help out with them," Will assured her.

"I'm a functioning member of the Krewe," Kat said.

Sean was watching her intently. "Every one of us needs the others to watch our backs—and whatever you're learning may be very important. What Kelsey saw in dreams led us to the truth at the Alamo, remember?"

Kat didn't argue. She studied the water, her blond hair streaming around her, blue eyes as deep as the lake and sky.

But that day, Will needn't have worried. Kat paused by the salon, then turned to him and shook her head. Nothing was happening. They followed everyone else to the hold.

The real difficulty was fitting themselves and the chains that were attached to the crane above inside the hold. The hull was broken out, but it was jagged in some areas and, in others, zebra mussels could cause serious damage to dive suits and equipment. Jimmy didn't attempt to help. Amanda managed to be just as authoritative with her hand signals beneath the water as she was with her voice on top. Tyler, Sean and Will moved as directed, trying to maneuver the large, tarp-covered crate through the broken area of the hull and onto the lake bed. Will noticed the big block writing that indicated it contained the valuable sarcophagi. Once they had it out, he and Tyler handled the crate while the others worked with the chains at Amanda's command. Finally, the crate was secured, the massive hook set into the center ring and two more on either side, and it was time to raise it. Jimmy gave the chain a tug, indicating to his uncle and the two interns above that they should start turning the giant winch, and the divers began to follow the slow ascent of the crate.

When they reached the boat again, the divers emerged while the weight of the water balanced the crate. They divested themselves of their tanks and regulators as they got the crate on board. Finally, the feat was accomplished, and although Amanda wouldn't allow anyone to touch the crate once it was positioned, she was beside herself with jubilation, certain they had, at the very least, obtained the sarcophagi.

Amanda was happy; she didn't want to dive again that day, she wanted to get her treasure back to the center where it could be opened in a climate-controlled room under the right circumstances.

"And without any fear of a curse!" Jon said cheerfully.

She was immediately dismissive. "Oh, please! Newspapers started all that. Sure, the pharaohs warned people away from their treasures. Who wants to go to the world of the gods without a lot of jewels and servants? But did the lights in Cairo go out because Tut's tomb was discovered, or did they *always* go out in Cairo at the time? I'm pretty sure that was the case. Some people did die naturally, or through accidents that would have occurred, anyway. It's like…even a broken clock is right twice a day. People can make events look like a curse. I mean, Howard Carter lived for years and years—and he's the one who actually found the tomb."

"Didn't someone die when the sarcophagus was opened?" Tyler asked.

"If so, it had to be that some kind of organic matter in the corpse was toxic. Anyway, we take precautions in the laboratory," Amanda said. "There's no curse, and you know that!" she said, glancing around at the others. "Let's go back. This is a triumphant day!"

Earl Candy stared at Will and Sean, and Will said, "A few of us are going to board the security boat for the day and set up a remote camera, Amanda."

"What? Why? You already have a boat standing guard," Amanda said.

"To keep an eye on everything below. We want to guard your treasures," Will told her.

"That's great!" Jon said with undisguised eagerness.

"I'm still confused." Amanda frowned. "You're not bringing anything up, right? It's illegal. The Preservation Center is the only entity approved to handle the recovery."

"Amanda, I swear, we're not going to touch anything," Will said. "We're just trying to safeguard what you're doing."

"Fine," she agreed, although she was clearly unhappy about it. Then she looked at her crate again, and Will wondered if she'd ever be capable of giving a lover such a look of absolute adoration.

Alan contacted the security boat, and the two vessels brought out their bumpers, linking up long enough to transfer men and equipment.

Will paused, feeling anxious as he thought of Kat.

He felt a hand on his shoulder. It was Tyler Montague. "I'll stick with Kat like glue, I promise."

Will nodded, ready to resume his work. But then he felt another touch on his shoulder and turned to see that Kat was smiling.

"I'm okay. You take care, huh? And don't let Sean get too carried away with his filming." She stood on her toes and kissed his cheek, then waved as he and Sean joined the film crew on the security boat.

With an uneasy feeling, one he couldn't explain, Will watched the *Glory* head back to dock. But he gave himself a mental shake and listened to Earl describe the camera; he even joined in on the discussion about where he and Sean should set it.

As he prepared for the dive, Will thought about the uncomfortable feeling that seemed to be gnawing at his gut.

And then he knew why.

It was the mummy.

Amun Mopat's mummy was going into Chicago.

And, according Austin Miller's revenant, *the mummy did it*.

10

Kat wasn't worried about getting back to the hotel or wherever she needed to go; she could always call a cab.

But when they reached the docks, she found that Tyler had gotten Will's keys to the rented Honda, and they could leave whenever they were ready. Alan King and the film crew would bring Sean and Will back.

"Want to watch them unload?" Tyler asked Kat as they looked at the ship and everyone milling around.

"I think I'd rather watch Amanda when they open that crate," Kat told him.

He nodded. "They'll open the crate in a climate-controlled room at the Preservation Center. And it won't be for a while. They have to get it off the boat now, into a truck and then get it to the center." Tyler gestured down the dock. "And all hail! The press is here."

Media had come in droves. Kat could see TV reporters and cameras from all over the country—and the globe. She recognized some of the major networks: CNN, BBC, NBC and more.

Apparently they'd all gotten word that the mummy

of Amun Mopat was coming in. Kat wondered if some-one—Amanda?—had purposely alerted them.

"Hey," Kat whispered to Tyler. "How come they're here *today?* This is the third day we've been out on the lake, and Brady actually discovered the wreck and died on Monday!"

"Either they learned that the *Glory* went out this morning, or they got a heads-up that something major was happening." He grimaced and indicated Amanda.

"I wondered about that myself," she murmured.

"They're here!" Amanda announced grandly. She looked like a queen about to meet her people.

"We don't know what's in there yet," Jon warned her. Obviously he hadn't been party to this media scrum.

Amanda leaped from the boat to the dock and started down its length to the gate, where the reporters had been held at bay.

Questions shot out at her.

"You've brought up the first of the treasures!" one man cried. "Is it the mummy?"

"Do you have visual proof that it's the *Jerry McGuen?*" a woman with an English accent asked.

"Are you afraid of the curse?" someone else asked.

"Did the ship kill your coworker?"

"Did the curse kill Brady Laurie?"

"Do you think the death of Austin Miller is con-nected?"

"Do you believe in the curse?"

"When will you report to the scientific community on your discovery?"

"Will you be filming when you open the crate?"

The questions came in a flurry from all directions. Amanda raised a hand. "Please!" she said and laughed pleasantly. "Yes, it's the *Jerry McGuen*, and King Productions—working on a documentary about our historic find—will have footage for the media soon. I'm a scientist, and I don't believe in curses. I'm heartbroken that both Brady and Austin are dead. Brady's excitement led to his carelessness, I'm afraid, but I'm sure he's watching over us as we continue his work, and that he's thrilled! Austin must have died knowing that, as well. We've followed through on his dream! Now, I believe we've found—"

Jon Hunt had been standing quietly behind her. He stepped forward at that, cutting her off. "We believe we have definitely found a major artifact from the tomb, but exactly what it is, we don't really know yet. As soon as we do, we'll have a press conference, and tell you all about it. We have to ask you to clear the way, however. We're going to unload and get our find to the Preservation Center."

Captain Bob and Jimmy were maneuvering the crane again, carefully lifting the crate from the deck of the *Glory* to the dock and onto a dolly, held tightly by the two interns. A large truck lettered with the Preservation Center's name waited beyond the group of reporters.

"I'm going to give them a hand with this. That's a

heavy crate for two skinny scientific types to handle," Tyler said.

"You go, cowboy," Kat told him.

The media didn't disperse; meanwhile, Captain Bob, Jimmy, Tyler and the interns managed to move the crate while Amanda continued to talk to the press. Jon hovered behind her, listening closely for what she might say. *It was actually an amusing spectacle,* Kat thought.

"When will you open the crate?" one of the reporters asked Amanda.

"As soon as possible!"

"We'll open it when the conditions are right—and the film crew is there to document every step," Jon corrected.

"Quite a show, quite a show!" Captain Bob said. He'd finished his work with the crane and had come to stand by her. "By the way, someone left a cell phone in the galley. Is it yours? Or maybe one of your coworkers'?"

"I'll go see. Thanks, Bob."

Kat hurried down to the galley. The phone on the table wasn't hers, which she'd known; hers was in her bag. When she turned it on, the picture on the screen was of King Tut's death mask.

It was Amanda's phone.

She scrolled through the numbers called recently but none of them meant anything to her.

Then she paused. Looking at Amanda's phone like this wasn't legal.

Of course, it *was* in plain sight. Kat told herself that

she was only taking it to return to its rightful owner. Any information gleaned from it without a warrant couldn't be used in court, but...

They were searching for a killer.

She took out her own cell phone and started snapping pictures of the numbers called over the past few days. But then she heard voices. She quickly checked Amanda's last few emails, and snapped pictures again, then hurried up the galley stairs in time to innocently hand the phone to Amanda.

"Oh, thank goodness it was here!" Amanda said, accepting the phone. She was flushed with pleasure from her moments in the spotlight. "Thanks!"

"Don't mention it."

With the crate packed in the van and on its way to the center, the media finally scattered.

"Shall we go back to the hotel?" Tyler asked Kat.

"I'm afraid to let that van out of our sight," Kat said.

Tyler grinned. "Not to worry." He pulled out his cell, calling Logan. When he ended the call a minute later, he said, "They'll be met by one of our people."

"It's great to be part of a team, isn't it?" She smiled wearily. "I am *so* ready for a hot shower!"

They returned to the hotel and split up, agreeing to meet in thirty minutes. Kat was greeted by Bastet at the door to her room and stopped to give her some attention. "I wish you could speak," she said. "I'm sure you knew it wasn't a mummy coming after your master!"

Showered and changed, she met Tyler across the hall

in the suite as planned. "Have you spoken with Logan again?" she asked.

"He's at the center himself. He said we have a few hours. Amanda won't let anyone touch the crate until the film crew's there, which could be two hours. And I'm just here to serve. What do you want to do while we wait?"

She grinned, removing her cell phone with a flourish. "In her enthusiasm over the press, Amanda forgot her phone. I took pictures of her recently called numbers and some of the emails she's received. I'd like to see who she's been calling and emailing."

"Let's do it," Tyler said.

Kat connected her cell to one of the laptops on the table. Then she brought up the photos on Tyler's screen.

"You're not going to win any photography contests," he said.

"Hey! I was in a hurry!"

"I'll take the phone numbers. You can work on the emails."

They set to work. Kat was disappointed. Amanda had written to her cousin in Phoenix, to a superior on the board at the Preservation Center to assure him that she was following protocol and to someone she'd met at an online dating site, telling him she'd be too busy to see him for the next few months.

The next email written, however, was intriguing. "Listen to this," she said to Tyler.

Tyler looked up.

"'Please be advised,'" Kat read, "'that legal action will be taken with the State of Illinois should either of your companies seek to investigate the *Jerry McGuen,* find artifacts or in any way hinder the efforts of the Chicago Ancient History Preservation Center. We will prosecute any interference to the full extent of the law.'"

"Who was she writing to?" Tyler asked.

"Landry Salvage *and* Simonton's Sea Search," Kat said.

Tyler nodded grimly. "Strange. She's still on speaking terms with someone at Landry Salvage—she's made calls to their switchboard every day for the past two weeks. Guess who else she'd been calling? Austin Miller."

Will and Sean went back down to the wreck to adjust the position of the remote camera, trying to make sure it wouldn't be caught in any debris and that it would focus on the hold. Earl had rigged the mechanism so the divers could see up to the control station on the security boat, while anyone at the desk could view the dive site.

Will held up a thumb to Earl Candy. Earl grinned and raised a thumb in return. Sean moved to Will, and they both waved at him in approval. Earl seemed pleased with his success; he had all the training and equipment he needed but didn't customarily film in the depths.

Before ascending, Sean studied the wreck again. He could look all the way over to the starboard side, since so much of the massive steel hull had been ripped out.

Of course, it was astonishing that the ship had gone down in one piece. It appeared to have sunk quickly—with greater speed than the *Titanic!*—and flooded evenly. If one section of the ship had filled with water first, it was likely that the *Jerry McGuen* would have broken in two. As it was, she lay with her port side jagged and exposed, at a slight angle, the aft section with the storage holds almost ten feet deeper than the deck and the grand salon.

Sean tapped him on the arm. Time to surface. The two of them did so, following safety procedures.

On deck, Alan King was pacing anxiously. "We need to get back to town. How did I *ever* become associated with someone like that woman?" He groaned, shaking his head.

"What's going on?" Will asked.

"Dr. Amanda Channel. She's got ants in her pants. She can't stand waiting. God, the woman doesn't have an off switch!"

"There is a board of directors," Earl said. "We could go to them with our complaints." He grinned. "I have video to show them!"

"Or," Bernie suggested, "we could take the high road—at least for now." He explained to Will and Sean. "Amanda just called Alan. The crate's at the center. They've removed the outer tarp, and the wooden box inside seems to have withstood the wreck, the water and the ravages of time. She sounds as if it's all her doing. Yep, it's all her doing. Anyway, she knows she can't go any further without us, but she's threatening to do exactly that."

"Someone in the Krewe must be there," Sean said, frowning.

Bernie nodded. "Oh, yeah. Your man Logan, and he's keeping her down. But we need to head back immediately."

Will and Sean looked at each other. He wasn't sure how they were getting back, because the security boat had just been rigged to maintain the remote camera.

"We have help coming," Bernie told them. "Captain Bob and Jimmy should be here in about five minutes."

"I'll take a look at the computer, see how our remote's doing," Will said.

The brawny young security guard on duty gladly relinquished his chair at the computer to Will. "Boring, really," he said. "But don't worry. We know our jobs."

Will sent him to take a break, to the guard's evident relief.

Once the guy had left, Will studied the footage and understood what he meant—the camera was focused solely on the hold. Then, unexpectedly, something in the corner of the screen caught his attention. He could just see the grand salon and, for a moment, it seemed that ghostly images danced by him. He blinked; they were still there. He wasn't sure what he was seeing with his eyes and what with his mind, but he saw the water in a horrible maelstrom. There were women in beautiful long dresses and men in tuxedos and suits, scrambling, fighting the roiling rush of the water, spinning and turning....

"What do you see?" Sean asked him.

Will almost jumped. He'd been so intent he hadn't heard Sean behind him.

"I'm not sure. I had an image of the ship wrecking. I wish we could learn more about what happened that night. As far as I know, there wasn't even a Mayday sent out. The *Jerry McGuen* had reported her estimated time of arrival the next day—and then she was never heard from again. That's the way I understand it, anyway. I've got to do more reading."

"I went through all the files, too," Sean said, "and that's my understanding, as well. Nothing. She was coming in and then she disappeared. A terrible storm had struck, with blinding snow and sleet. Search parties went out as soon as possible, but nothing was found. Not so much as a floating deck chair."

"She must have gone down really fast—as if a plug was pulled on her," Will said.

"Half the port side is missing."

"You'd almost think she was rammed by something like an icebreaker," Will mused.

"Say there *was* an icebreaker out on the lake... Wouldn't they have tried to save any survivors or at the very least reported what happened?"

Will shrugged. "You'd hope so," he said.

Earl took a step into the cabin. "Transport is here," he told them.

Will had no idea how Captain Bob and Jimmy managed to stay calm while working with Amanda, but they were pleasant and ready to move with their usual speed and competence when they picked up the film crew, plus Sean and Will. Two of Alan King's security guys remained on the control boat, including the young man who'd resumed watching the screen.

Will stood with Captain Bob as he took the helm.

"Press has gone wild." Bob rolled his eyes. "The dock was a zoo when we came back in."

"I guess it'll be frenzy for a while. This is pretty momentous. Finding a ship in one of the Great Lakes would be enough, but the *Jerry McGuen* held a mummy," Will said. "I assume the crate made it safely off the dock?"

"I make sure things like that happen, you know. This is our living," Captain Bob said with a grin. "And your friend, Mr. King, pays very nicely."

"Glad to hear it," Will said, grinning back.

Thirty minutes later, he and Sean were dropped off at the hotel. Will's cell rang as they left the elevator—Kat, saying that she and Tyler had just reached the center, and Amanda and her team were waiting for the documentary crew to arrive. Kat spoke quietly, and he knew she didn't intend to be overheard.

"Will, I got some interesting information off Amanda's cell phone. Tyler and I have been checking out her recent communications. She sent a threatening email to both of the major salvage companies who had contact with the Sand Diggers. But she also called Landry Salvage—every day!"

"Who was she speaking to?"

"The switchboard. We can't track calls to specific extensions, only to the main number."

"There's something...fishy about that woman," Will said drily. "We'll have to look into it. Does Logan have a report on anyone who might have a diving motor device?"

"Both Landry and Simonton have one. He found a few others that were privately owned, but he's already gotten alibis on those. Oh, and a few companies up in Wisconsin have them, but from what he can discover, they can't be connected to what's going on here."

"All right, thanks. Sean and I will be there in about thirty minutes. Don't start the party without us."

The crate was going to be opened in a climate-controlled clean room and everyone present had to be suited up—face masks, booties, hair in a gauze cap.

The area was kept cool to avoid degradation that might set in with any kind of heat. Even a speck of dust could harm certain instruments or damage artifacts that had been underwater for years. They wore masks to avoid contaminating the objects...and to protect themselves from any ancient bacteria or microorganisms that might have survived.

There were sterile stainless-steel tables to receive the treasures in the crates, but everything, including the crowbars, had been sterilized first. Earl's camera and the microphone and boom had to be cleaned and covered, as well. If she wasn't consumed by the fact that they were looking for a murderer, Kat would have found the whole procedure fascinating.

She was already gowned and masked when Will and Sean showed up, but Will came right over to her. She raised a brow and he grinned behind his mask. "At last—all shall be revealed." And although she couldn't forget the murders for a second, Kat suddenly felt excited.

Despite all the precautions and the machinery, pure brawn was needed at times. Will, Sean and Tyler were called upon to help as the giant crate was dismantled. There was layer after layer of packaging, which was in itself a historic find. Canvas and wood chips had been used for waterproofing inside the crate and under the tarp; another box was beneath those, and it took well over an hour to get through the packing to the real treasure. But then they reached it.

The outer sarcophagus was the size of a coffin and a half. It had been carved out of granite and was staggeringly heavy. Even with the use of robotic arms, winches and small cranes, it took real effort by all the men to maneuver it.

Jon Hunt was as much in awe as Amanda, remarking on the preservation of the sarcophagus, the beauty, the design.

Extremely carefully, the seals were broken, and the lid was finally removed.

Beneath it lay another sarcophagus.

Earl moved the camera close, and Bernie wielded the microphone while Amanda explained the intricate designs and what they signified. Amun Mopat had seen himself as perhaps greater than the pharaoh he'd served, and that pharaoh had been one of the most powerful ever to rule. She spoke briefly about the New Kingdom and the glorious reign of those pharaohs and their priests. Toward the end of her talk, she pointed to hieroglyphics on the coffin depicting creatures who'd had so much significance in Egyptian life, such as the cobra, the jackal and the cat.

Then it was time to open the inner sarcophagus. There was silence when the lid was lifted.

Kat almost gasped aloud.

Amun Mopat wore a gold and bejeweled death mask, which depicted him in the prime of life.

His face, on the mask, was the face she'd seen in her dreams.

Will knew that he and every member of the Krewe tried *not* to stare at Kat.

But, of course, they'd all seen the picture Jane had drawn from Kat's description, and now…there he lay.

In death.

Kat didn't move; she barely blinked. She didn't give away a thing in front of the others. Will was impressed by her lack of reaction. Eyes were the most telling feature on the human face, and her eyes were all that was truly visible.

Amanda noticed nothing at all wrong. She marveled at the discovery for the camera and the microphone and went on to say how they wouldn't disturb the mummy further until it had been CAT scanned, X-rayed and all the noninvasive work possible was done. At the end, she preened for the camera, Earl Candy shot the mummy from all angles and Amanda announced that they were done for the day.

But when Earl turned off the camera, she was still staring at the mummy.

"What?" Jon asked her.

"We haven't lifted the mask," she murmured. "But…I thought the scepter would have been in the sarcophagus."

"Amanda, are you *ever* happy?" Jon burst out. "We've found the mummy. The *mummy,* Amanda. And it's in excellent shape, and all the outer trappings are just about perfect. I'm going out for a drink to celebrate. Who's coming with me?"

"I'm in!" Earl exclaimed. "I am so in!"

"Let's get out of these bunny suits and take a little time to relax," Bernie agreed. He appeared to be extremely happy.

Will glanced at Alan King.

Alan was more cautious, but he nodded. "It's late, no

one's eaten since lunch, and I'd say we owe ourselves a celebration."

"I've got a bottle of fifty-year-old tequila in my office. I bought it off a Mexican. I'm not stealing any treasures!" Jon said. "Shots all around!"

"Out of the clean room—and out of the bunny suits!" Amanda said, joining in, if rather belatedly.

Will stayed close to Kat as they exited first into the alcove, where they removed their "clean" covering, and then into the lobby. Jon Hunt led the way to the conference room and excused himself while he went to get the tequila. One of the interns entered, bearing platters of snacks, and the receptionist hurried in, too. She was looking at her watch, however—anxious to leave for the day. Will had the feeling that momentous discoveries didn't mean as much to her as the fact that she was already in for massive overtime.

"I am one of the few who loathe tequila," Kat whispered to him.

"Just raise the glass!" he told her.

Soon, they were assembled and the shots passed around. Earl balanced his while he held the camera; he wanted the celebration on film.

"To Brady Laurie and his vision. May he rest in the heaven of his choice! Brady, we are so grateful to you. Wherever these treasures may go, your name will be held in high esteem," Alan said.

"To Brady!" the others chorused.

For a while, the group remained seated around the

table, chatting. Will asked Jon Hunt about the security they had for the center.

"We have a state-of-the-art alarm system," Jon said. "And a guard on duty at the reception desk through the night."

Logan stepped over to join them. "We'll have a team from the Chicago office of the FBI watching the building tonight, too," he said. "And the Chicago police are aware of the discovery—and the risk of fortune-seekers breaking in." He looked at Jon. "I'd say it's time to get it all locked down for the night."

Everyone seemed to agree. The visitors were ushered out, waiting in front while the center employees closed the offices. Will met with the guard who came in for his shift. The man tried to seem assured, but he obviously hadn't expected to be guarding a place that might be under siege.

As they stood on the lawn in front of the center, Will stepped over to Logan. "Should one of us stay here through the night?" he asked.

Logan sighed. "Not you or Kat. She's the key on this, and you've been working with her. You two need the rest. Like I said, we've got a couple of local agents who are going to be watching, but I'll have Tyler and Jane on lookout for a while. Kelsey and I will hold it down while they get some dinner, and then they can take over. I believe there's a break in the diving tomorrow?"

Will nodded. "Amanda wants to play with her new toy," he said.

Logan drew closer. "Kat's vision was of Amun Mopat himself." He spoke in a low voice.

"Yes, but I don't believe the ancient ghost of a priest caused a ship to sink."

"And you don't think the storm caused it to sink?"

"No, I don't. Today I studied the way she went down. My guess is she was rammed."

"Sunk on purpose?"

"Yes."

"And you think that might have something to do with what's happening now?" Logan asked him.

"I don't know how or why, but yes."

Logan didn't argue with him. "We have to find the connection, but we're not going to do that tonight. People have to sleep. We'll meet tomorrow and figure out where we're going. Get Kat back to the hotel, and both of you…get some sleep."

Will was glad to do as ordered. Kelsey and Logan stayed out front; he left with Jane, Tyler, Sean and Kat, so that they could all grab something to eat before Tyler and Jane started their nighttime stakeout.

They returned to the hotel, having grown accustomed to the restaurant there. Not only was it a comfortable place, the other diners had already finished due to the lateness of the hour, so the group could speak freely. But as they sat down, Will found himself remembering that it was only a few days ago that someone—*someone in the hotel*—had been prowling around their floor.

Leaving *authentic* mummy wrappings smudged on the wall.

He made a mental note to ask Logan if the guest roster had been thoroughly checked out for the night in question. One thing was certain; their visitor had not left the hotel after being on their floor that particular night.

"Steak!" Jane said. "A steak. I'm starving. And Chicago is known for its steak!"

"Italian food, too," Tyler reminded her.

Kat had been quiet. Jane placed a hand over hers and Kat started, looking at her friend. "Kat, I'm not surprised that the image you've seen is that of Amun Mopat. When I was researching today, I came across similar images. But, according to what I read, the priest wasn't popular with one of Ramses's descendants, the boy king, Tutankhamun. During that era, his images and statues were all broken or marred. But, of course, his image does remain in places where those who came after him didn't know who he was. You must have seen it somewhere."

"Icebreaker," Will said.

"Icebreaker?" Tyler glanced at him. "You want a drink?"

Sean laughed. "No. Will thinks that an icebreaker rammed the *Jerry McGuen*."

"Why?" Jane asked.

"Because," Kat said, "someone didn't want the *Jerry McGuen* making it to Chicago," she said with certainty.

"Interesting concept." Will looked at the others thoughtfully. "All right, we've been going at it from what would *seem* to be the obvious angle—someone out there ready to kill for the treasure. But what if someone is killing others so the treasure *won't* be found?"

"Someone who believes in the curse of Amun Mopat," Kat said.

"After a hundred-plus years?" Tyler asked skeptically.

"I think it's possible," Will said.

"That brings us back to the Preservation Center itself, the Egyptian Sand Diggers or *perhaps* one of the two salvage companies." Jane counted them off on her fingers. "The connection is what we need."

"We'll figure it out," Will said.

"I'll go to the library tomorrow and look at their newspaper archives for 1898," Jane said.

"We can find out who was in business with icebreakers at the time, too," Sean added.

"That'll be important," Will said with a nod.

"How does an icebreaker fit with my…vision of a giant Amun Mopat coming to swallow up the *Jerry McGuen?*" Kat mused aloud.

Will noted that Tyler squeezed her hand. They were good friends; they'd known each other a long time.

He envied Tyler.

"We'll figure it out," Will said again.

Kat was silent for a minute. "We're all quite accustomed to the fact that souls can stay around. We try to make contact. There are rare occasions when the dead saw what happened, when they can help an investigator uncover clues that can prove the truth. So…would it be so ridiculous for Amun Mopat to be…somewhere?"

"You're saying, what? His soul's been haunting the lake for all these years? And before that, his soul was haunting…his own tomb?" Jane asked.

Kat shrugged. "I don't know. I do know that I saw his face   or the mask of his face—*before* we saw him." She paused. "There was something odd about the face. It had no animation. Now I know that's because it was a death mask." She smiled ruefully at Will. "Usually, when we meet a ghost, even a new ghost, there's an animation about him or her. Austin Miller, for instance—I could see him just as he must have been before he died. But he was animated. He was like he'd been when he was…alive."

They finished their meals, Kat managing to eat a Greek salad, while Will ate English-style fish and chips.

Jane, done with her steak, yawned and stretched, then eased her chair back. She tapped Tyler on the shoulder. "We should go spell Logan and Kelsey. We need to let them get back here."

"Yep," Tyler said. "But, come on—we're taking it until six in the morning."

"What happens at six?" Sean asked him.

Tyler grinned broadly. "You come on!"

"Oh. Well, then, excuse me, I'm going to get some sleep."

"We're right behind you. I'll just sign for dinner," Will said.

The others waved. As Will smiled and made a motion in the air to indicate he needed the bill, he saw that Kat was still frowning.

"What's the matter?"

She glanced at him and managed a quick smile. "I'm just being obsessive. Now I have it in my head that there's something wrong with the face I see coming to devour the ship."

He slipped an arm around her. "One thing Logan is right about—we need some sleep. Maybe it'll all seem clearer in the morning."

She nodded.

And going to the room with her was so natural, so easy. Kat had to be exhausted; he was, too. His muscles were sore from all the diving he'd done and from straining as he hauled the crate.

But when they entered his room together and the door was closed, he suddenly felt a new surge of strength. She turned into his arms, and they were entangled in a long, hot kiss. He pulled back and looked into her eyes. "And I thought you'd be tired."

"You worked harder than I did."

"I was hurting all over, but now..."

They lunged toward each other again, and their clothing began to fly around the room. As his shirt landed on the bed, they were startled by a plaintive meow. They paused, staring at each other, and then laughing. Will walked over to the bed and lifted the shirt.

A very indignant Bastet lay beneath it.

"Ah, poor kitty!" Kat laughed again as she stroked the sleek head. "She's got food?"

Will checked on the bowls. "The cat is fine. Water and plenty of food."

"Then, Bastet, I promise you more attention in the morning. For now…well, it looks like you have your own room for the night." She turned away from the cat and leaped into Will's arms. "Actually, it's not a good use of government money," she said, "a cat having a room of her own."

He smiled at Kat and kissed her, then carried her through the connecting door, still kissing her. They'd scattered their clothing throughout the two rooms by the time they reached the bed, and they were breathless when they fell on top of it. The thrill of being together was so new. He was in awe of the delicate, pale beauty of her skin and the blond silk of her hair as it fell over the bronze of his chest and arms. Whatever was happening between them was something he'd remember all his life. They had a bond, he knew, that was deep and real and unforgettable. But where it would take them he didn't know. Still, he wondered if any children they had would be dark or light, or light with his dark eyes and her sunlit hair or…

He stopped wondering as her kisses ran down his chest and below, and all he could think of was the desire burning fiercely through every part of him. He brought her close, found her lips again, rolled with her on the expanse of the bed—and then paused, despite the urgency of his passion. His fingers curled over hers as she gazed into his eyes. She smiled at him, and he trembled. He lowered himself, thrusting into her, and in minutes they were so entwined they were nearly one.

Climax came with a shattering impact and they lay together in silence. She nestled against him, and his fingers brushed the curve of her hips. They didn't speak. It was so easy to be together and—even better—it was easy to wake together. He turned to her, and he saw that while he was feeling the sizzle inside once again, her lashes were closed. Her breathing was even.

She was sound asleep.

He smiled, lay back and stared at the ceiling.

There was nothing as sweet as the comfort of deep sleep.

Kat drifted in that sphere for hours. When she dreamed, it wasn't of the current time or place. She felt safe and secure, and she thought she was at home. She'd had wonderful caring parents who had worked hard. Her father, naturalized when he was ten, hadn't forgotten his own family, and as aunts and other relatives came over from Russia and Soviet Bloc countries, they were made welcome in their home.

While her dad had quickly become a chef to help support the family, her uncle Nick had gone through medical school, and he was the one to open the world of medicine to her. When she was young, he and others were often at the house. She'd loved it; the kitchen would smell delightfully of pastry baking, and when she came home from school, she'd curl up on the couch and watch television, listening to them in the kitchen. Her aunt Olga often visited her mom in the afternoons to teach her Russian. Kat would hear them greet each other, and then her aunt would say, "Okay, now. In Russian. *Privet!*"

Talk to me. It was an all-around greeting. *I pray you. How are you doing? What would you like?*

Home was a good, safe place to be.

She missed her parents. Her mom had moved to Florida after her father's death. Of course, her mom had become part of her dad's family so sometimes everyone still gathered for reunions in San Antonio, reunions filled with delicious food, with conversations and laughter and love and so much warmth.

But all at once she went from that place of warmth and safety to another, somewhere else. It was as if she'd suddenly been drawn to the television screen, and then into it.

She was part of *The Mummy*—now in living color.

It really didn't frighten her at first. It was so silly! The mummy moved slowly—all anyone had to do was outrun it!

She'd often thought so. Only silly girls screamed,

did nothing and fell down while staring at the mummy and walking backward.

But now, she wasn't in a movie anymore, and it wasn't a movie mummy lurching awkwardly toward her. Instead, there were dozens of mummies, and when she turned to run, there were more of them, behind her and on either side.

There was nowhere to run.

She was suddenly fighting them, smashing at them, kicking them, wrenching and tearing. She was an M.E., for God's sake, and she could make them all fall apart. In the early days of Egyptology, she knew, mummies had been so plentiful they'd been used as fuel for home and cooking fires. She could beat them.

But they were strong....

So many...

And coming through them, one who wasn't a mummy, one who seemed to be a living, breathing human.

Amun Mopat.

"Not in my name," he cried out to her. "Not in my name!" he said again. "Don't they understand? You put something in a man's mind, and he believes it. But I will have it no more. Not in my name."

She stopped because she was so astounded. And then she could feel the *things,* closing in on her, touching her. She twisted and turned, and saw that Amanda Channel was walking toward her from one direction and Amun Mopat from the other.

And then, her strange realm was pierced by a loud shrieking.

It was Amanda. She was screaming in terror.

Kat woke with a start.

At her side, Will instantly woke, as well. Alert to danger, he sat up, reaching automatically into the drawer at the side of the bed, as if he'd forgotten they were in her room. It didn't matter, though. That was where she kept her service Glock, too.

"What?" he asked. His voice was thick; he'd been sleeping soundly. "Are you okay?"

She nodded. "Did you hear a scream?"

"No."

She jumped out of bed, racing around to find fresh clothing.

"Kat?"

She grabbed panties and a pair of jeans from her drawer. "Will, come on! We have to go."

"Where?"

"The Preservation Center. Something's happening there."

"Kat, it's not even six. Tyler and Jane are in a car, watching the place. There are two other agents and the cops are going by constantly. Are you—"

"Sure? Yes, positive. Will, *something* is happening there. Please come with me."

She didn't have to ask again. He was out of bed, hurrying to his own room to dress and retrieve his weapon.

There was very little traffic. They parked directly in

front of the center in a no-parking zone, but Will didn't care and neither did she. Tyler got out of his rental as she ran toward him.

"Kat! What's the matter?"

"Have you seen anything? Has Amanda come back here?" she asked.

"No, nothing. Those are the other feds right over there and the police have been around every fifteen minutes, like clockwork," Tyler said.

Jane, looking slightly disheveled from sitting up in the car all night, was beside them a moment later.

"We've got to get that guard to let us in," Kat said urgently.

She led the way, almost running as they all followed her.

At the door, she paused. Beyond the plate-glass doors, she could see the guard.

He lay on the floor in a pool of blood, his gun in his outstretched hand.

11

The center's glass front doors were still bolted shut.

Although the guard, lying by the shadow of the reception desk, appeared to be dead, they couldn't wait. If there was a chance he was alive, they had to get in.

Will tried ramming his shoulder against the door to smash it, joined by Tyler, but the heavy safety glass didn't break. "Stand back," Will said. He raised his Glock and shot out the glass. He noted in the back of his mind that the center's alarm didn't go off. He heard the sound of glass shattering and emergency sirens approaching the center, which meant someone had called 9-1-1.

He wrapped his hand in his jacket and reached in, undoing the bolts. They were inside the center in a matter of seconds. Kat immediately went to the man on the floor, feeling for a pulse. She looked up. "He's got a pulse—it's faint, but he's got a pulse!"

Will hunkered down by her side. "Gunshot wound to the chest," she said. "Missed the heart...we need an ambulance...like ten minutes ago." She had taken off her jacket and used it to apply pressure to the wound. She nodded at Tyler, who'd had some paramedic training. He got down on his knees and listened to her quick words of instruction, taking over from her, applying pressure to stop the bleeding while she ripped off the man's tie and wrenched open buttons. She looked over at Will. "Go—someone is in here. Amanda's here for some reason…I just know it. Please, Will, *go*."

Will indicated that Jane should take the conference room while he moved toward the climate-controlled area. The two agents who'd watched the center from a distance had entered behind them. The older of the two, a tall, dark-haired man of about forty, nodded at him and then at his partner. The older agent accompanied Will, while the younger man followed Jane.

Will and the other agent passed the entry and turned to the left. They paused at the first workroom, positioned themselves on either side of the door. The agent counted off three with his fingers and Will kicked it in.

It didn't take long to see that the room was empty, except for a statuette on the work stand in the process of being cleaned.

They went down the hall and reached the climate-controlled room. Heavy plastic barriers guarded the area where the "bunny" suits were kept; steel racks held boxes of gloves, masks and booties. The plastic barriers could have hidden a person, and the two men held back again, communicating silently. The agent pulled back one of the plastic slats while Will stepped forward, Glock tightly gripped in both hands.

Will passed through the dressing area and came to the next plastic barrier, just before the entry to the clean room. The other agent was behind him.

A double sheet of plastic hung in front of the clean room itself. He moved it, looking in, thinking of the care they'd taken that day and aware that he wasn't at all clean. The preservation of history, however, had to take a backseat to the protection of the living.

The giant outer sarcophagus lay as they'd left it twelve hours before; the inner sarcophagus was on the stand, also exactly as they'd left it.

There was nothing else in the room other than the steel racks of sterile equipment and the two giant sarcophagi.

Will stepped carefully forward to look in both. The first was empty.

He went to the second, where the death mask lay over the mummy of Amun Mopat.

And that was where he found her.

Dr. Amanda Channel—wedged next to the fragile mummy, eyes closed, arms crossed over her chest.

The paramedics arrived in less than three minutes.

Still, Kat knew the guard had suffered a great deal of blood loss. Without causing further trauma, the best she could do while waiting was staunch the flow of blood and ease his breathing and that, with Tyler's help, she'd accomplished. When the emergency techs rushed in, she told them her findings and stepped back. Tyler stood at her side.

A couple of minutes later, she saw Jane returning from a search of the conference room to the right of the entry. A young FBI man in a suit was with her.

"Anything?" she asked.

Jane shook her head.

Kat heard the med techs talking to one another, their voices quiet as they assessed the victim and worked on him before transferring him to a portable gurney. Then she saw that Will and a second FBI man were walking toward them.

Will looked tense.

"Amanda Channel," he said.

"She's…here?"

"She's dead."

"Dead? No pulse, nothing?" Kat asked. "Where?"

She pushed past him before he could stop her.

"The clean room, Kat. And she is dead. Believe me."

She believed him; still, she had to check for herself. The guard stood a small chance of surviving, so, even knowing that Will was probably right, she hurried to find Amanda.

Giving no thought to dust or germs, Kat rushed through the layers of protection to get to the clean room.

"The sarcophagus," Will called from behind her.

She came to an abrupt halt, staring in shock at Amanda tucked into the sarcophagus with her beloved mummy. The woman had been as slim as a reed, which was the only reason she fit. She was wedged beside the preserved remains of the long-dead priest. No ancient linen wrap covered her, but her arms were crossed in the typical fashion of ancient Egyptian burial. Kat took a shaky breath and ran over to check for a pulse or a sign of breath. She felt Amanda's cooling flesh and knew, before using any instruments, that the woman was far beyond medical help.

Will came to stand by her side. "How long?" he asked softly.

"Core body temperature drops at an estimated rate of 0.8K every hour from the time of death," she said, "But there are variables, this room being one of them. A number of factors can be part of determining the exact time—humidity levels, air movement and, in Amanda's case, the fact that there are very few fat cells in her body. Rigor mortis has just started to set in, so…"

"Rigor mortis can set in soon after death, right?"

"Right. In half an hour or less. We'll know more at the morgue."

"Can you tell how she died?" he asked.

There were no visible signs of trauma on the body. Kat examined her eyes for petechial hemorrhage, then shook her head. "She wasn't strangled. I'm assuming it has to be from some kind of toxin in the body. I'm not seeing any blood or signs of outer damage."

"So, the guard shot himself and Amanda crawled into a sarcophagus to die?" Will asked wryly.

"That's what it's *supposed* to look like," Kat said.

Will moved away from her, speaking into his cell. Cops and emergency medical personnel had arrived in numbers now. They stood outside and she heard him directing officers to guard the perimeter but to let the crime scene detectives in to do their work. She remained by the corpse, staring at Amanda. Had the woman been part of what was going on? Or had she and Will misjudged her entirely?

She stood in the clean room, wishing that Amanda or Amun Mopat would appear in the mist around her. Or that she could look down and imagine Amanda's eyes opening, and that she'd hear what her soul was saying that her lips could not.

She was in a clean room, now compromised by dust motes and germs. The environment around here still seemed pristine, but she knew it wasn't. The noise rose as conversations sifted through to her, as she heard footsteps and the sounds of the investigation beginning.

She waited, feeling a little numb, until the crew from the morgue showed up. She was glad to see that Cranston Randall was there to represent the coroner's office. He stood by her side for a moment, gazing down at Amanda and then turning to Kat.

"Ah, yes," he said. "The curse. Those who disturb the dead and all."

"Those who practice a 'curse' are living," Kat responded.

"We know that, of course," he said. "The papers will have a heyday, however. I can assure you of that. So,

Dr. Channel is lying here dead, but the guard might survive?"

"They took him to emergency. I believe his vital organs were missed. I didn't stop to look for the shell, although I'm almost certain the bullet went all the way through."

"Let's pray the young man makes it," Dr. Randall said. He beckoned to someone, and she saw that police and forensic photographers were waiting to do their work.

Randall smiled grimly at her. "So, will you accompany me to the morgue?"

Kat nodded, glancing around. Will and Logan were talking to the Chicago homicide detective who'd come in with the crime scene crew. She stood back, still feeling that oddly numb sensation while work went on around her. At some point, Jon Hunt was called in; she could hear him crying hysterically—in both grief and terror. He kept wailing Amanda's name and talking about his own fear that he'd be the next to go.

It was hours before she and Randall were ready to leave. And when they did, Chicago had woken up. Traffic clogged the streets, horns blared and people were on their way to work.

As they drove along Lake Michigan, Kat contemplated the beauty of the sunlight on the water. Early sailboats caught the breeze, and it looked as if they were dancing across a horizon studded with diamonds.

But she knew how treacherous the water could be....

* * *

Will had been the first person on the case, so he wasn't surprised when Logan asked if he'd act as their spokesman and speak with the press. It was now almost two in the afternoon.

Standing before the mob that thronged in front of the Preservation Center, he gave a brief overview of what they'd discovered. Then the questions bombarded him.

"How did you find the guard?"

"Isn't it bizarre that it happened the first night the mummy was at the center?"

"Is this the 'curse'?"

"Who is dead?"

"What about the guard?"

"Why didn't anyone hear the shot?"

He lifted a hand; he didn't say a word but waited, and in time, his silence brought them all to silence, too.

"A *curse* did not shoot a man," he said dismissively. "We're praying first and foremost that the guard survives. Perhaps when he's conscious, he'll be able to help us. At this stage, we don't know the cause of death in the case of Dr. Amanda Channel. As to the curse? Once again let me say that not one of us believes that a curse kills. People kill. Whoever has perpetrated this heinous crime is flesh and blood and after something— and that murderer will be found. We're following up various leads in the city now, and we'll report more as soon as we have it."

"Will salvage on the *Jerry McGuen* continue?"

"It's a shipwreck and it's now been discovered. I can't imagine it'll lie there without further effort being made to retrieve the treasures and eventually provide divers with another tourist location," he added drily.

"*Everyone* will want to dive it now!" one reporter mumbled. "People are such ghouls!"

He was probably right. Will went on to field more questions, being very careful and circumspect in his answers. They had information, and they had clues that suggested certain avenues of research, but at the moment, they weren't prepared to point a finger in any one direction.

He was glad when it was over. He'd spent much of the past few days and nights diving and investigating, but the press conference was the most exhausting thing he'd done. The early-morning hours had passed quickly at the Preservation Center. Then they'd gathered what they could find before the forensics team began their work—and now the press conference.

Afterward, he was able to meet with the Texas Krewe at the police station. Logan was busy writing on another one of those white boards he was so fond of, listing what had been discovered by the forensics team.

The guard, Abel Leary, had survived surgery, but was still unconscious. Jane was maintaining a vigil at the hospital should he awaken. The shot wouldn't have been heard by any of the police who happened to be driving by for two reasons: the small caliber of the bullet and the fact that it had been fired directly against the guard's body. Thus far, fingerprints in the reception area had led them to no one but employees and board members. The alarm had been disconnected, possibly by Amanda herself when she'd returned to the center. She hadn't been seen entering because she'd used a back entrance that had supposedly been sealed off long ago.

Logan was irritated; he'd asked about other entrances and Amanda had told him there were none, that the only other one had been closed off maybe fifty years before. Jon Hunt had reported, in his hysteria, that it wasn't considered an "entrance" at all anymore. To the best of *his* knowledge, it *had* been sealed.

But Amanda had lied to them about its being sealed, probably because she knew it was still a viable entry. Jon couldn't tell them why Amanda had sneaked inside in the middle of the night.

"Here's what we know," Logan said. "At some point during the night Amanda Channel went back into the Preservation Center through a delivery door in the back—a door that hadn't been used in years. Evidently she'd found a way to open it. She turned off the alarm system to get in and someone must have followed her, although I think it's supposed to look as if the guard shot himself and Amanda crawled into the sarcophagus to die, unlikely as all of that sounds. Whether the guard's shooting is meant to resemble an accident, we can only speculate. I spoke very briefly with Kat before she and Dr. Randall accompanied the body to the morgue. They both figure it's some kind of poisoning because there's no outward sign of trauma. Whoever entered the museum did so through the same hidden entry as Amanda, since no one was seen anywhere near the front entrance and police were patrolling every fifteen minutes. Plus we had our agents watching the front."

"*Someone* had to know about the rear delivery entrance," Will said. He stood up to join Logan, who handed him the marker. "We're looking for someone with the ability to dive, who's familiar with the lake and has an interest in the treasure—or in the *Jerry McGuen* itself. This person knew Austin Miller, his house and his habits very well, just as he was familiar with the Preservation Center. It seems to me that as far as suspects go, we've always felt we needed to investigate Landry Salvage and Simonton's Sea Search. We know that Amanda was communicating with someone at Landry, and we know that both of those companies have access to motorized diving devices. We're certain that someone other than the center's people, the film crew and our own team members have been out to the site. While the local police might have initially doubted conspiracy or murder when they had a drowning victim and an elderly man dead of a heart attack, the city's law enforcement is now fully involved."

"I can investigate the preservation company's computers," Sean said. "We shouldn't have any difficulty getting access now."

"All right, Sean, that's perfect," Logan said. "Jane

will wait at the hospital. Kat's at the morgue, but I expect she'll be ready to leave soon."

"I'll pick her up," Will said. "I think we should pay the Egyptian Sand Diggers a visit. I'd also like to stop by both salvage companies again with what we know. And, after that, we should try to find out more about the *Jerry McGuen,* perhaps at Austin Miller's house."

Kelsey said, "I'll go over to the library and keep going with the research on Lake Michigan shipping, travel and icebreakers."

"The library is going to close in a couple of hours," Logan noted. "I'll make arrangements for you to have extra time there this evening," he said, "if you feel you need it."

She nodded. "The research on Chicago and the lake at the turn of the twentieth century is monumental. Tyler, you want in with me?"

"Anytime, Kelsey."

"Good," Logan said. "I'll handle communications here and work with the local authorities. Everyone—" he began, but his team finished his sentence en masse.

"Report anything, even if you think it's minor!" they chorused.

"Yep, that's it," Logan said. "So…get going!"

Like Brady Laurie, Amanda Channel had been in excellent physical condition—until she died. Her autopsy was duly carried out, and when it was complete and they were stripping out of their gowns and washing up, Dr. Randall said, "We'll have to wait for the toxicology reports. She reacted to something, and I know they'll find it."

Kat thanked him.

She hadn't expected Amanda to speak to her in the middle of a Y incision, and Amanda hadn't. Dr. Randall's diener was sewing up the incision. Amanda might speak to her in the days to come, but Kat didn't expect it.

She was worn-out when she left the morgue, and stunned to see that dusk was falling.

Before she left the building, she called Will, who said he'd come and get her.

"No, no, don't bother. I'll just grab a cab," she told him. "There are dozens on the street. I think we should head straight over to see what's going on with the Egyptian Sand Diggers tonight."

Will agreed. "That's what I had in mind, too. Today's events must be really traumatic for them. I'm sure there'll be a gathering."

"See you there."

"I'll come—" Will said.

"Will, I'm staring at three cabs!" She hung up before he could protest; she didn't want to waste time.

Still, she paused before walking out to the street.

The city was moving into nightfall, which brought a beauty of its own. There were lights on in abundance, and the place seemed to sparkle. From somewhere she could hear jazz music, and people meandered along the streets, laughing and chatting.

Kat looked back at the morgue, then hailed a cab, anxious to get on her way.

She gave the driver the address for the Egyptian Sand Diggers. As they moved through the traffic, she gazed out at the city in its evening finery.

Once she'd arrived and paid the cabdriver, she glanced around for Will's rented Honda. She didn't see it.

She stared up at the exquisite—and exquisitely maintained—Colonial Greek manor. While she waited for Will, she decided to walk around the building.

Kat could hear the low murmur of voices coming from the parlor. Slipping around the side of the house, she saw that there was a summer room in back and that, for modern Chicago, the yard was large. She immediately noticed a small entrance guarded by two sphinxes—an entrance leading into some kind of maze. A sign in English and hieroglyphics warned Enter If You Dare!

A rustle in the trees startled her and she turned quickly. She wasn't afraid of the living, not while she was armed and alert. Her service Glock was in the holster beneath her jacket, and she could draw it in a second.

However, she couldn't see anyone. She didn't really want to announce herself, since she was wandering around private property, uninvited and unaccompanied.

She was definitely intrigued by the maze, but with darkness descending, taking a stroll there wouldn't be wise.

Hearing a car door, she walked around to the front. Will had arrived, and she hurried forward to meet him.

"Hey!" he said, greeting her with a hug. There was tension in his muscles; she lowered her head, smiling, because she knew he worried about her when they were apart. It was natural. She did the same thing.

Kat liked the way he treated her, concerned but with respect, and always deferring to her now when he knew that her knowledge of a particular subject was greater than his.

"I'm okay," she assured him.

"And Amanda?"

"We have to wait for the tox reports."

He nodded.

"There's a maze in back," she told him. "Very cute. High bushes, Egyptian sculptures."

"You went out in the back *alone?*"

"I just took a look. It's private property and I'm well aware that we need imminent danger or a search warrant to prowl."

He arched a brow, offering her a half smile. "You *were* prowling around."

"But not a lot. I was admiring the landscaping."

"That wouldn't stand up in court. Anyway, shall we?"

Side by side, they climbed the steps and Will rang the

bell. Nothing happened. They knew there were people inside, so he banged on the door. When nothing happened then, either, he tried the handle. The door was unlocked.

They entered the grand old mansion off Michigan Avenue.

The hallway itself was empty. Will shrugged and they moved toward the parlor. A few members, two men and a woman, were sitting there, deep in discussion. They were all clad in loose white robes, as if they were acolytes getting ready for a religious ceremony.

The discussion stopped as soon as they noticed Kat and Will.

The woman rose. "May I help you?" she asked coolly.

Kat introduced herself and Will by their names only—not mentioning the FBI. "We were hoping we might see Dirk. Is he here?"

The woman nodded. She glanced at the men and forced a smile to her lips. "I'm Samantha Willard, and these are Bill Bartholomew and David Gleeson. Dirk is up in the study. Are you prospective members?" she asked.

"We're friends of Dirk's," Kat said.

"I'll bring you upstairs." Samantha waved at the two men. "Be right back!"

As they headed for the stairs, Will exchanged a quizzical look with Kat. There had to be a number of people in the mansion at the moment; they could hear voices coming from the kitchen and dining areas, as well as the parlor.

At the upstairs landing, Samantha led them to the first door on the left. She tapped on it lightly, and Dirk Manning called, "Come in."

He was sitting by the fireplace, also clad in one of the white robes, reading from a journal. He looked sad and drawn, but if he was surprised or dismayed to see them, he didn't reveal it. He rose, smiling. "Welcome. Welcome back. Sorrowful times, I'm afraid, but of course that's why you're here. Can you tell me what happened? Amanda Channel killed herself and a guard shot himself? Is that true?"

"I don't believe any of it, not for a minute, and that's *not* what I said at the press conference," Will told him.

Dirk Manning studied him for a minute and then smiled. "No, that's not what you said. Some of the stations actually showed you talking. Most of them only used a few words of what you said and added their own commentary. So…someone is killing off anyone connected to Amun Mopat's treasure and the salvage of the *Jerry McGuen?*"

"Frankly, it's a mess, Mr. Manning," Kat said. "You threw a party to get people interested. Brady Laurie was the most excited because he believed he had the answer—which he did. But Brady's dead, and so is Amanda."

"What did she die of?" Manning asked her.

"We think it was some type of poison," Kat said,

"but we don't know what. There was nothing obvious, but I'm positive that with the tests we've ordered, we'll find out."

"Brady Laurie was drowned, Austin Miller was sent into heart failure, a guard's been shot. And now Amanda is dead, apparently by poisoning," Will said.

"Maybe there is a curse." Manning sank back into his chair before the fire. "Maybe there really is a curse."

"And maybe the curse is greed," Will muttered.

Manning shook his head. "What kind of greed would cause someone to kill like that? Maybe, when it was just Brady, it *could* have been greed. Someone who wanted to get the treasures for him- or herself. But the location of the ship is now well-known. However, Amanda died at the Preservation Center."

"That's why we need your help." Will sat in one of the chairs by the fire, facing the old man. "For starters," he said, "what's going on here tonight?"

Manning raised his hand absently. "A farewell to our dear friend Austin Miller. A ceremony to say good-bye. The morgue has told us that they don't know when they'll release his body. These people, all of us, loved him. We will give him an Egyptian ceremony that is intended for the comfort of those left behind. We offer up food and gifts at the altar in the center of the maze. Nine of us will speak, each to a certain god of the ancient world, asking for Austin's speedy flight to the heavens above. It's a memorial," he said simply.

"That's fine, Mr. Manning. That's fine. Will other people, nonmembers, be here tonight?"

Manning nodded. "Everyone who was on our invitation list the night we had the party—the night Brady Laurie told us he thought he'd found the location of the *Jerry McGuen.*"

Will looked over at Kat. "May we attend, Mr. Manning?"

Manning was silent for a moment. "You want to attend our ceremony?" he asked, astonished. "You didn't know Austin."

"We didn't know him," Kat said, deciding she shouldn't tell Manning that, in a way, she *had* met Austin, just not when he was alive. "But we want justice for him."

"How involved do you want to be?" he asked.

"As involved as you'll let us be," Will replied.

Manning shook his head again, a look of confusion in his eyes. "I...I can't believe *we* might have brought this about, that I might be responsible for the death of my best friend. For *all* these deaths... Is it possible?"

"No, it's not," Kat said firmly. "You are not responsible for the depravity of another person, Mr. Manning, not at all. But we're pretty certain that someone who's been here *is* responsible for these deaths."

Manning straightened his shoulders. "You seem to think I'm acquainted with a killer. But I will not help one! Yes, you must stay and be involved, if you believe I can assist you any way—or if you think you might get

a shred of information from being here. Absolutely!"
He stood. "Come along," he commanded. "It's time to
prepare."

An hour later, the Egyptian Sand Diggers' clubhouse
mansion was filling up.

Will was impressed by the number of Egyptologists,
scholars and old friends who arrived for the special trib-
ute to Austin Miller.

He was equally impressed that he and Kat were
dressed and ready for the evening. They, too, were clad
in long white robes; they had brass torches to resemble
the wooden ones that would have been used during the
time of the New Kingdom.

Kat was to read a passage as Mut, or Maut. The
Egyptian word for *mother* had come from her name,
and she was the daughter of the sun god, Ra—the all-
seeing, vengeful eye of Ra. Kat had been given the Mut
headdress, which was that of a vulture, one of the forms
in which Mut could sometimes be seen.

"Cool, huh?" she whispered to Will, holding a glass
of wine as they stood casually in the dining area, meeting others as they came in.

"I think Mut is also sometimes depicted as a cow,"
he told her, grinning.

She frowned. "At least I'm not reading as a schizo-
phrenic god," she retorted.

He was reading a passage for Aker, an ancient earth
god honored in the New Kingdom and often depicted

as two lions facing away from each other. Aker was the god of the horizon—day to night, and night to day.

Kat's phone rang. She glanced at Will, fumbled through the robe to find the phone in her pocket and started to answer it.

Samantha walked by, frowning. "No cell phones once the ceremony starts!" she chastised.

"Of course," Kat murmured.

She turned away from the crowd and spoke so softly that not even Will could hear. When she turned back, she touched his cheek, as if in a gesture of affection. Of course, he hoped it was real, but she was gesturing for him to bend down.

"Saxitoxin," she whispered.

"What?"

"Saxitoxin," she said a little louder. "It's a toxin from shellfish. Amanda must have had an allergy— and someone must have known it."

"That's what killed her?" he asked. "But…how did she get in the sarcophagus with Amun Mopat?"

She shook her head. He looked away, and took a sip from his glass of "ceremonial" wine. He set the wine-glass down and, to Kat's surprise, took hers, as well.

He raised a brow and saw the comprehension in her eyes.

Nothing to eat or drink here!

Hearing someone greet a new visitor, Will stepped into the parlor and saw Andy Simonton. He was alone, but he seemed to know most of the people there.

Samantha walked toward him. Her stride had changed; it was suddenly sultry, her hips swaying beneath the robe. "Andy!"

"Sam."

"I'm so, so glad you could make it," she gushed.

Andy shrugged. "Hey, Austin was a good guy. If this is how he'd want us to say goodbye, so be it." He sighed. "That awful business at the center today—boy, I'm glad I stayed away from that ship. It sure looks like it's cursed!"

"The cops claim someone else had to have been in there—at least that's what I saw on the news," Sam said. "Personally? I think Amanda was a flake. She was in love with that mummy. She probably offed the guard herself, then climbed into the sarcophagus."

Andy Simonton shook his head. "I'm just glad I had nothing to do with that damn ship. It's scary—Brady Laurie, Austin...and now Amanda and a *guard?*"

"The guard isn't dead," Samantha said.

"Maybe the poor guy will survive to tell the tale." Simonton looked past Samantha and saw Dirk Manning. "Dirk!" he called, walking past Samantha. He set a hand on Manning's shoulder. "Hey, I'm so sorry. I know what good friends you and Austin were."

"Thank you, Andy, thank you. Samantha, I do believe just about everyone's present, is that correct?" Dirk asked.

"We're waiting on just one more—Landry. He's on

his way with a date or a friend or something," Samantha said.

As she spoke, the door opened in the hallway; Stewart Landry was there. He was accompanied by his attractive receptionist, the blonde Sherry Bertelli. She smiled vaguely when Dirk Manning came forward to greet them. "Thank you, thank you for coming. It would have meant a lot to Austin."

"We were still reeling from the news of his death when we heard about Amanda," Landry said.

"She really wasn't very nice," Sherry noted.

Manning cleared his throat. "Yes, well, it's very sad, all the same."

Andy Simonton had been standing still, watching Landry and Sherry. Landry noticed Simonton and seemed slightly surprised. "Simonton, how are you?" He strode forward, offering his hand.

Simonton took it. They behaved in a cordial manner, but both men seemed tense. "Hello, um, Ms. Bertelli," Simonton said.

"Sherry. Yes, hello, Mr. Simonton."

"Andy, please," he told her.

"Let's get started, shall we?" Manning said. "We have our nine to read in honor of our friend Austin Miller. We shall begin. If everyone will gather in the yard?"

As he spoke, Simonton caught sight of Will and Kat. He seemed curious, but not dismayed. "Hello." He walked over, gesturing at their robes. "I wouldn't have thought you were members or associates of the Sand Diggers."

"We're here because of Dirk," Kat said. "He was with us when we found Austin Miller, so…I guess we have something of a bond."

"I figured you'd be busy at the Preservation Center," Simonton said. "That's all very tragic, but…" He grimaced. "Both Brady and Amanda were obsessed. I feel bad for poor Jon Hunt, though. He must be suffering big-time. I mean, they have a guard, a receptionist… interns, but those three were the ones who really held the fort down, you know?"

"Yes, Jon isn't coping too well."

"Poor boy!" Simonton shook his head. "Well, I guess we should get into the yard."

He joined the stream heading out. Will held his reading in one hand and took Kat's hand with the other. He almost walked into Sherry Bertelli. She looked up at him and her eyes widened.

"I know you!" she said.

"Yes, hello, Ms. Bertelli."

"You're the agent. Oh!" She'd noticed Kat beside him. "And you're the other agent."

"Tonight," Kat told her, "we're just mourners."

"Did you know Mr. Miller?" she asked.

"Only in death." Kat smiled. "But he was a lovely man."

Sherry seemed perplexed; at her side, Landry paused, frowning as he saw Will and Kat.

"Good God! Do you people hold nothing sacred?" he demanded.

"Actually, we hold a man's life sacred above all else," Will said pleasantly.

"Is there a problem?" Manning called from the back door.

"We're on our way, Dirk, on our way!" Landry called, frowning again as he looked at Will.

They continued out.

In a long trail, they began the procession through the winding maze. Will knew that, alone, he'd find it difficult to orient himself. But Dirk Manning, at the head of the line, was sure of every step.

"I speak for Ra!" he intoned, waving an incense burner in front of him as he walked. "Although our brother Austin lived in a different time and place, we pray that in his new life he may forever know the warmth and nurturing power of the sun."

Samantha had the next reading. "I speak for Isis," she said. "Isis, who represents healing of all that hurts and bears down upon a laden soul. Austin, may you be relieved of the pain that is the lot of man. May you feel the grace of freedom, the health of the soul, in your new life."

By the time Samantha finished speaking, they'd come to the center of the maze. There was an altar guarded by two stone lions; in the center was a large obelisk.

Will was touched to see that many of the mourners had brought flowers, which they laid on the altar.

Other members of the group read as their assigned gods or goddesses. The first of the two men he'd met in the parlor, Bill Bartholomew, read thoughts as Khepra, god of creation and change, and talked about the new life. David Gleeson spoke words of wisdom from Seker, god of light, and the god who protected souls as they passed from this world to the next. It was while Gleeson was speaking that Will saw Kat staring hard at the altar. He focused in the same direction. After a moment, he could see the vague image of an elderly man, and then, bit by bit, Austin Miller, became more visible to him.

He stood next to Dirk Manning, his hand on his old friend's shoulder. If Dirk felt his hand in any way, he didn't show it.

Next it was Kat's turn to speak. She said the words written for her as Mut, telling the soul of Austin Miller that a mother's love would guide him. She looked straight into his eyes as she spoke. The spirit of Austin Miller looked back at her, smiling, his eyes a little moist.

Will heard Austin so clearly when he said, "Thank you, my dear," that he was certain others must have heard him, too. But they hadn't. Other speakers, including Will, read their speeches and the service continued.

"Tell my friend, please, that my old meerschaum pipe he so admired is in the pocket of the smoking jacket I left in the closet here. I want him to have it. I want him to have the pipe and to take care of himself, and I don't want him at my house or at this house alone. Tell him I fear he is in danger. There *is* a curse. I saw the mummy."

Will glanced around, wondering if anyone else could possibly see and hear Austin Miller. He seemed so clear and strong and loud. But they were all paying attention to the next speaker.

"I will," Kat said softly.

Austin Miller was still next to Dirk Manning when he brought the ceremony to a close. "Ancient Egypt is my passion," Dirk told the crowd solemnly. "Christianity is my religion, but mine is a God of love and kindness, and He understands what we did here tonight. Some scholars now consider the polytheistic beliefs of the old Egyptians as the practice of seeing one god in many ways. And as we all know, methods of worship changed over the fifty centuries that passed within the many kingdoms and periods of the people we study. Thank you all for being here. Thank you for this sendoff to our dear friend. Mortal remains, we know, mean nothing. Austin's soul is with us tonight."

Will was startled when Kat walked forward, tiny but so regal, to speak to Dirk Manning across the altar. "Dirk, Austin really *is* with us tonight. He is truly appreciative of all that you did. He wants you to know that his meerschaum pipe is in his smoking jacket, in the pocket." She stopped speaking and turned around, looking at the gathered guests. "He says there is no curse. He reminds you that you love Egyptology, but you're not superstitious fools."

Will watched her with curiosity, crossing his arms over his chest.

"But he warns that you are all in danger because of a psychotic human being, so he wants you to be careful," Kat finished.

What the hell is she doing? Will wondered.

The ghost of Austin Miller was staring at Kat. "That's not what I said, my dear. I told you—the mummy did it!"

She turned again to look straight at Austin Miller. "Someone here tonight knows what happened—what's *been* happening," Kat said.

Stewart Landry's secretary suddenly gasped. "Oh! She sees him! She sees Austin's ghost! I think…oh, there's something there, Dirk, right by you!"

Dirk Manning twitched, turning with a frown.

Obviously, he saw nothing.

"He is! He is with us!" Samantha said, raising her arms to the night sky. "We have given this ceremony in his honor, and he has become like a living god!"

Andy Simonton started laughing. "Oh, please! What a crock of shit!" he exclaimed. "I'm going to honor old Austin, all right. I'm going to have a Scotch and toast to his honor. Join me inside!"

"Hell, I'll join you!" Stewart Landry said. "We'll honor the old fellow in the way he would've liked!"

He turned. Others, confused, turned to follow him, as well. People were ready to go back to the house.

Dirk Manning looked at Kat with tears in his eyes.

"Why?" he asked her. "Why would you do such a thing, say such things—make a mockery of our ceremony?" he asked.

"Mr. Manning, I wasn't mocking you, but I'll admit I *was* using you tonight. Someone here does know what's going on, and I'm hoping I managed to unnerve that person. I'm sorry if I hurt you." She inhaled a deep breath. "I used you, yes, but I do have a…way to hear the dead."

"Of course. You're an M.E.," he said.

"That's true, but I also have a strange sixth sense." She shook her head, smiling. "What I said about the pipe was true. Austin Miller loved you like a brother. He wants you to have his pipe and I'm sure you'll find it where I said you would."

His expression was troubled. But whether he believed her or not, they would never know, because they suddenly heard shouts coming from the maze.

"Hey! Manning, how the hell do we get out of here?"

It was Andy Simonton calling to him.

"Here, Andy, follow my voice. I can get you out!"

That was Samantha, calling back.

But before anyone else could shout that they, too, were lost, there was a desperate scream and Sherry Bertelli began to sob.

"Help me, help me, oh, God, help me! It's…it's the mummy!"

12

Kat turned to stare at Will. He was already pulling his robe over his shoulders, yanking it off, ready to go in search of Sherry Bertelli.

Landry was shouting in desperation, calling her name over and over again.

Kat instantly got out of her own robe and asked Dirk Manning, "Which way? Which way would have gotten her lost?"

Manning pointed to one of the paths. Kat tore down it and crashed straight into Samantha, who looked at her with wide, terrified, eyes—speechless for once.

"Get back to the house!" Kat said, pushing her aside. People were shouting from all over the maze, and it was impossible to get a bearing on Sherry's location. At last, she went silent.

Kat envisioned the worst, but she kept running through the darkness and the shadows, guided by the moonlight that filtered down and the occasional flash of a torch carried by one or other member of the group.

She made a hurried turn to the left—and practically tripped over Sherry. The woman was lying on the ground. Kat fell to her knees just as Will reached her, too.

"Oh, Lord!" he exclaimed, hunkering down beside her. "Is she—"

"She has a strong pulse and she's breathing evenly. I think she just passed out," Kat said, relieved.

"Let's get her to the house." Will slipped his arms beneath the woman, cradling her before rising carefully to his feet. "Which way?"

"We came from that direction." Kat pointed behind them. "If we can just get to the altar…"

"Sherry, Sherry!" they heard Landry cry in anguish. "Where are you?"

"We have her! She's all right!" Will shouted in reply.

They could hear Landry babbling his relief as they approached the altar. Dirk was still standing there, as if stunned. When he saw them, he came to life again. "This way. Follow me."

He led them out of the maze. Will carried Sherry past Landry, who tried to stop him and touch Sherry.

"Mr. Landry, let's just get her inside."

"A doctor, we need a doctor!" Landry said.

"She probably scared herself after all that ridiculous ghost talk," Andy Simonton muttered. "She needs a whiskey!"

"Mr. Landry, I am a doctor," Kat said.

"Hell, yeah! A doctor for the dead!" Simonton snorted.

"I assure you, I finished my residency in a hospital working with the living," Kat told him. "Ms. Bertelli will be fine."

Will wasn't a man to be stopped easily; he'd barely slowed when Landry accosted him and he continued his long strides, carrying Sherry back to the house. He brought her to the parlor, where he placed her on the sofa. Her eyes were already opening as he did.

"Oh!" she gasped, her lashes fluttering.

"Sherry, Sherry!" Landry rushed to her side and fell to his knees, taking her hand. He smoothed her hair. "Where are you hurt?"

"I'm not hurt. I'm not hurt. I'm fine, Stewart. I'm just scared and shaken and—" She broke off. By then, everyone had come in and they were all staring at her. Her voice was tremulous. "I swear to you, there was a mummy in the maze. It walked toward me. It was terrifying!"

"I'm going for the whiskey!" Simonton said.

"They need to stop. They need to stop right now," Samantha exclaimed. "Honestly, someone should make them throw that mummy back in the lake and forget the *Jerry McGuen* was ever found. Three people are dead and one more may be dying…because there's a curse. Such things *can* exist."

"I'm afraid," Will said, "that once a discovery is

made—it's made. I sincerely doubt the mummy will be cast out to sea. And surely you know there's no curse."

"But there was a mummy in the maze," Sherry insisted.

"Then we'll search the maze," Will said quietly. "Whoever might've been there is probably long gone. Sherry might even have been startled by running into one of us in the darkness. Still, we'll search the entire maze."

"Oh, hell, no! We're not going back out there," Landry said.

"I wasn't expecting you to, Mr. Landry. We'll have the authorities do the search," Will told him.

Andy Simonton grinned. "I thought *you* were the authorities."

"We are," Kat said in an aloof voice. She pulled out her cell phone. "And we will investigate the maze."

"You…you can't. You…can't!" Sherry cried. "There was a curse. It was written on Amun Mopat's tomb. Just because it was unspoken doesn't mean it doesn't exist!"

Simonton shook his head and laughed. "Unspoken? It's all anyone talks about, writes about or puts on the news. And Ms. Bertelli, I'm sorry, I don't mean to be cruel, but there is no mummy in that maze. We all scared ourselves—*she* scared us!" he said, pointing at Kat. He walked over to her. "You may be all kinds of gorgeous, honey, but you're a freak!"

Kat could feel Will's tension; it would have made

her smile if she hadn't been afraid he was ready to deck Andy Simonton.

She rose swiftly to her own defense. "It's Special Agent Sokolov, not *honey,* Mr. Simonton. Or Dr. Sokolov, if you prefer. I'll be happy to answer to either. And I wasn't creating an illusion or a freak show. Dirk, would you be so good as to find out if I'm right or not?"

Manning hurried to the closet. It was a big walk-in closet and it took him a few minutes to rummage through the many jackets there.

He stepped out of the closet and stared at Kat in utter disbelief.

"Well?" Simonton demanded.

Dirk produced the exquisitely carved meerschaum pipe.

There was an audible gasp.

"She planted it there," Simonton said.

"No, she didn't." The whisper of incredulity in Dirk's voice made those around him fall silent.

Kat looked around the room, letting her eyes settle on Stewart Landry first, and then on Andy Simonton. "The dead do speak to me," she said quietly. "And someday soon, one of the dead will tell us who was behind all this."

"What?" Sherry gasped.

Simonton scowled at her. "She's pretending she talks to ghosts!" he said.

Kat smiled. "Actually, I was referring primarily to the fact that I'm a medical examiner. And the dead speak through their remains. They speak to me," she said again. "There isn't a killer out there who doesn't make a mistake, and a dead body will eventually tell us just what that mistake was. There's so much we can learn." Of course, they hadn't learned much on the scientific front yet, not from Austin or Amanda, but none of these people knew that.

Sherry let out a little sob. "Please, Stewy, I want to go home now!" she said.

Her words began the exodus. Most of the crowd looked warily at Kat as if they were more than a little afraid of her, but no one approached her or said a word.

The fact that Will was standing behind her—tall, broad-shouldered and fierce—might have had something to do with that.

At last they were alone with Dirk Manning.

"Mr. Manning," Will told him, "we are concerned for your safety. I'm getting some of our fellow agents out here with good lights and we'll go through the maze. But I don't think you should be alone tonight. I'd like you to stay at the hotel with us."

To Kat's astonishment, Manning didn't blink an eye. "You're sure you can get me a room? I can be on the same floor with you agents?"

"I'm sure we can arrange it." Will pulled out his phone and turned aside. Kat could hear him speaking with Logan, but she gave her attention to Dirk.

"Mr. Manning, I need you to think hard. If any of your associates have behaved strangely in the last while, if any of them have seemed either uninterested or too interested in what's going on, we need to know."

Manning groaned. "I'm numb right now. I can't seem to think of anything."

"Don't worry. Maybe after you've had some sleep..."

"You really saw him—Austin. You really saw him?"

She nodded.

"So there *is* something more!" he whispered.

Will walked over to them. "We'll have other Krewe members here in a few minutes. Kat, you want to stay with Mr. Manning until then? I'll get started in the maze."

"You won't know where you're going," Manning protested. "If there's anything out there..."

"If there's anything out there that would hurt me, it's human—and I have a gun," Will assured him.

"I don't know what's going on," Dirk said when Will had gone.

"We'll find out," Kat told him. They would; she just prayed it would be before anyone else died.

"Sherry Bertelli must have *imagined* she saw a mummy," Dirk mused. "I think—"

"You know," Kat broke in, "maybe Andy Simonton's idea wasn't so bad. I'm going to get you a drink. What's your preference?"

"Scotch," Dirk said. "A good shot of Scotch!"

She went to the kitchen and fixed him a drink. When she returned to the parlor with it, she sat across from where he perched on the sofa.

"I do miss Austin. So much," he said. "We used to run this place, plan events, bring in speakers, write out invitations…."

"Speakers? Do you have other people involved—other than the list of forty members you gave us?" Kat asked him.

"Well, we have what we call 'associates'—when they allow us to call them that," Dirk replied. "Scholars, people in the field…people we find interesting. Adding names like that helps when you have events or you're fundraising," he told her. "We hold events to raise money for children's charities. We're quite a humanitarian organization."

"I know. But could you get me a list of those associates? Before we leave tonight?"

He nodded. She rose, certain that she'd heard a car door.

She had. Opening the front door, she saw that Logan and her Krewe had arrived.

"We need to search a maze?" Logan asked. They'd come prepared; everyone carried a high-beam flashlight.

She quickly explained much of what had happened. "I'll show you out," she said, looking at Logan and indicating Dirk, who still sat on the sofa.

Kelsey walked past her. "I'll stay with Mr. Manning," she said. Entering the parlor, she greeted Dirk, reminding him that they'd met under sad circumstances. Kelsey was charming, as always, and Dirk seemed fine.

"Come on, I'll take you out to the maze. Will's already there."

In the yard, she shouted so Will would hear her and know that the others had come. "I'm almost at the end to the right. So far, nothing!" he called back.

"We should be sticking together," Logan said. "Tyler, you're with me. Kat, hang with Sean."

She followed the two men. It was hard going in the dark, and a little eerie, since at practically every turn there was a statue of a god or goddess in the form of whatever creature was usually linked with him or her.

She almost walked past a life-size marble Bastet. But something about it caught her eye and she walked back.

There was a pale smear at the base of the tail. She trained her flashlight on it.

"What is it?" Sean asked, circling back to her.

She dug in her pocket for an evidence bag and removed what she'd seen.

"What the hell?" Sean muttered.

"More of the gauze—or real mummy linen. Like the stuff we found on the wall at the hotel—and at Austin Miller's house."

There was nothing else in the maze. There was no real proof that the gauze was disintegrating fabric from thousands of years ago, but since the other pieces had proven to be just that, Will had little doubt that they'd found more of the same.

The night grew long. Because Chicago Homicide

was now involved, Logan felt that they needed to at least report the evening's strange events to Sergeant Jenson and the detective who'd been at the Preservation Center. Both officers arrived at the Egyptian Sand Diggers' mansion and added notations to their records. Will meant to keep control of the piece of mummy evidence, and he was glad the officers were appreciative of being in the know—despite not being in control.

Jenson told Will, "I'm not sure what we'd investigate even if you handed it over to us. A woman who thinks she saw a mummy in the middle of a whacked-out memorial? Or a shred of mummy fabric at a clubhouse for Egyptian scholars?"

Jane called in a report to Logan from the hospital. Abel Leary, the guard who'd been shot, was still unconscious. He had fallen into a coma. Doctors were encouraged that his vital signs seemed stable, but he wasn't yet capable of providing them with any information.

The crime scene techs had retrieved gunshot residue from Abel Leary's hands, but that fact was being withheld from the public for the time being, as were the results of Dr. Amanda Channel's toxicology report.

When they returned to the hotel, the Krewe members were exhausted. There was no meeting. Will and Kat had taken Dirk to his home to collect an overnight bag, and a room was found for him on the same floor as the agents. Then everyone retired for the night.

Kat seemed small and fragile, and when she headed for the shower, Will thought she might want to be alone.

He drew out his notes, thinking that if he studied them for a while, it might lead to a better night's sleep. He was surprised when Kat appeared outside the bathroom, clad only in a towel. "Too tired to join me?" she asked.

He looked at her and smiled. "Maybe one day. When we've weathered a few more very long days and nights together," he answered. "But not yet."

There was something about being together in the heat and steam of the shower that erased exhaustion. Maybe it was the wonder of life itself, the excitement of the sensations and feelings that could arise between two people.

Maybe it was finding a woman who was stunning and complex and beautiful beyond measure. A woman who'd found him, too. Making love in the shower seemed so natural, and when they were finally out and dry and in bed, sleep came quickly and easily. He woke up hours later, and she was cradled in his arms. He held her, just watching her. Watching her breathe and the rhythmic motion of her heartbeat. He felt her warmth, and he lay there for long moments savoring the feel of waking with her beside him, suddenly and perhaps ridiculously certain that this was the way he'd like to wake every morning of his life.

Then the alarm rang, and it was time to start the day.

They didn't go down to the hotel dining room that morning; Logan had ordered food for the suite.

He stood by his boards, going through points he'd

written down. "Saxitoxin—that's the poison that killed Amanda Channel. But she should have suffered before she died. She should have shown some signs of trauma. In short, she shouldn't have been able to crawl into a sarcophagus, curl up with her favorite mummy and die. And, once again, we're left with a dilemma. This is a poison she might have acquired herself from eating shellfish. But, according to Jon Hunt, Amanda *knew* she was allergic to shellfish, so why would she have eaten it? There were trace elements of lobster in her stomach contents so, somehow, the woman ate lobster. East-coast ocean seafood." He paused. "Of course, it could have been concealed in a stew or a soup…"

"Someone must have tricked her into eating it," Will said.

"Yes. It takes effect quickly, so I believe beyond the shadow of a doubt that someone was in the Preservation Center with her."

"Amanda probably wanted to get back into the center, even after it closed for the day," Kat said. "She was obsessed with that mummy. I don't think it would be difficult for anyone to guess she'd go back."

Will glanced up; he'd been reading the invitation lists of "associates" Dirk Manning had given them before they'd left the Sand Diggers' mansion the night before.

"The Preservation Center doctors are on this list. All three of them—Brady, Amanda and Jon Hunt," he told the others. "The heads of both salvage companies—Stewart Landry and Andy Simonton—are on it, as well." He looked at Kat. "There's also a name I wasn't expecting."

"Who?" Logan asked him.

"Dr. Alex McFarland."

"I'm lost. Who is McFarland?" Kelsey asked.

"Dr. Alex McFarland is the medical examiner Kat and I met when we went to the morgue to view Brady Laurie's remains," Will answered.

"McFarland?" Kat repeated. "He did know all about the ship, the lakes and a lot about the Chicago Ancient History Preservation Center."

"He wasn't at the ceremony last night," Will said.

"All right," Kat began. "So suppose Sherry Bertelli did see someone in a mummy suit last night, someone carrying around one of those swatches of real mummy cloth. McFarland wasn't there, so he could've slipped in before us, ready to 'haunt' someone in the maze once everything broke."

"Would McFarland have access to real mummy wrapping?" Kelsey asked.

"Someone who worked at the center might have," Kat said. "We've been focused on the *Jerry McGuen* and Amun Mopat. But many museums have mummies, and I'm sure the center has worked with plenty of Egyptian relics. That's probably true of the Sand Diggers, too. If Dr. McFarland is one of their 'associates' and a reputable pathologist, he might have had access to a mummy at sometime."

"Motive," Logan said. "What would McFarland have wanted?"

"Motive seems to be the main problem with all our suspects," Kat pointed out. "Yes, the *Jerry McGuen* holds untold riches. So, if someone was trying to throw off the salvage—in killing Brady Laurie—that would make sense. But it's not going to matter how many people die, or how many times someone shouts 'curse.' That treasure has been discovered. The world at large won't forget. If the center pulls out, if the film crew pulls out—someone else will go in."

"Either Landry Salvage or Simonton's Sea Search could be the company given the right to go in," Logan said.

"So how would that involve a Chicago M.E.?" Tyler mused.

"We figured that more than one person has to be in on this," Kat said. "It looked like Amanda might be part of it, but Amanda is dead."

"McFarland was the M.E. who wanted to sign off so quickly on Brady Laurie's death. He was adamant that it had been an accident," Will explained. "Maybe he knew exactly what happened to Brady Laurie. And maybe he knew that whether or not he pulled the Miller autopsy, a heart attack was a heart attack, and no one could prove otherwise."

"That sounds like a stretch," Logan said.

"Maybe we should pay him a visit," Tyler suggested. "Shake him up a bit."

"I think we should go a step further." Kat looked at Logan. "Have the police go and get him. Bring him down to the station and ask him questions there."

"Will gave the man a hard time at the morgue, right?" Logan said. "Then Will should interrogate. With Tyler. You can play desperate lawman needing information, Tyler. And Will, you continue knocking his ability." Logan took out his phone. "I'm going to have Sergeant Riley bring him in, since he was the first one called in on the accidental death. Will, Tyler—get down to the station. See what we can get out of the man…if anything. He could just be a pompous jerk, but at this point, we need to start real interrogations. Kelsey, spell Jane at the hospital so she can get some sleep."

"I'd like to bring Dirk Manning the files we took from Austin Miller's house and return there with him," Kat said. "I still think that we're missing something we should be seeing."

"Good idea." Logan made a note. "Sean will go with you two."

"There's another thing," Will said slowly. "I don't know if it means anything or not."

They all looked at him.

"The filming has stopped, if only temporarily. Dives to the wreck have stopped. If that's what someone wanted, it's happened," he said.

Logan nodded thoughtfully. "Will, call Alan King. Tell him that tomorrow you'll dive to get more footage of the entire ship. We'll assure the Chicago authorities and the Preservation Center—that's Jon Hunt now, unless we go to their board—that nothing will be touched until an Egyptologist is back down with us. But, Will, you're right. The diving *has* stopped. And we shouldn't let that happen. There's still something down there that someone wants. Either that, or it's at the Chicago Ancient History Preservation Center."

"And I can't help believing the clues are at Austin Miller's house," Kat said.

Dr. Alex McFarland seemed to believe he'd been brought down to the police station to be helpful; after all, he was an M.E.

He sat in one of the interrogation rooms, idly looking around, then playing with his cell phone, slamming it down when it didn't work. Will and Tyler watched for a while with Sergeant Riley.

Riley shook his head. "The man may have medical degrees up the wazoo, but he doesn't seem that sharp to me. I mean, he doesn't strike me as the mastermind behind three deaths and an attempted murder."

"He might still be part of this," Will said. He glanced at Tyler. "Want to show him that list of 'associate' Sand Diggers?" he asked.

"Okay, I'm moving in."

Although Tyler was imposing—tall and Texan, with his service pistol visible at this side—he introduced himself to McFarland in a friendly fashion. The two chatted for a while. Tyler explained that he'd been with the Texas Rangers before joining a unit of the FBI. He complained about the amount of training he'd had to do all over again, drawing McFarland's sympathy.

Then he showed him the roster.

McFarland looked startled. He thrust the roster back at Tyler. "Those Sand Diggers think they can put anybody on their list! I didn't attend their 'raise the *Jerry McGuen* party.' I like Egyptology, but if I was going to support anything, it would be the Chicago Ancient History Preservation Center. Those folks know what they're doing."

Will chose that moment to go in. McFarland was immediately hostile, getting to his feet when he saw Will.

"Those folks did know what they're doing," Will said with a smile. "But they're mostly dead now, aren't they?"

"I don't even dive!" McFarland protested. "I did nothing to harm anyone."

"I'm not so sure. It seems to me that you might have been involved somehow. You wanted to put Brady Laurie's death down as accidental, but it's starting to look like you were way off base with that."

McFarland leaned forward. "You still don't *know* that's true. There are a bunch of could-bes with what you tried to sell, Agent Chan. And there's still a bunch of maybes. I didn't do the autopsy on Austin Miller but I read the reports. There was a bruise on the back of Miller's arm. *As if* he'd warded someone off. But he could have gotten that bruise anywhere. And even with Amanda Channel—hell, I've seen way too many people die under similar circumstances. She could have died of anaphylactic shock from shellfish at any time."

Will had taken a seat across from him. Listening, he turned a pen over and over in his fingers. McFarland had realized he wasn't at the station as an expert witness, after all. He was looking intimidated, but Will figured Logan had bargained on that.

He smiled. "I don't know about Amanda, and I don't even know that much about Brady. But I do know about Austin Miller."

"What do you mean?" McFarland asked.

"I know he was sitting in his den, relishing the idea that the *Jerry McGuen* and Amun Mopat's treasures were about to be found. And while he sat there, about to turn on his alarm and go to bed for the night, someone walked through the patio doors and approached him— someone dressed as a mummy. I know that when Austin reached for his pills, that so-called mummy slammed them from his hand."

"How do you know that?" McFarland demanded, his face growing red.

"Because Austin told us," Will said.

"Austin is dead!" McFarland screamed.

"Yeah, ain't that a bitch?" Tyler asked quietly.

"Yeah? You talked to a *dead* man?" McFarland jeered. "You people are just as big a bunch of loonies as those Sand Diggers!"

"No, Dr. McFarland," Will told him. "You think it's

only the body that can tell us what happened. What you don't see is that there's so much more. We study a man's habits—and his home. And the evidence tells us that he was visited by someone dressed up as a mummy."

McFarland looked as if he was about to explode and, at that moment, Will agreed with Riley that McFarland was no mastermind. The people behind these deaths weren't afraid of a curse and didn't believe in ghosts. They would've been startled that the Krewe had worked out exactly what happened, but wouldn't have given themselves away so easily.

But McFarland was somehow *involved.*

"Look, I swear to you, I don't know anything about what's going on. The only time I've ever been to that society was when I gave a lecture on ancient embalming techniques. And—"

He stopped speaking abruptly.

"And what?" Will snapped.

McFarland let out a breath. "We, uh, talked about the mysteries of Ancient Egypt. How some of the pharaohs and other high-ranking people died. The kinds of things that wouldn't have been obvious to the medical field a century ago. Tooth decay, poison, allergic reactions…"

"Like…*shellfish* allergies?" Will asked.

McFarland nodded. "It was just a lecture. People give lectures like that all the time. To police units, criminology students, clubs and societies. Look, I didn't tell anyone how to do it! And if someone used that information, it's not my fault!"

* * *

Kat stood in Austin Miller's office. A number of the files and journals the man had kept lay open on his desk, but she'd become fascinated with a picture on the wall. She'd been in the room with Dirk Manning for a while, reading. Sean Cameron, who'd accompanied them, had brought along the computers belonging to Brady Laurie and Amanda Channel. He was to crack all their codes and passwords, find out if either had been doing business or communicating with anyone of interest—current suspect or not.

He worked near the entry. The patio doors were locked; the alarm had been set.

As Sean worked, he kept an eye on the house itself, watching over Kat and Dirk Manning. He'd told them that the alarm was functioning perfectly, but promised to remain on guard.

Manning had been nervous about the whole idea, but she and Sean had managed to reassure him.

The ship in the painting rode the high waves with majestic beauty.

"The *Jerry McGuen*," Dirk Manning said, standing behind her.

"She was a beautiful ship," another voice said.

Kat turned. Manning looked at her, and she smiled. "He's here, Dirk. Austin is here. I can't explain how to see him or feel him, but he's here."

Dirk sat down in the chair behind the desk, hard.

"He can't see me, can he?" Austin asked her sadly.

"No, not now, but he may," she said. "Later on."

"He who?" Dirk asked, his expression lost. "Me?"

"Yes. But Dirk, I swear to you, he's here with us."

Tears stung Dirk Manning's eyes. "My old friend. My good friend!" he said softly.

"You be careful." Austin set a hand on Dirk's shoulder. "You be careful, my friend."

Manning trembled. "I feel…something. Like a little chill," he whispered.

"Austin's standing right behind you," Kat told him. "That's what you felt, Dirk. His presence."

Austin frowned at Kat. "And you, young lady! You repeat my words just as I say them, do you understand? What were you up to last night? You said things I didn't!"

"Mr. Miller, I'm trying to lure your killer into the open."

"You might have gotten a young woman killed!" he said indignantly.

"If that young woman and the others hadn't rushed off in such a fright, nothing would have happened. All right now, both of you—what can you tell me about the sinking of the *Jerry McGuen?*"

Dirk gave her a half smile. "I'm old—but not that old."

"But you two know so much. What do you think of this? Will Chan believes the ship might have been purposely sunk—rammed by an icebreaker on the lake. Have you ever heard such a story?"

"An icebreaker..." Dirk murmured. "Of course, many shipping companies were using icebreakers on the Great Lakes by the turn of the century. So was the Coast Guard."

"Why would an icebreaker have been used to sink the *Jerry McGuen?*" Austin muttered with a frown.

"I don't know. That's why I'm asking you two," Kat said.

"Is Austin *speaking?*" Dirk asked.

"Yes."

"You can see him? You can have conversations with him?"

"Yes. And you can feel him. I see that you do," Kat said. "Okay, listen. This is what we think. Whoever is doing this isn't after treasure. Any treasure belongs to the State of Illinois, or probably to the Egyptian people. Our theory is that the person or persons behind this followed Brady's steps and actually reached the *Jerry McGuen* first, but they didn't go down to get various little pieces or even big pieces that they might put on the black market. I believe they're after something specific for reasons that have nothing to do with money or with Egyptology, per se. Someone purposely sank the *Jerry McGuen* because of whatever this object might be. And someone is killing now, with the express purpose of recovering that object. Someone or several someones," she added.

Dirk stared at her blankly. Then he said, "Ask Austin. He has a book somewhere with pictures of ships from the late 1800s, including the icebreakers of the time. Maybe you can find what you're looking for there."

Kat wasn't sure *what* she'd discover by studying the ships, but it was worth a try.

"Where is the book, Austin?" she asked.

"Under the golden jackal in the display case," Austin told her. He walked to the case and pointed. "Here."

Kat pulled it out and brought it to the desk, sitting in the guest chair across from Dirk. She began to flip through the pages, wondering what she could see in a photograph.

Then she froze. The picture had been taken more than a hundred years ago and it was grainy and unclear, but it gave her what she wanted.

She turned the book to face Manning and shoved it toward him.

"She was called the *Egyptian,*" Kat said.

"Yes, yes, I've seen pictures of her. But she went down, too."

"When?" Kat grabbed the book back.

"The same year the *Jerry McGuen* went down, but she was discovered decades ago. She's in deep water, below two hundred feet. And she's completely wrecked—pieces scattered all over the lake bed," Manning said.

"But she was an icebreaker, right?"

Manning tapped the book impatiently. "That's what it says, is it not?"

"Look at her closely. What's that on the bow?" Kat asked.

"A figurehead. Ships back then had figureheads."

"Look at it *closely*," Kat insisted.

Manning bent over the book. "The figurehead's an Egyptian man. It's a myth, really, that all figureheads were female. I've seen stunning examples of figureheads that were carved as males. That one is of—"

He looked up at Kat.

"That's Amun Mopat," she finished for him. "That's the exact image of the death mask on the mummy."

13

Will was eager to speak with Dirk Manning. Now that he knew the medical examiner had given a speech that was, for all intents and purposes, on *ways* to kill without being detected, he wanted to know precisely who among the Egyptian Sand Diggers and their so-called associates had been at the lecture.

But when Kat answered his call, he noticed that her tone was odd, and before he could make his request, she told him what she'd learned.

"So, there really was an icebreaker, and it was named the *Egyptian* and it went down the same year," he summarized.

"Yes, and the figurehead was Amun Mopat," she said.

"Well, it explains your dream."

"I'm looking up more information on it now," she told him.

"Great. Find out anything you can. And tell Dirk Manning what I need the names of all those who were at Dr. McFarland's lecture."

"I'll do that."

"Ask him to write up a list for me," Will said. "And in the meantime, ask him if Stewart Landry and Andy Simonton attended. I think it's time to bring them in for questioning, as well."

He heard Kat speaking with Dirk; a moment later she came back to the phone. "Yes, Will. Both men were there. The lecture was presented at a barbecue luncheon at the Sand Diggers' mansion."

"Thanks, Kat. I'm going to see that both men are now invited down to the station for a bit of discussion."

"We still don't have any proof," she said.

"Yes, but those two are looking more and more suspicious. They both have small boats that would work well as dive boats. Both men own diver motor devices, and both have been with the Sand Diggers. If they were connected with Brady Laurie or Amanda in any way, they'd know about the facilities at the Preservation Center, and if Amanda had relationships with either of these men, she might have thought she was encouraging help while she was giving away information she shouldn't have been. I don't know how it all fits together yet, but I feel we're making progress. And questioning the men in a police station might get more out of them, just as it did with Dr. McFarland."

"You go for it," Kat said. "I'll keep reading."

"Keep me posted on whatever you learn."

"Okay. Oh, anything from Jane or Kelsey about the guard?"

"Not that I've heard," Will replied.

They rang off a minute later.

"Who should we bring in first?" Tyler asked him. "Landry or Simonton?"

"I say we bring them both in," Will said. "Make sure each knows the other is there, and then we'll see if any accusations fly."

Tyler nodded in agreement. "I'll tell Riley to send out escorts with our invitation."

"Your grandfather would have been a talented journalist," Kat told Austin Miller.

"My grandfather?" Dirk asked her blankly.

"Sorry. Austin's grandfather," Kat said. "Austin, can you show me which of these might have been written *after* the *Jerry McGuen* went down?"

Austin tried to push the journals toward her, but his spectral fingers went right through them. Impatiently, he tried again.

A book moved half an inch.

Dirk Manning jumped to his feet, staring at the journals and then at Kat.

"He's really here. I mean...*really*," he said, his voice a mere breath.

"Yes, and I think this is the book I want," Kat said, picking up the journal he'd indicated. It was dated late February, about two months after the sinking of the *Jerry McGuen*.

Since the two men were with her, she read aloud.

"'The *Egyptian* was lost today—the news was terrible. Twenty-two men on board, and not a survivor among them. But then, I always thought Captain Ely was more of a fanatic than any man on a dig. He was a *believer*. His wife told me once that he adhered to spiritualism and that he had an intense belief in magic, in ghosts—and in curses. I spoke to him once, soon after the loss of the *Jerry McGuen*. He told me that men were fools if they did *not* believe in a higher power. I assured him that I was a good and active member of the Episcopal Church. He shook his head and said I did not begin to understand all the powers we could not see. He told me that day that the *Jerry McGuen* had gone down because of the curse, that no man should have interfered with the tomb of Amun Mopat. I should've known, he told me. Amun Mopat had been a powerful sorcerer. He had maintained vast power through his scepter. Of course, I had seen the scepter—I was there the day it was found in the tomb. It was a beautiful piece, a rod or staff of the most valuable ebony, carved with vultures and lions and cobras and topped with the largest, most fantastic ball of crystal I have ever seen. I knew, from what hieroglyphics I could decipher in the tomb and the painting within, that Amun Mopat had used the scepter in his ceremonies. He had raised it to the sun, and when the sun caught the crystal, it seemed that the entire sky lit up, and whenever it did, people kneeled before him. I held the scepter myself, and I tried to explain to Captain Ely that it was a beautiful artifact, nothing more. But legend claimed that it was the scepter that gave Amun Mopat the power of the gods. He could save lives with it, and he could take lives away. The power was so great that he was beloved of Ramses II. Riches came to him, and people bowed to the ground when he walked by, as if he were himself a god or a pharaoh. Captain Ely seemed to believe that I was the crazy one. I do not understand precisely why he was so determined to retrieve the scepter, whether his intent was for good or ill. They say that after the sinking of the *Jerry McGuen,* he became worse and worse, more and more deluded. Men were afraid to sail aboard his ships, and on the night his *Egyptian* went down, many had warned him that was not a night for even an icebreaker to be out on the water.'"

Kat set the book down. "That's it," she said quietly. "I believe that whoever is doing this is after the scepter, and that's why the center was broken into, why Amanda is dead and why the guard was shot. But the scepter wasn't in the sarcophagus."

"Well, of course not," Dirk said, frowning. "You just read from the journal. Austin's grandfather was there when it was discovered in the tomb. It must have been packaged and crated separately."

"So," Kat said. "It's still down in Lake Michigan."

"And Captain Ely went down to the bottom of Lake Michigan, too," Dirk said, shaking his head.

"He did die because of the curse," she said, and when both men looked at her, she said, "It was in his head. He let himself believe in the evil of it, and he brought it to life. Curses are only real when we allow them to be."

As Will and Tyler watched from their vantage point behind the glass, Landry and Simonton met each other in the hallway leading to the interrogation rooms.

Both men came to a sudden halt. Landry spoke first. "Simonton. What are you doing here?"

"Same as you, I imagine." Landry shrugged. "Trying to help them figure out what's going on with the salvage on the *Jerry McGuen*."

"Yeah," Simonton said. "They asked me down."

"Think we were really *invited?*" Landry drawled.

"What difference does it make? We're here, right?"

Will remained behind the one-way glass of the interrogation room. As arranged, Tyler came up to the two men. "Mr. Landry, if you will? The room right here. Mr. Simonton, can you accompany me down the hall, please?"

Landry sat at the table in the small interrogation room, and Will decided to let him wait there for a few minutes.

Landry drummed his fingers on the scarred wooden table, leaned back in his chair, then sat forward again.

He looked impatiently at his watch and fidgeted some more.

Finally, Will went in to join him, dropping his file on the desk between them.

Landry frowned. "*You?* I thought the cops wanted to talk to me."

"Despite what you might see on TV, the FBI and the police are after the same outcome, Mr. Landry."

"I'm at a total loss as to what you want from me. An idiot diver drowns, and an old man has a heart attack. Then that crazy Egyptologist at the center tries to kill a guard or whatever and offs herself—and you think *I* might be involved?"

Will smiled. "Mr. Landry, you were very upset last night when you believed Ms. Bertelli was being attacked by a mummy."

"By some fake mummy, yes. Not by me!"

Will didn't reply.

"Hey, you could see me almost every second—and I sure as hell wasn't dressed up as a mummy."

Will pushed the folder forward. "Mr. Landry, you own an Aquasport Explorer and an Osprey, along with two Sea Ray boats. You also own a UPD—an underwater propulsion device. And you attended a lecture given by Dr. Alex McFarland on ways to kill."

"*What?* That lecture was on Egyptian embalming!"

Will shrugged. "According to Dr. McFarland, he also talked about poisons that weren't easily detected—or that might be accidentally ingested."

Landry waved a hand in the air. "I attended that lecture for the lunch!" he said. "And what the hell—I like the Sand Diggers. You people are so busy looking for evil, you don't look at the good that group does for the community."

"I like the Sand Diggers, too," Will said pleasantly. "But here's the thing. Let me show you one more document."

Landry stared down at the paper. "What the hell is this?"

"Amanda Channel's phone log. You'll see the number for your company multiple times over the past few months."

"She wasn't calling me."

"Who runs your company, Mr. Landry?" Will asked. "I do!"

"Yes, that's what Mr. Simonton said," Will threw in.

"Simonton! He's probably guilty!"

Will ignored that. "Would you know if any of your possessions—personal or corporate—were being used?"

Landry leaned forward. "I've had my UPD under cover at the boat dock on my *private* property. It hasn't been used this year. I haven't been out on the water at all."

"Getting old? That's tough, when you're in love with a sweet young thing like your receptionist."

He straightened in his chair. "I'm married, Agent Chan," he said indignantly. "I care about Ms. Bertelli and she attends many business functions with me. I'm not *getting old*—I'm a CEO and I have staff to do the day-to-day work. But guess what? None of them have used my UPD. It's in the boat hangar, along with my private pleasure boats. You want to go see?"

Will rose. "I think that would be a great idea, Mr. Landry. I'd very much like to see the inside of your hangar and your boats."

It was late afternoon when Logan called Kat. He told her quickly that Jane had slept for a while and had awakened and was back at the library, researching the icebreaker *Egyptian* and her captain.

"But I'm really calling you about our shooting victim—Abel Leary. Kelsey just phoned me. The doctors say he's taking a turn for the better. They believe he'll wake up soon."

"I'll go over there," she said.

"Have Sean drop you at the hospital and then bring Manning to me. He'll be safe. Kelsey can keep an eye on him, and I'm sure they'll entertain each other."

"We'll head out right now."

Manning didn't want to leave the house; he wanted to believe that eventually he'd see Austin Miller.

But even more than that, he didn't want to be alone where a mummy had stalked his friend, so he was willing to go with Kat and Sean. He clearly felt relieved that Sean would stay with him until he could deliver him to the safety of more agents.

Kat liked Dirk Manning, and she liked the ghost of Austin Miller. She assured Manning she'd be with him as much as possible and would see him later. He watched her as she got out of the car at the hospital.

"You be careful!" he told her anxiously.

She found her way to the floor where Kelsey had been sitting outside Abel Leary's room, reading a book on Egyptology.

"Decided I should do some research," she said. "I always thought of Ramses II as the Yul Brynner character in the old movie. And I hated him, of course, because he was enslaving people. But this is a fascinating book. We're looking at millennia. Most people believe that Ramses II was king at the time of Moses, but it's not really certain, and it's not specifically stated in the Bible. And all the evidence says that Ramses II was truly a great ruler. Egypt prospered under him. So, if Amun Mopat was one of his priests, maybe he wasn't as evil as he's been portrayed."

"Maybe not," Kat agreed, but she told Kelsey about the icebreaker, the *Egyptian,* and how it had carried a figurehead of Amun Mopat. "Which sounds crazy. Apparently, Captain Ely, who had Amun Mopat for a figurehead, believed in the curse. Why have the man as a figurehead if you thought he was capable of such evil?"

"Maybe he felt evil warded off evil?" Kelsey suggested. "Or maybe he was avenging what was done to Amun Mopat's tomb?"

"Yes, I suppose."

"Do you really think the man would have been

crazy enough—or obsessed enough—to ram the *Jerry McGuen?*"

Kat nodded. "Yes. I believe he had his icebreaker ram the ship and that's why she went down, not because of the storm. There *was* a storm, of course, but the *Jerry McGuen* was an impressive ship. It would have taken an impact like that of an icebreaker to tear out her hull."

The door to Abel Leary's room opened and his doctor stepped out. Kelsey introduced the young man as Dr. Gilliam, and she introduced Kat as Dr. Sokolov instead of Agent. Kat grinned; when the title worked, they used it.

"He's conscious and he's stable, but…five minutes," Dr. Gilliam said. "He's still floating in and out, and on top of his injuries, we're pumping him full of medication, several of them for pain."

"Has he said anything to you?" Kat asked.

"He's tried, but I honestly have no idea what he's babbling on about. Perhaps he'll make more sense to you. Five minutes," he repeated emphatically.

"Of course," Kat said.

She slipped into the room, aware that Kelsey had followed and stood just behind her.

Abel Leary was probably in his late twenties. There was an IV in his arm, heart monitor attached, the instrument panel at his side humming its watchful rhythm. His eyes were closed when they entered, and Kat said his name very softly. His lids flickered for a moment, then his eyes opened and he stared at her.

"Hello." His eyes closed and he winced. He slowly opened them again. "Are you an angel?" he asked in a raw, husky voice.

"Mr. Leary, I'm Kat Sokolov and I'm with the FBI. This is my colleague, Kelsey O'Brien. We're trying to catch whoever did this to you. We're desperate for any help you can give us."

His eyes closed once more.

"I shot myself," he said. "Didn't you see? I shot myself."

"Why would you shoot yourself, Mr. Leary? Did you see Amanda Channel when she came in?"

He winced again, obviously in pain.

His eyes met hers. "No," he said. "I didn't see Amanda Channel."

"What *did* you see, Mr. Leary? What did you see that caused you to shoot yourself?"

He was silent again for a minute. "No one will believe me," he said.

"We'll believe you, Mr. Leary. We're trying to get to the bottom of this."

"They said it was cursed," he murmured.

"What happened? We're open to anything you have to say, I swear," Kat told him.

He looked at her again and seemed to really focus on her. "Are you sure you're not an angel? Hey, if I get out of here, do you want to have dinner?"

"Please," Kat said. "We need to be serious."

He looked away, gazing at the heart monitor. "I heard

something and I got up. I was stunned. It was coming from the climate-controlled room."

"What was coming?" Kat asked.

"*It* was coming. It—it didn't stumble…. It came toward me, moving slowly. Steadily. I got up from the guard desk. I just stared at it. And then I drew my gun, but not fast enough. It was on me, and was strong…so strong. It got hold of my hand and the gun and I was trying to shoot it…but it was stronger. It twisted the gun. I remember the pain…."

"What was *it,* Mr. Leary?" Kat persisted.

He curled his lips in a sardonic expression as if mocking himself. "The mummy. It was the mummy. Old Amun Mopat must have crawled right out of his coffin thing. It was the mummy, and it made me shoot myself. It was the mummy."

Before they could leave the station, Will received a call from Earl Candy.

"You're not going to believe this," he said.

"What?" Will asked, bracing himself.

"The remote. The guys called in from the security boat. They were watching the remote and the screen went dark—and then it cleared again. But there was no movement, and one of the bozos finally realized that nothing was changing down there. Like, like the fish were in the same spot forever. They played with the lens but didn't get anything. Someone was down there, Will. Someone was down at the wreck site, and they destroyed my remote!"

"What time was that?"

"Damned if anyone knows. The guys didn't. And the time on the film footage was stopped. They realized it about twenty minutes ago, called me and I'm calling you."

"We'll get down there and check on it in the morning," Will said. "Can't do it any earlier than that."

"Yeah, it's almost dark. I wouldn't want anyone dying over a remote, but what the hell? Someone's been down there."

"We'll get on it first thing, Earl," Will promised again.

He speculated as he watched Landry. The man didn't act as if he was afraid he might have been the object of a conversation. Of course, Will had been careful.

"Let's go," Will said. He collected Tyler, who'd finished with Simonton and let him go. As they drove to the dock, he tried to calculate the timing. The remote camera *could* have been disconnected hours ago. That would have given Landry all morning to be out at the wreck.

At the dock in the boathouse, Landry seemed almost impatient to bring Will and Tyler over to his underwater propulsion device. On the way to the heavy steel shelving where he kept a number of his diving toys, they passed Landry's various pleasure boats.

He could see water on one of the Sea Ray speed-boats, *Lake Shark*.

It looked as if the boat had been out—and not long ago.

But Landry didn't even notice it; he was leading them to the steel shelving.

"There. It's right there. Where it's supposed to be. And it's—"

He stopped dead, his hand reaching toward the motorized device.

"It's wet," Tyler said.

"I wasn't using it! I'm telling you, I haven't had the damned thing out all season. Look, I don't even keep this boathouse locked. There are always too many people working in and around here who need access. I mean, we lock up at night, but during the day…"

He stared at the faces around him.

"I think we need to go back to the station," Will said.

"I think I need to call my lawyer."

"Fine. He can meet us down there."

Kat returned to the hotel with Kelsey; it was seven o'clock and they were due to gather in the suite, where Logan had arranged for room service.

Dirk Manning seemed happy. He had a room adjacent to the suite, so he knew that Kelsey or Logan or both could reach him in less than a minute if necessary. He was in bed by the time they got back to the hotel.

Only Will and Tyler hadn't shown up yet. Seated together, the others went over the events of the day.

They realized by then that a search warrant had been executed on Stewart Landry's home, his office, car and property.

Strips of ancient linen had been hidden in a secret compartment of his glove box. That seemed the clincher, despite the fact that Landry continued to bitterly disclaim all knowledge of anyone using his UPD or his boat. Or, for that matter, his car. What they'd found had nothing to do with him, he said.

He had never killed anyone. He'd never caused anyone to suffer an accidental death, and he was completely innocent.

But he was being held overnight while charges were prepared against him.

Kat didn't know why she didn't feel relieved, but when Will returned with Tyler Montague, she saw that he didn't seem particularly relieved, either.

While they ate, the conversation revolved around Landry.

"How did he get hold of linen wrapping used for mummy preparation that was thousands of years old?" Kat murmured. "Even if he claims he didn't know anything about it…"

"It's possible that he was in on it with Amanda," Logan said. "We know she called his company countless times during the past month."

"Okay, so we think Amanda supplied him with

Brady's information regarding his search for the *Jerry McGuen?*" Kat asked.

"She really didn't have to," Sean told her. "I studied his social networks and his website today. Not long after that party the Sand Diggers had, Brady published his reasons for believing the ship could be found. He'd used weather reports from the era and pertinent weather and lake information throughout the following decades. In other words, he made his theories public. And, using what he wrote, someone who knows the lake—like a salvage diver—could have gone through his calculations and come up with the same approximate findings."

"Which brings us back to Landry," Will said thoughtfully. "The guy must be one hell of an actor, though. He really looked shocked when we found his gear wet—and that his boat had been out."

"How did it go with Andy Simonton?" Logan asked.

"Simonton was forthright and told me he'd been at the lecture and that it was 'tremendously interesting'—his words. He said, though, that Dr. McFarland was a jerk, pompous and full of himself," Tyler replied.

"Well, Landry's being held overnight," Logan said. "We'll see what a night in lockup will do. Maybe we'll learn more tomorrow."

"Someone tampered with the remote camera today," Will reported. "I'm going back down in the morning."

Kat frowned. "Here's what I don't see. All right, so say Amanda was Landry's Egyptologist and that she got him the mummy wrapping, which she must have had access to at various points during her career. Then he starts to worry about her for some reason. He gets into the center because she lets him in. He kills her, and then goes for Abel Leary, the guard. But, according to Abel, the guy who made him shoot himself—the supposed mummy—was strong. Landry isn't that young. Could he be that strong?"

"I guess he's got lots of stamina," Tyler said in a wry voice. "He has a wife—and he's apparently having an affair with his young receptionist. Although how he thinks he's hiding it from his wife, I don't know. Hey, has anyone talked with Mrs. Landry?"

"Yes, I spoke with her this afternoon," Logan said. He shrugged. "She figured out that her husband worked the hours he worked because he was having an affair with Sherry. She's ready to throw him to the wolves. She said that nothing she knew pegged him for a murderer, but she couldn't alibi him for any time period."

"Couldn't—or wouldn't," Sean added.

"There's just something that doesn't feel right." Kat looked at Will. "If you're going down tomorrow, I am, too."

She talked to them about the icebreaker, the *Egyptian,* and how the captain had believed that Amun Mopat's scepter had been the source of his power. He might well have rammed the *Jerry McGuen* with his ship and suffered a bout of madness before setting out on another stormy night soon after—and meeting his own demise.

"Still...could anyone believe that today? That an *object* could be the source of incredible power?" Kelsey asked skeptically.

"Hey, could anyone believe that a mummy—rotting for thousands of years—could possibly attack them?" Tyler countered.

"Maybe the scepter did have power, but not the way ancients Egyptians thought it did," Kat said. "That kind of crystal could catch sunlight. It could even have been used to start a fire on a bed of dried tinder. The thing is, Captain Ely accepted it. And I have to conclude that the scepter is what our killer considers the greatest treasure of the *Jerry McGuen*." She paused. "Precisely why, I don't know."

They discussed that and various other possibilities, then broke for the night.

Kat and Will didn't even pretend they were doing anything other than going to one room.

Kat wanted to spend a little time with the cat, but Bastet was no longer in either of their rooms. Before she could worry, Logan appeared at her door to tell her he'd come to fetch the cat and her equipment earlier. Bastet seemed to bring Dirk Manning a measure of comfort, so he was letting the cat stay with him for now.

When Logan was gone, Kat grinned at Will. She didn't have to speak. They showered together, made love and lay still, talking quietly. The next day would be a long one.

Stewart Landry was being held in jail. They'd found his UPD and his boat wet—both had been out on the lake. It fit; someone had tampered with the remote that day. And mummy wrappings had been recovered from his car. All signs seemed to point to him. She should have rested well.

But she didn't.

The dream began, but this time, when the wall of darkness turned into the face of Amun Mopat, he was real, and he spoke to her again.

Even in her dream she paused to wonder how an ancient Egyptian spoke English so well. She didn't understand that, but they communicated with ease.

"Stop them. There is no power. There is no curse, and there is no power. People kill for what they believe, not for what is real."

As he spoke, the wall of water started coming toward her, closer and closer.

"We've found the man," she said. "It's over. A full-blown salvage effort will begin, and all the treasures will come up. No one man will claim them. They'll eventually be returned to the Egyptian people."

The water was still coming.

"I have tried. I have prayed," he said. "My scepter was nothing but a way to keep the laws of a good man, perhaps harsh at times, in a different world."

The water poured over them.

Kat heard screams, and realized she was the one screaming.

Will was at her side, holding her, shushing her, whispering that she needed to breathe.

As she felt his warmth and his strength, she looked into his dark, concerned eyes. "It's not over, Will," she told him. "It's not over."

"How do you know?" he asked gently.

"The mummy told me."

14

The next morning, Will and Kat went out to the dive site with Sean and Tyler. They met Earl, Alan and Bernie at the dock, where they boarded Captain Bob's boat.

The night Amanda was killed, Jon Hunt had been in such a state that he'd been sedated for the past few days. He didn't ever want to go back to the wreck, he insisted. He didn't know what would happen now, but he wasn't going back down.

Bernie, too, seemed depressed. On the way out to the site he told Will, "I love Alan. He's a great guy. He likes to film and preserve history. But all these people dying—I can't take it. I think I need to go back to working on frivolous comedies, the kind full of silly fart jokes and sexual innuendoes."

Will wasn't sure what to say to him, so he just patted him on the shoulder.

At the site, they all went down together, including Jimmy Green. Will noted that Kat paused at the salon, but when she saw that he was waiting for her, she shook her head, eyes enormous behind her mask.

They dived deeper, and he joined Earl and Sean at the remote camera. Earl was maneuvering it, irritated as he showed Sean and Will the switch that had been jammed, freezing the image of fish swimming around the hold.

Will motioned to him to fix the switch and leave the camera there. Earl frowned, but then shrugged.

Will realized that Bernie had taken over with one of the underwater cameras while Earl worked on the remote.

It might all be worthy of a documentary, although not the one that had originally been planned. He had a feeling that the documentary was no longer going to focus on ancient treasure.

Instead, it would focus on the lust for power.

Kat was hovering in the hold, barely moving, and staring at one of the doors. He swam toward her, and she pointed, but he wasn't sure what she saw.

They swam to the door. There, with the power of the water, the door had been solidly wedged shut. It seemed to fascinate Kat, however, so he worked at it. A moment later, Tyler and Sean came to help.

Between them, they shoved the door open against the force of the water and the rusted hinges. They could hear the creaking, even in the water, as it moved.

Tyler flashed his headlight into the hold room that was now open as Will gave a slight kick and eased himself in. At first, he saw nothing other than more crates, piled on top of each other.

Then he saw something that gleamed beneath the light.

He swam down to retrieve it. He turned the object over in his hands. It was no great artifact from the age of the pharaohs.

It was a dive knife, shiny and new.

They might have had difficulty with the door, but it had been opened before—and then closed, jammed tight against the hold. He gestured at Tyler, and they returned to the others just as Jimmy Green tapped his wrist, indicating that they'd run out of time.

They surfaced, using the same care they'd taken with their descent.

Back on the boat, Will produced the knife and they all studied it. Even Captain Bob came over to look. "Oh, that's a local manufacturer," he said. "It's an Everstone." Everyone stared at him. "Everstone Dive Accessories. They're just off Lake Shore Drive, near the park," he said. "They sell spear guns, compasses, suits, regulators—you name it. They manufacture for the entire lake region. See—there's their little insignia on the back."

"Well, I think we found out how Brady Laurie was 'helped' to drown," Kat murmured.

"We'll get over there as soon as we're back," Will said in an equally quiet voice.

Later, as they were on their way to shore, they sat near the bow, where they had at least a little privacy.

"How did you know?" he asked her.

She gave him a lopsided grin. "Okay, even for us,

this sounds crazy. Last night I told you about Amun Mopat being in my dream? Now, none of us is really sure we've hit the mark with Stewart Landry, and that kind of worry could cause a dream—or a nightmare. I know that. But today, when we were down there…I could swear I saw him again."

"Him? Amun Mopat, you mean?"

"Yes. He's not some ugly wizened creature with an evil look on his face, the way he was portrayed in the movies. He was relatively young when he died, or young for us—about forty. He has the face you see on his death mask. Intense dark eyes…" She paused. "A bit like yours, really, although he wears much more makeup."

"Ouch. I don't wear makeup at all!" he protested.

She smiled. "I know. You have a similar dark coloring—but don't worry, I'm not seeing you as his reincarnation or anything. I'm seeing him, I think, because he *wasn't* evil, he didn't bring about death. He just found his place at the pharaoh's side, and tried to serve him and their people. Anyway, he was trying to make me see the door. That's why I knew there had to be something behind it." She smiled again. "This is one thing that makes me crazy. You know how in movies about aliens they're always familiar with English? Well, either that or they've come down to kill us all. The thing is, I understand him when he speaks."

"Maybe language doesn't matter when we're dealing with the sixth sense."

"I guess. But I feel that the real Amun Mopat has been hovering around *my* sixth sense from the beginning. Maybe I only saw him in nightmares because after our experience with the *movie* version of Amun Mopat, I thought he had to be purely evil."

"You're probably right."

"I just feel he's trying to tell me something."

"Then he will do so," Will told her, "when he's ready."

He rose; he was still in his swim trunks but he could hear his phone ringing from the helm, where he'd left it.

"Landry is out," Logan told him, not bothering with a greeting.

"What? How?"

"Ms. Sherry Bertelli. She came into the office, tearful and swearing that he couldn't have been out in his boat or using any kind of device yesterday morning. He was closeted with her, working on…work," Logan said.

"Did anyone else verify that?"

"Well, Landry swore he'd been working."

"Why didn't he give Sherry as his alibi before?" Will asked.

"Maybe he thought his wife really didn't know. Maybe Landry thought it was better to be held on murder charges than to admit to a very angry wife that he was having an affair," Logan said. "Or…maybe he was waiting for Sherry."

Will gritted his teeth. "She's lying for him. She's sleeping with the guy, and he's probably paying her to lie for him. Logan, they found the mummy wrap in his car!"

"He swears it was planted there."

"We're on our way back," he said. "See you soon."

He hung up and told Kat the news.

"But they're lying. They're obviously lying."

"Well, at the moment—despite the mummy wrap—everything we're looking at is circumstantial evidence. Remember, a district attorney, or a federal attorney, has to prove the accused party's guilt beyond a reasonable doubt. So far, it seems evident to us that Brady was drowned, and while we know that Amanda was poisoned, she *could* simply have eaten shellfish without being aware of it. And Austin Miller *did* die of heart failure. The only witness we have is going to sound crazy, because he says a mummy made him shoot himself, and he has Landry's wide-eyed mistress to back him up on that because *she* believes she saw a mummy at the Sand Diggers' maze. Which, of course, we believe, too—though we don't think it was an actual mummy," Will said.

"Where does that leave us?" Kat asked.

"Continuing to investigate." Will hesitated. "And, probably, now that two of the center's experts are dead and the third is an emotional wreck, the board of directors will have to hire new experts and arrange for serious equipment to move forward with the salvage. Unless they choose to give up their bid to work the site."

"No one will do that," Kat said with certainty.

"So, we keep looking," Will said. "We just go back over all of it until we find out what we're missing."

"Or…we find the scepter."

At the hotel, the divers showered. Logan and Kelsey were at the police station reviewing all the information that had been gathered, and Jane was at the hospital, keeping watch over their gravely injured eyewitness.

Dirk Manning was with Kelsey and Logan, refusing to be left alone. He sat in their borrowed office, calmly reading the paper.

Kat had to wonder what would happen with Dirk if they were forced to give up their investigation before the case was completely solved.

"I'll get started on the research," she told Will. "I still think there's something from the past that we're missing. I'm assuming you're going to Everstone Dive Accessories to find out about our knife?"

"Yeah, I'd love to know who bought it," he said.

It was decided that Tyler would stay at the hotel, ready to move in any direction when needed, and Sean and Will would go to Everstone to learn who'd purchased the knife.

Kat leafed through more of the journals and read about Austin Miller's grandfather's adventures, but she felt restless and couldn't concentrate.

Tyler was reading over the many computerized sheets matching up who'd been where and who could've had access to Egyptian knowledge or the Preservation

Center when Kat looked up. "I'm spinning my wheels here. Let's go to Landry Salvage."

"You think Landry will welcome us?" Tyler asked. "We need something else if we want to bring him back in or even talk to him."

Kat smiled. "I don't want to go after Landry. I want to go after Sherry Bertelli."

"Sherry?"

"She's lying. She's lying through her teeth," Kat said.

"Gee, you don't believe they really spent the morning working—or shacked up together?" Tyler asked sarcastically.

"Come on, what can they do? Kick us out? People rarely do, not when we go in with Federal shields."

"All right," Tyler agreed. "I'll just tell Logan where we're going."

They drove out to Landry Salvage with Logan's blessing. When they entered, Sherry, who was at her desk, saw them and immediately stiffened. "Mr. Landry is not available," she said.

"We didn't come to speak to him. We came to speak to you," Kat told her.

"Me?" she squeaked.

"I think you're lying to protect your boss."

"Oh, you people are terrible!" Sherry said. "I'm not lying. I wouldn't protect anyone involved in this. You forget, the mummy came after *me!*"

"I'm going to ask you to call all the employees out here," Tyler said, leaning on the reception desk. "And then we'll find out if anyone can vouch for the fact that you two were together."

"Most of the staff is out now," Sherry said regally, tossing back her hair. "Why don't you leave him alone? He's innocent. I swear it."

"So who's guilty, then, Sherry?"

"Go after that Andy Simonton!" she yelled. "He's a creep! And he's rude and obnoxious, too."

As they spoke, Kat heard the sound of a floorboard creaking and turned to see a door opening.

Someone was sneaking out the back.

She drew her gun and hurried through the hallway, with Tyler close behind her. When they dashed out the door, they found themselves at the boathouse.

"Hey, careful!" Tyler warned. "We don't have what we need on Landry."

Kat nodded, but she clicked off the safety on her Glock. "Mr. Landry, if you're innocent, why are you running from us?" she demanded.

She moved past the speedboat called *Lake Shark,* and as she did, a bullet whistled by her.

"Down!" she shouted to Tyler.

She ducked low herself, trying to determine where the shooter was. Landry had to be hiding behind a cabin cruiser, she decided. She carefully made her way over there.

Another bullet whizzed by, but she was low and the aim was terrible. She fired back in the direction of the shot.

"Put down your weapon! Throw it out here! Come out with your hands high!" she ordered. "Come on, Landry! You don't want to die here!"

Another shot exploded. Kat bent low and inched around the speedboat.

Then she stopped.

"Kat?"

"Here!" she called to Tyler.

He ran over to her. Landry was on the ground, bleeding out from a hole in his forehead. Eyes wide open, he stared into space.

"Son of a bitch!" Tyler said, turning to her.

"I didn't hit him."

Tyler looked at her incredulously. "If you didn't shoot him..." He paused, studying the scene. "There's his gun...beside his hand. He shot himself in the forehead rather than speak with us?"

Kat shook her head, scrutinizing Stewart Landry where he lay, eyes open, blood pooling beneath his head. "That's impossible. The angle is impossible." She frowned. "He didn't shoot himself, Tyler. Someone else was out here with us. Someone who killed him and wanted it to look like *we* did—or like he killed himself."

Will knew he didn't have the right to feel upset. Kat Sokolov was fine. She'd done the necessary training, passed the tests, and she had the skill to handle a firearm.

He and Sean found out about Landry's death as they

returned from the dive store, when Logan called to inform them. Instead of going back to the hotel, he and Sean drove straight to Landry's and the boathouse. Tyler and Kat were there, speaking with one of the local agents, giving their reports of the incident. Neither of them was suspected; the bullet that killed Landry had come from his own gun, a 57-Magnum. But a man was dead, and that meant paperwork. Lots of paperwork.

The body had yet to be picked up, and Dr. Cranston Randall had been called to the scene. Perhaps because of his seniority—or perhaps because he'd pissed off a superior—it seemed they now had Dr. Randall on all the deaths associated with the *Jerry McGuen*.

Will paced near the body. He couldn't help realizing that there'd been a lot of bullets, and Kat could easily have been hit. He tried to reason with himself.

"Poor bastard should have stayed in jail," Logan said. He was close to the activity, ready to step in if a team member needed him.

"Yeah, I guess he should have." Will sighed. "We're falling deeper and deeper into this quagmire." He stopped pacing and looked at Logan. "I forgot to tell you—Stewart Landry bought the knife we found in the *Jerry McGuen*. The salesman remembered him perfectly, even though he bought it about a year ago. Landry bought a lot of his dive gear there."

"And now Landry is dead. He didn't kill himself and we're running out of suspects," Logan said. He nodded at Will. "You're acting like a caged tiger."

"It's just that—"

"Oh, you don't have to explain," Logan told him, smiling. "Except that you'll have to get used to it. Usually, it won't be this bad. In this case, Kat seems to be the catalyst. Naturally when she's the one out there the most, you'll worry about her. It's not a bad thing—it's instinct. But, trust me, if you want any kind of a future…well, you can't change what someone is, what she wants to be, and what she wants to do with her life. Kat isn't going to sit home, ever, while you take off to chase evil. She's not the delicate creature the he-man protects. Under our current circumstances, every member of the team will rally around her. She is the one in greatest danger on this case. So, yes, go ahead and worry. But if I were you, I'd keep that worry to myself. She is what she is, and she'd never understand that you'd want to take risks that you feel she shouldn't."

Will looked at Logan for a minute, recognizing the wisdom of his words. "Can it work?" he asked quietly.

Logan smiled again. "So far, it works for me. I just keep remembering that we have one another's backs at all times. That helps. You never walk into danger if you don't have to, and when you do, you use your training. And you trust all your team members to do the same."

"I do know that trying to stop people from what they feel they need to do is a mistake. And," Will said, shrugging, "I know that because I found where I was meant to be—with the Krewe of Hunters. If you took that feeling from me, from anyone, a relationship would be doomed."

"Hard to live with sometimes," Logan said. "But… yeah."

However, when they finally gathered back at the hotel, Will asked as evenly as he could how Kat and Tyler had ended up at Landry Salvage when he'd left them doing research at the hotel.

"I was sure that Sherry Bertelli was lying to save her boss. I'm still sure of it. Except that Landry is dead now," Kat said.

"You came out to talk to Sherry, but Stewart Landry wound up dead?" Will asked.

"We were at the reception desk, talking to Sherry, and saw someone slipping furtively out the back door— Landry," Kat explained. "We followed to find out why he was running away. He started shooting. We started shooting. But someone else was out there. Someone who's growing careless, because the position of the bullet hole—the angle of entry—would have been almost impossible for him to achieve on his own. The idea was for us to find Landry and either believe we'd killed him, which means the killer didn't pause to think about different weapons, bullets and shell casings, or that he killed himself. But a bullet dead center in the forehead isn't logical because of the way our thumbs and fingers fit on a trigger. There's always an angle." She hesitated, looking around at the Krewe. "I'll go in when Dr. Randall does the autopsy tomorrow, but imagine the length of your hand and a gun. Imagine manipulating your fingers and taking straight aim. Also, if he'd killed himself, there would've been a darker stain of gunpowder."

"It feels like we're back to square one," Jane said. "Everything points to Landry. Except that now Landry is dead."

"Great." Kelsey shook her head. "We have one survivor who swears a mummy tried to kill him. We have four dead. And two of them, Landry and Amanda, *might* have been involved."

"Back to the drawing board," Logan said. "We also have the Sand Diggers, most of whom wouldn't have any inner knowledge of the Preservation Center. But would that matter if Amanda had been the liaison? With Landry dead, the next closest salvage company is Simonton's Sea Search—whose owner attended lectures about the ship *and* Dr. McFarland's discussion on methods of death. Including methods that aren't easy to trace.

"Tomorrow we'll get a search warrant for Simonton's home, boats, car and place of business," Logan said. He looked at Will. "I think it's important that we continue the dive, whether Jon Hunt's with us or not. Because the film crew's documentation of the wreck is all we have left. Everyone, get some rest now."

When they were together later that night, lying in bed, half-asleep and half-curled together, Will rose up on his elbow, stroking the sleek line of Kat's back.

She rolled over, touching his face. "You seem different," she said.

"Shaken," he told her.

"Will, I know how to duck," she teased.

He nodded slowly. "I have to get used to it."

"Can you?" she asked him. "Will you always feel as if you have to protect me?"

"It's not easy to ignore that impulse, Kat, but will I try? Yes."

"It's no different, really," she said softly. "I feel the same about you. But I trust you not to take unnecessary or foolish risks. I know you can look after yourself."

"Hey," he said gruffly. "I'd like to see *you* not worried if you found out someone sent a hail of bullets my way."

"It wasn't a hail of bullets," she said.

"It only takes one."

"I know."

She searched his eyes in the dim glow of a night-light and reached out for him, bringing his lips down to hers. The kiss began as something very simple, something to seal the words between them. It grew far more impassioned and he found himself wide-awake again, sliding along her body to caress her with his tongue. Soon they were breathless, writhing in each other's arms, and later lay spent and exhausted, ready for much-needed rest.

In the morning, Kat answered a call from the morgue; as she'd hoped, she was invited to join Dr. Randall for the autopsy.

Will left with Tyler and Sean, keeping his thoughts to himself.

He had to accept the fact that bullets could fly at either one of them, but for today he was glad she'd be safe among the dead at the morgue. The wreck of the *Jerry McGuen* seemed like a very dangerous place to be.

"So many healthy people dead," Randall said as he and Kat worked on the corpse of Stewart Landry. "What a beautiful heart. The man was fit, toned and other than having a brain that's just about turned to mush…"

"Whoever shot him was only a couple of feet away," Kat said. She shook her head. "Why did he run from us? There was no reason for him to do that. He had his lawyer on the case, he'd been released…."

"Maybe he believed that since you showed up at his place again, some other evidence had been found against him."

"That's possible," Kat agreed.

"And you didn't see anyone else in the boathouse at all?" Randall asked.

"No, just Landry. I stayed with the body while Tyler searched. When the police arrived, they searched, too, but…there were at least a dozen ways of getting into or out of the boathouse. You're on the water, there are entrances in front and on either side.… The killer could have been waiting in the boathouse or come in after we chased Landry." She paused, looking at the corpse.

Landry wasn't speaking to her; she hadn't expected that he would.

There was nothing else Kat could do at the morgue, so she cleaned up and called Logan. He and Kelsey, she discovered, were with the police executing the search warrant on Andy Simonton's property. Sean and Tyler were diving with Will, and Jane was at the main branch of the public library with Dirk Manning, researching Captain Ely and the *Egyptian*.

Kat put a call through to Jane, telling her she'd join them at the library. She found the two of them sitting side by side at library computers, and she drew up a chair at the third.

Jane passed her a piece of paper with a website address scrawled on it. "Try this one. There's an article on Ely. His full name was Josiah Brentwood Ely. He joined the Union navy at the age of seventeen, near the end of the Civil War, and when the war was over, he did a lot of traveling—including some time on ships coming and going from Egypt. He was a strange man who got involved in the spiritualist craze of the late-nineteenth century. And later, he became a fundamentalist Christian. There's more on him. I haven't gotten to all the links yet."

Kat thanked her and started on the computer herself. It wasn't long before she'd connected to the site Jane had suggested. One of the links took her to an article discussing "the strange case of Captain Josiah Brentwood Ely." Ely, according to the article, preached against dabbling in the occult, mysticism and other uses of "magic." He told friends, family and followers that he knew of objects, physical objects, in the world that were Satan's tools, capable of destroying entire civilizations.

He claimed that among those objects was the scepter that had belonged to the Egyptian priest Amun Mopat. Mopat had used it to countermand the plagues that hit Egypt, and to help the godless survive when Moses led his people to Israel. If it hadn't been for Mopat and his scepter, Ely said, the New Kingdom of Egypt would have dissolved, and the Egyptian people would have been free to become believers in the one true God.

"Pretty crazy, huh?" Jane said to Kat.

"Yes, but it makes me even more convinced that whoever is doing this is after the scepter."

"You think someone *really* believes the scepter could control the world?"

"We've heard crazier beliefs or, at least, just as crazy," Kat said. She shut down the computer and stood. "The police are still at the Preservation Center?"

"Yup. It's still under lock and key, and surrounded by crime scene tape," Jane said, turning off her computer and rising, too. "I'll check in with Logan. We can go there if you want."

"To the center?" Dirk Manning asked anxiously.

"You don't need to come with us," Kat replied.

"You want me to stay here *alone*?"

Kat smiled. "We'll leave you with one of Chicago's

finest," she told him. "Maybe he'll let you turn on the siren."

"Very funny, young lady," Manning said. "But, yes! *I* will sit outside in a police car."

Just before going down to the wreck, Will called Kat.

The autopsy had been completed, he learned; they'd discovered nothing they hadn't expected. But they'd confirmed that Landry couldn't possibly have shot himself.

"It's a pity the boathouse isn't a more confined space," Kat complained. "Whoever was in there took off before we realized there *was* anyone else."

"I still think that one or more of the dead had to be involved," Will said.

"Yes. But the only one talking is Austin Miller, and Austin can't tell us anything except that he believes a mummy killed him. Anyway, Jane and I are going to the Preservation Center. I want to prowl around there some more."

"Be careful," he said.

"There are still plenty of cops out front. I'll be with Jane, and we'll be very careful," Kat promised.

They said goodbye, and Will told himself that this was her job. He reminded himself again that he couldn't stop her from doing it.

"Everything all right?" Tyler asked him.

Will nodded. "Kat and Jane are heading over to the Preservation Center. They're going to start tearing the place apart, since we haven't got anything to move forward with."

"Maybe they'll find something," Tyler said with a shrug.

Sean walked over to him. "Kat has worked with cops in law enforcement for a long time. She's smart as a whip and she knows what she's doing," he said.

"Can't blame you for worrying, though," Tyler put in. "We always worry most about the key person on any case." He pointed at Will. "That's you as well as Kat, so stay close by when we dive, huh?"

Will grinned. "Yeah. Thanks."

Thirty minutes later, they were down at the *Jerry McGuen.*

Will instinctively paused near the grand salon and looked in, trying to imagine what Kat had seen there. The ship at sea—the realization that a storm was coming and worse....

They were about to be rammed by an icebreaker.

But the salon held nothing for him. He joined the film crew and Sean and Tyler in the hold. They were inspecting the darkened space behind the hold door, searching for anything that might tell them another diver had been down there. Will hovered in the main section, looking at the crates. He turned, hearing something, and was startled to see what appeared to be a wavy image in the water. He blinked.

There, before him, was the shape of a man.

An Egyptian with handsome sculpted features and a look of dire warning in his eyes.

He didn't speak; he lifted his arms to Will and seemed to form a single word with soundless lips.

Danger.

The image was that of Amun Mopat.

And Will wasn't in danger.

Kat was.

He stared at the image, about to rise as quickly as possible to the surface, but the figure of Amun Mopat seemed to be gesturing at him, beckoning him to the wall. Wedged between one of the massive crates and the wall was a slender, narrow box, perhaps six feet long. As he struggled with it, he saw that Earl was filming his movements and Bernie was trying to attract the attention of the other men. A moment later, Tyler and Sean swam over to help him. Together, they managed to ease the heavier, larger crate far enough back to free the tarp-covered box. Will gestured at the surface and they agreed to go up.

On board, they took off their dive gear and studied the box, now removed from its tarp. Alan King was the one who suddenly exclaimed, "Look at the markings on it! There are lions and jackals and—Will, that's it. That's got to be the scepter of Amun Mopat. The source of all his power!"

15

Dirk Manning was happy to sit with the police.

The Preservation Center, empty of life and sound, with the auxiliary lights burning, seemed an eerie place as they walked in.

"I wonder what's happening with the rest of the employees," Jane said. "From what I understand, the place is actually governed by a board, but Amanda Channel was the boss. Brady and Jon reported to her, and there was a receptionist, the guards hired on by the center, and a bunch of interns coming and going."

"I doubt any of the interns are eager to get back in. And Jon Hunt is a total basket case, so who knows if he's even returning to work?" Kat responded.

"Where should we start?" Jane asked.

"Why don't you take Brady's office and I'll take Amanda's," Kat suggested.

"And at this point, we're looking for absolutely anything, right?"

"That's about it."

They parted ways in the hall, going to the separate

offices. Kat began to rummage through Amanda's drawers. She was surprised and somewhat saddened to see that Amanda had stashed away a bag from a chic lingerie shop, together with gift wrap and an unsigned card that read "To my Best Friend." Kat didn't have time to consider the pathos of that. Because behind the bag, as if caught there when the drawer was opened and closed, she found a crumpled piece of paper. Kat straightened it. The paper had a phone number on it and a quick notation: "7:30 p.m. S.B."

Frowning, Kat studied it. She dialed the number, using her cell phone.

She had a suspicion as to whose number it might be, and she was right. Landry Salvage. Her call was answered by an automatic message that said the offices were closed.

Kat set the paper down and tapped her fingers on the desk.

S.B.

Sherry Bertelli?

Landry was dead; he'd been killed by someone who had known or guessed why she and Will wanted to talk to him again—that they still had unanswered questions. Sherry had seen them run after Landry. She must have assumed they'd discovered something else that would implicate Landry, and perhaps Landry had been ready to point the finger at her.

Sherry had access to everything that was Landry's.

Landry was madly in love with her, and would have never questioned anything she did.

And now he was dead.

She automatically tried Will on her cell phone but, of course, he didn't answer. He was down on the dive to the *Jerry McGuen*.

She should call Logan, and she did that next. He answered on the first ring. "We need to pick up Sherry Bertelli," she said.

"The receptionist?"

"Yes. Logan, it makes sense. We didn't find anyone in the maze when she was supposedly attacked by the so-called mummy. I'm positive *she* was the one who left that swath of wrapping. She was definitely dealing with someone at the Preservation Center—I just found a note in Amanda's desk with her initials and a time on it. Plus Amanda was calling Landry Salvage constantly. I think that Amanda was involved with Sherry, maybe hoping to be her friend, and Sherry had access to this place because of her. She was with Landry when Dr. McFarland gave his lectures." She paused to take a breath. "We didn't look at her because we were too busy looking at Landry. And, frankly, she didn't seem bright enough to carry out this plan. Talk about stereotyping, huh?"

She paused again; she thought she'd heard movement down the hall, although she and Jane should have been the only ones there. Unless it *was* Jane, coming to talk to her about something she'd found.

"Logan, get someone to bring in Sherry Bertelli. We'll finish up here and meet you at the station."

"We'll get her," he said. "I'll send out some officers to find her right now."

There was no further sound in the hallway. Kat stood up, about to head into Brady's office and find out what Jane was doing and share her suspicions. Her phone rang; she saw it was Will and answered quickly. "Hey! You're out of the water fast."

He hesitated, and she knew he was about to say that he was worried about her.

But he managed not to. She smiled. "I'm okay, Will. I'm with Jane at the center. Listen, I just talked to Logan. Will, I think Sherry Bertelli had something to do with all this. She was everywhere with Landry, and Landry would do anything in the world for her."

"Then we've got to bring her in—now. She may realize that with Landry dead, she'd be next on the suspect list."

"Logan has detectives going for her now."

"Good. Hey, I've got news for you, too. We found the scepter. Amun Mopat's all-powerful scepter."

"You're kidding! You sure?"

"Alan is certain of it. He read what could still be seen on the box…but we didn't take it out. None of us knows a thing about preservation, but…anyway, we're coming in. I'll drive over and meet you and Jane at the center."

"Once they've brought Sherry in, maybe you should

be the one to interrogate her," Kat said. "You've seen her, talked with her...."

"Maybe it should be you. A woman might react more honestly with another woman."

"Well, let's give them a chance to bring her in first," Kat murmured. "I'll see you soon."

She hung up, feeling hopeful. *Sherry Bertelli.* Right. Naturally, the men—the CEOs of the salvage companies—would be the initial suspects. And now that Landry was dead, anyone who might have known of her involvement was out of the way.

But what had she wanted? The scepter?

Kat stood, remembering how she'd thought for a moment that she'd heard Jane in the hallway. She stepped out. It was empty, just as it should have been. Then she walked down to Brady Laurie's office and looked inside.

Jane wasn't there.

Kat decided not to shout out her name, even if that would more easily assuage her sudden fear. If her colleague was in any kind of danger, Kat could amplify that danger by spurring someone into action.

Silently, she moved along the hall in the other direction. She passed the empty conference room and stopped, drawing her Glock and clicking off the safety. She peered through the plastic sheets that led to the clean room.

Someone was there. Someone was standing over the sarcophagus of Amun Mopat.

* * *

While the film crew had been perplexed by Will's determination that they surface before their time was up, Tyler and Sean had been willing to follow his lead.

He apologized to the others as the boat motored in.

"Maybe this is getting to me," he said. "I thought I saw Amun Mopat down there."

"Maybe you did see something—a vision of the past," Tyler told him. "We now know that Captain Ely was a quack—with a ship that had Amun Mopat for a figurehead—and we're pretty sure that he used his ship, guided by that figurehead, to ram the *Jerry McGuen*."

Will shrugged. "I thought he was warning me of danger. In fact, it almost seemed that he said the word. I was afraid he meant *Kat* was in danger, but I talked to her. She and Jane are at the center. She found some evidence there that incriminates Sherry Bertelli."

He explained the situation while they completed the return trip to the dock. He was still puzzled. "I see where we might have missed something with Sherry. She could definitely be part of it. But whoever killed Brady Laurie was strong—probably *very* strong. Sherry may be fit, but judging by her size, I don't see how she could have had the strength to kill Brady. And the guard, Abel Leary—he struggled with his attacker. With the 'mummy.' Maybe they were in it together. Maybe Sherry took care of Amanda and managed to befriend her for access to the Preservation Center, and Landry was the muscle behind it all."

"It's a theory," Tyler said slowly, "and maybe her involvement was with—*and because of*—Stewart Landry. Maybe he was the one who wanted to destroy the center's involvement in hopes of being next on the list of companies to salvage the wreck. Or maybe he wanted a specific object that was on the ship. Sherry just did what he asked to her to, but when it looked like he might put the blame on her, she felt she had to kill him. Amanda was already dead, so if everything pointed to Landry, then she'd be an innocent bystander."

"All right, so Sherry befriended Amanda," Will said. "She then had access to the center, and she might have met with Amanda before she died."

"If that was the case," Sean continued, "she could have somehow gotten Amanda to eat the shellfish. She must've known Amanda was allergic but she could have slipped it into something else Amanda was eating. Of course, they'd have had to get to the museum really fast after their meal—that kind of poison can act quickly."

"Or they met at the Preservation Center for dinner, and when Amanda was dead and the guard taken of, she took whatever plates she'd used and escaped out the back, the same way she and Amanda both entered," Will said.

When they arrived at the dock, Will decided he'd go straight to the center. Sean and Tyler would make their way to the police station and help out if they discovered that Sherry Bertelli hadn't been brought in yet.

As he drove, Will kept thinking about Sherry Bertelli, Stewart Landry and the strange night they'd spent with the Egyptian Sand Diggers at the memorial service, when Sherry had been screaming in the maze. Landry had seemed truly devastated that something might have happened to his mistress. Was he really that good an actor?

Someone other than the petite woman had been involved. And someone other than the very slight Amanda Channel, as well.

Landry. That was where it all pointed.

Except for that one night.

So who else? Simonton? The police had spent the morning searching his home and office, boats, car. Will had heard nothing back. Simonton was big; he had the necessary strength. If not Simonton, then...Dirk Manning? No. Manning was in decent shape for his age, but he *was* in his late seventies. Not as old as Austin Miller, but not young enough to take down a guard in the prime of life.

It suddenly occurred to him that many people could be excellent actors. And there'd been a great deal of knowledge about the ship and Egyptology associated with recent events....

He stepped on the gas, anxious to reach the center.

When he got to the entrance, he saw that a police car was stationed in front, just as it was supposed to be. He should have felt at ease.

But as he got out of his car and approached the entrance, he felt the chill of fear. Before going in, he called Logan's number.

"Get over here, please," he said quietly.

"What's wrong?" Logan asked.

"We've been missing one suspect all along."

Kat saw the figure bending over the sarcophagus of Amun Mopat that lay on the steel table. At first it was impossible to tell who it was; the person was dressed in a bunny suit, gloves, booties, hair cover and mask.

After everything that had gone on here, Kat figured a clean suit was probably pointless and she wasn't going to bother with one herself. Fingers curled around her Glock, she moved through the different layers of plastic, walking into the clean room.

The figure looked up at her. She recognized Jon Hunt.

"Hi," he said. Then he frowned. "What are you doing here without a suit on?"

"What are you doing here, period?" Kat asked him.

"Working. I work here," he said.

"Jon, I thought you were taking time off. You were a mess after we found Amanda."

"I was, yes. But work is good therapy. And when I was at home, I remembered that we never lifted the mask—or examined the mummy."

"Jon, Amanda was found dead in the sarcophagus. It's still considered evidence," Kat said.

Jon walked around the sarcophagus, looking down at

the death mask and the mummy. He seemed especially intrigued. She couldn't see what had so thoroughly attracted his attention, but he seemed protective.

"You don't understand. The scepter is here somewhere. Everything hinges on the scepter. There's some kind of power in the crystal head. Men bowed down before the priest because of the scepter."

"They bowed down before him because otherwise he could have them killed," Kat said. "Look, it was the way they governed. Jon, I'm shocked that you—a scientist—can put that kind of belief in an object. Anyway, you're not supposed to be here," Kat told him. "The place is closed until the deaths are solved."

"No, *I* can be here, but you shouldn't," he said. "I have to find the scepter. I *will* find the scepter."

The deaths of his colleagues seem to have unhinged him, Kat thought.

"Jon, the scepter isn't in the sarcophagus with the mummy. The divers found it today."

"What?" he asked, spinning to face her.

"I just talked to Agent Chan. He and two other agents were down with the film crew. They believe they've brought up the scepter."

He stared at her in horror. "No!" he said.

She holstered her Glock, walking over to him. "Jon, you need to go home. You need to get some rest. You need—"

She broke off; she had reached the sarcophagus and she saw what had attracted his interest.

Jane.

Jane lay in the sarcophagus just as Amanda had, arms crossed over her chest.

Kat sprang into motion, terrified that she wouldn't find her friend's pulse, but when she pressed her fingers to Jane's throat, she felt the beat of her heart. She stared at Jon. "What in God's name—help me! Help me get her out of here!"

Jon stepped back. Kat ignored him and reached in for Jane, trying to discern what had made her lose consciousness. She had to get an ambulance quickly. Watching Jon, she searched for her cell phone, but she'd left it on the desk in Amanda's office.

She struggled with Jane's body, getting her out of the sarcophagus and onto the floor, then stood, realizing that Jon's mind was far gone. She leveled the gun on him. "Jon, move away from Jane and the sarcophagus. Give me your cell phone."

He looked back at her, a puzzled expression on his face. She shook her head. "You didn't kill Brady Laurie, did you? It couldn't have been you *or* Amanda, because you were the ones who were supposed to *discover* him. But, Jon, you did dress up as a mummy, didn't you? You caused Austin Miller's heart attack, and you caused the guard to shoot himself. Did you kill Amanda? Or did Sherry Bertelli do it?"

Jon smiled at her. "You don't understand. I've read everything there is, and if you know the proper rites and incantations and you possess the scepter, you can rule the world."

"Give me your cell phone," she said again.

Jon stood there smiling at her. She realized that he was looking past her, and there was someone else with them.

Kat didn't turn around. "Sherry, welcome to this little truth-telling get-together," she said. "By the way, it's over. The police are coming for you."

"You bitch!" Sherry screamed. "How the hell—never mind. Drop the gun. Do it now, or I'll shoot you in the back."

"I can shoot Jon, you know," Kat said.

"That's fine," Sherry told her.

"Sherry!" Jon protested.

"Oh, quit whining, will you?" Sherry snapped. "She isn't going to shoot you in cold blood. You're not even armed."

"I'd be careful, Sherry. If I'm in danger, I just *might* shoot Jon. And don't forget—you've already turned him into a killer. He could turn on you."

"Don't kid yourself. *I'm* the killer," Sherry said. Her voice was like ice. "I watched people. I *studied* people. I knew their habits and schedules. I climbed up the wall and walked right through those open doors and into his office and gave that old bastard Austin Miller the scare of his life. When he went to get his pills, I smacked them right out of his hand. Actually, I didn't mean to lose any mummy wrapping there, but that happened when

I was climbing back over the wall—when I dropped that statue. I was going to plant it in Landry's office… oh, well. I *did* mean to lose some of the mummy wrapping when you two were in the hotel that night, because I wanted to warn you that you'd be dead real fast if you messed around with Laurie's death. Do you know how easy it is to get false identification and dress up as someone else and check into a hotel? Of course, I wanted to do more." She shrugged. "You didn't totally suck as an agent."

"Wow, thanks. What about Brady Laurie? He did die from drowning. He was just helped. But that wasn't you, was it? You're not that good a diver," Kat said.

"I'm good enough," Sherry insisted. "But, no. Landry was so easy to manipulate. He wanted the salvage rights on that dive."

"So, do I understand this correctly? Landry came at Brady with some kind of weapon. He scared him half to death, then held Brady, tore his regulator from him and kept him down there until he drowned?"

"Something like that. I wasn't there," Sherry said. "I was waiting for him on the boat. I'd already become friends with Amanda. Good friends. The best of friends. She called me for everything. What a loser. She didn't have any real friends, big surprise, and, of course, she was so obnoxious it sure could look like she was guilty of everything. Ah, well, information. That's what I got from Amanda. Silly, naive, pathetic woman! She thought everyone just loved history! She fell for everything I said. Obviously. In case you were wondering, we ate here, and I dropped lobster pieces into her salad. I knew she'd have a severe reaction. Happened almost immediately. And no one knew she'd been with me."

"Oh, someone out there saw you. *Someone* will always see you."

"But I was *in disguise,*" Sherry told her. "I told Amanda I liked to dress up—that I'd be on stage one day. She totally believed me."

"Every move you make, you give something away. You leave something behind."

"Yes, well, prove it. Oh! You aren't doing very well with that, are you?" Sherry taunted.

"Let's see, you pulled all those histrionics at the Sand Diggers' mansion to look like an innocent woman in terror of the mummy."

"I did look like a terrified victim, didn't I?" Sherry asked, preening a bit. "Maybe I *should* go on stage. I was really good."

"Only to those who enjoy overacting." Kat rolled her eyes.

"Ha-ha. Very clever. Now drop the gun or I'll shoot you," Sherry said. "Put it down and kick it to me."

"But if I drop the gun, Sherry, you'll shoot me in the back."

"Well, how about if I shoot your friend in the heart?"

Kat could hear her coming closer. She spun around, aiming at her. "So, which of us is the better shot?" she asked. "I've had extensive training."

"I won't aim for you. I'll aim for concussion girl on the floor."

"It's over. The cops are onto you, Sherry," Kat said.

Sherry stared at her, still pretending absolute assurance. But she hesitated; she had to know that Kat had training and that she was a crack shot.

Kat heard Jon move behind her just a second too late. Something suddenly hit her in the head. Turning slightly before the lights seemed to go out, she saw that Jon had wrenched the precious death mask from the mummy.

And that he had slammed it over her head.

She managed to squeeze the trigger on her Glock as she went down, and she thought she heard Sherry cry out in rage and pain.

Will got to the center and saw where Jane and Kat had slit the crime scene tape to slip through to the door. When he opened it, he stood still, listening.

He walked as silently as he could, looking into the conference room and then the offices, his sense of alarm growing with every footstep.

He could find no one.

He turned and hurried back across the entry toward the climate-controlled room. Squinting through the ribbons of plastic, he saw nothing except for the sarcophagus. It lay on the steel table, as it always had, and the larger outer sarcophagus hadn't moved, either.

He started to walk by, but then waited. He made his way through the layers of plastic and found himself striding toward the sarcophagus. His heart seemed to rise in his chest as he did.

He almost tripped when he reached the other side of the table.

The mummy of Amun Mopat lay on the floor—on top of Jane Everett.

In the sarcophagus itself lay Kat.

He began to reach in for her, desperate for her to be alive. The sound of gunfire startled him; he heard and *felt* the thunk of bullets as they hit the wood of the sarcophagus. He ducked down low, skittering around to the other side of the table. For a split second, he was distracted. The way the mummy had fallen, it was almost as if the wrapped eyes were looking right at him.

He couldn't tell the direction of the gunfire, except that it seemed to come from the far side of the climate-controlled room, from behind other layers of plastic. He noticed then that there was a trail of blood.

And Kat's Glock lay on the floor.

She'd gotten a shot off! He stared at the plastic, searching for movement.

"I see you," he said. "I see you through the eyes of Amun Mopat. I have held the scepter, and it has given me visions you cannot imagine."

He heard a whisper. "He's got the scepter!"

The plastic moved.

"Don't be an idiot! He doesn't have the scepter. We saw him come in."

Another shot shattered the silence, this bullet burying itself in the sarcophagus, as well.

Will rose and shot back; he didn't dare do anything else. He didn't know if the women were alive or dead. If alive, they needed help. He didn't dare think about the way Kat lay, like the dead....

There was a scream of pain. Suddenly, the plastic went flying outward. Sherry Bertelli, her face set in a mask of hatred, came at him, gun blazing. Will ducked and then straightened to return her fire, emptying his cartridge into the woman who came after him so hellbent on murder.

He caught Sherry dead center in the chest. Still, she whirled as she went down, screaming all the while, more in rage, it seemed, than in pain.

Before he could reload, he heard Jon Hunt screeching in fury. He turned; the man had gotten his hands on Sherry's cast-aside pistol and was rising to one knee to shoot.

He heard something...from the sarcophagus. It was Kat, struggling to rise.

She gripped the edge, crying out, "Jon! Turn around. He's here, do you see him? Amun Mopat is here, and he's furious with you. He wasn't evil, he wasn't evil at all. He never used his scepter for evil purposes. He used it to pray that the rains would come and that people would live."

Jon Hunt just stared at her. Then, slowly, he turned. He stared at the figure Kat began to describe.

"He was young by our standards, Jon. He wasn't even forty when he died. He spent his life trying to feed those who had nothing, and trying to guide the pharaoh to rule justly. He urged others to help the lepers and the sick and the lame. He never wielded that scepter in cruelty. Can you see him, Jon? He's walking toward you and he's so angry. He's furious with you!"

Will wasn't sure if Jon saw what he saw, or if Kat's description created the illusion, or if the ghost of Amun Mopat, historically wronged, had stepped through the veil between life and death to save him and Kat. He saw the priest, tall and straight, slim and regal, walking toward Jon. He saw him reach for the man—and send him sliding across the slick tile of the floor.

Will jammed a new cartridge into his service Glock. He rose and walked over to Jon, pulling the gun from his hand. He'd never realized until he'd seen him in a rage just how powerful Jon might have been.

He hunkered down beside him. "The cops will be on their way soon, Jon. Now, I'm going to go tend to my friends. If I were you, I'd stay there. I'd stay very still. Because do you know what's real? The human soul's quest for justice. You thought you could have all the power you ever hoped for in your strange, sick mind. I'm pretty sure Sherry was in it for the money. That doesn't matter anymore. What does matter is that if you move, Amun Mopat will strangle the life out of you, slowly and with malice." He gritted his teeth and managed a shrug. "And if not, may you rest in a urine-stained mental ward for the rest of your life!" Taking out his phone with one hand, he dialed 9-1-1, his eyes still on Jon Hunt. It seemed that he'd hardly hung up when the police came rushing in and he knew they must have heard the shots.

He and Kat, they were going to be all right. Jane, too.

He rose, jerking the cartridge from Sherry's gun and breaking it on his knee, then throwing the gun to a far corner of the room.

He couldn't help it; he rushed to Kat first. He helped her crawl from the sarcophagus and, before he could let her go to aid Jane, he held her for a second. "You had my back," he whispered.

"And you had mine."

"Jane?" he asked.

"Concussion," she said. "She needs an ambulance."

"And so do you."

"He hit me with the death mask. It wasn't really hard enough to do much damage," she told him. She pulled away, kneeling by Jane. Even as she did, Jane groaned. Her eyes began to flutter open and, in a minute, she was looking at Kat.

"Is it—"

"Over," Kat said. "It's really over."

Will found that he was studying the mummy that lay discarded and broken on the floor.

"Thanks," he said quietly. He could hear sirens blaring through the streets of Chicago. He thought they might sleep well that night, neither of them troubled by visions or dreams.

"Creepy, creepy, really creepy!" Kelsey said. She still shuddered when she heard Kat talk about having been laid out in the sarcophagus.

"It's just a box, nothing more," Kat pointed out. She pulled a loose thread off the robe that Kelsey was wearing. "You look great."

"Oh, yeah," Kelsey said. "I should run around in Egyptian robes every day."

"It's going to be nice," Kat told her. "We're doing it for Dirk Manning. Come on, he can't live with us forever, you know."

"True."

"Is everyone prepared?" Dirk Manning came into the parlor area of the Egyptian Sand Diggers' mansion. He seemed rested and relaxed for the first time in weeks. "Tonight, we set free a soul so that it may soar with the wind and ride the sun in the heavens," he said. "If everyone will follow me.... Those of you who will speak as the Egyptian gods and goddesses, please be ready."

They walked through the maze again.

Samantha was ahead of Kat in the procession; Kat had the feeling that she'd be taking on a bigger role with the society. She read her part in a clear, dramatic voice.

Others read, too, including Will. He winked at her as she recited her part. Kelsey, drafted into the ceremony at the last minute, did well, too.

"We, the Egyptian Sand Diggers of Chicago, wish peace and comfort to a man much maligned by history. A man who seems to have proven to all of us that he had nothing but a devout desire to help others. Around him, there were men, misled or filled with greed, who sought to steal his riches—riches they thought meant power, but his power was really the strength of his soul. Tonight, we swear to do the research to right his reputation in history. And we pray that his soul will find the heaven he has always sought."

Will came to stand by Kat, placing his arm around her. "Look!" he said softly. "It that my imagination?"

Kat squinted, looking past the altar and the obelisk, just behind Dirk Manning.

It seemed that Amun Mopat was indeed there, watching with approval. And at his side was Austin Miller. As if he was a guide, trying to explain the modern world to the ghost who'd been silent for centuries. Whose body had lain at the bottom of the lake for all these years.

Dirk Manning lit an incense burner, and smoke and scent rose into the air.

The Egyptian and the elderly American seemed to disappear in the smoke.

If they'd ever really been there…

They stayed and enjoyed the after-party at the Sand Diggers' manor for a while, but then Will and Kat slipped out early.

They had tickets to Second City, and then planned to enjoy some really great jazz.

The show was hilarious, and they were treated to an hour of the wonderful music for which the city had long been famed.

They drove back along the lake and stopped to look out on the water. "One day we'll come back and dive the wreck," Kat said.

He stood behind her, wrapping her in his arms. "Hmm, one day. But Simonton's Sea Search is now going to work with the new experts brought in by the Preservation Center's board. The filming will continue. But since the research and salvage will be managed by Andy, we may not be welcome for a while."

"I don't think he was that angry. In fact, he seemed fine when I spoke to him a couple of days ago." Kat reached up to stroke his face. "They were all in on it—Amanda, Jon, Landry and Sherry."

"All of them." Will nodded. "Jon was the least involved, I think—but, of course, he was the craziest."

"Obsessed," Kat agreed. "To the point of insanity."

"I think Amanda was kind of a patsy. She wanted a real friendship—and she wanted glory. Her relationship with Sherry seemed to be something she needed in a sad kind of way."

"On the other hand, Sherry just wanted money. From what she said that night, I believe she'd watched what was going on for a long time—and that she was the 'brains' behind the operation, if that's the right word.

I'm sure Landry thought *he* was in charge. Sherry might have been a better actress than I gave her credit for," Kat said.

"I agree, Sherry was in it for the money—and she played sweet, innocent and dumb extremely well. I think she learned a bit about high living when she went places with Landry, and that meant she needed cash to support the lifestyle she aspired to. Landry wasn't going to divorce his wife and Sherry wasn't going to play second fiddle forever."

"And Landry wanted the rights to dive the wreck," Kat said. "It all worked for them—for a while." She turned to look at him. "Murder does make for the strangest associations, not to mention bedfellows!"

"Murder and greed," Will added. "I'm not sure they actually wanted anyone to die. What they wanted was the *Jerry McGuen*. I just don't think they cared who had to die so they could get what they were after. Brady Laurie was so passionate about the ship and his work—he's really the one who was in the way. Knowing the truth now, it's easy to see how they created their plan. Amanda and Jon provided what was needed on the research end. Landry killed Brady, while Sherry played the mummy every time—and poisoned Amanda when she was afraid Amanda might start breaking because of our investigation."

"That's what Sherry told me, at any rate."

"Boy, she's the one who makes me shiver the most. She was stone-cold."

"Yep," Kat agreed. "She shot her lover without a second thought."

"Sad, truly sad. So many dead…"

"And, remarkably, it's over," Will said. "Bastet has a home with Dirk now. The research work will go on, and so will the documentary. There'll be pieces to pick up, and some people will still insist it was the curse written on Amun Mopat's tomb. In a way it was—a curse carried out through the living.

"Enough of that for tonight…" He swung Kat around to face him. "You know what we haven't done yet? The Shedd Aquarium and the Field Museum. The Field Museum, which has a really good Egyptian display."

"You're teasing me, and I know it! But guess what? Tomorrow, I think we should do a whirlwind shopping spree down Michigan Avenue, visit the Shedd Aquarium—and, okay, the Field Museum."

"Really?"

"I've actually acquired a fondness for mummies!" she told him.

He kissed her. "And tonight?"

"Let's get back to the hotel. I've actually acquired quite a fondness for you, as well," she whispered. "I thought I might show you just *how* fond I am."

He tilted her chin up. "Nice. Because I've acquired an adoration for you." He grew serious. "You do know I'm in love with you."

She smiled. "And you do know we'll work it out."

He nodded, turning away.

"Will?"

He laughed. "Well, come on, then! Let's start working it out."

She laughed and followed him.

The breeze was warm. The lake was sparkling like a sea of diamonds beneath the moon and the stars.

God, she loved Chicago!

* * * * *

REQUEST YOUR FREE BOOKS!

2 FREE NOVELS
FROM THE SUSPENSE COLLECTION
PLUS 2 FREE GIFTS!

YES! Please send me 2 FREE novels from the Suspense Collection and my 2 FREE gifts (gifts are worth about $10). After receiving them, if I don't wish to receive any more books, I can return the shipping statement marked "cancel." If I don't cancel, I will receive 4 brand-new novels every month and be billed just $5.99 per book in the U.S. or $6.49 per book in Canada. That's a saving of at least 25% off the cover price. It's quite a bargain! Shipping and handling is just 50¢ per book in the U.S. and 75¢ per book in Canada.* I understand that accepting the 2 free books and gifts places me under no obligation to buy anything. I can always return a shipment and cancel at any time. Even if I never buy another book, the two free books and gifts are mine to keep forever.

191/391 MDN FEME

Name	(PLEASE PRINT)

Address	Apt. #

City	State/Prov.	Zip/Postal Code

Signature (if under 18, a parent or guardian must sign)

Mail to the **Reader Service:**
IN U.S.A.: P.O. Box 1867, Buffalo, NY 14240-1867
IN CANADA: P.O. Box 609, Fort Erie, Ontario L2A 5X3

Not valid for current subscribers to the Suspense Collection
or the Romance/Suspense Collection.

Want to try two free books from another line?
Call 1-800-873-8635 or visit www.ReaderService.com.

* Terms and prices subject to change without notice. Prices do not include applicable taxes. Sales tax applicable in N.Y. Canadian residents will be charged applicable taxes. Offer not valid in Quebec. This offer is limited to one order per household. All orders subject to credit approval. Credit or debit balances in a customer's account(s) may be offset by any other outstanding balance owed by or to the customer. Please allow 4 to 6 weeks for delivery. Offer available while quantities last.

Your Privacy—The Reader Service is committed to protecting your privacy. Our Privacy Policy is available online at www.ReaderService.com or upon request from the Reader Service.

We make a portion of our mailing list available to reputable third parties that offer products we believe may interest you. If you prefer that we not exchange your name with third parties, or if you wish to clarify or modify your communication preferences, please visit us at www.ReaderService.com/consumerchoice or write to us at Reader Service Preference Service, P.O. Box 9062, Buffalo, NY 14269. Include your complete name and address.

SUS11

New York Times bestselling author

RACHEL VINCENT

Kori Daniels is a shadow-walker, able to travel instantly from one shadow to another. After weeks of confinement for betraying her boss, she's ready to break free for good. But Jake Tower has one final job for Kori, one chance to secure freedom for herself and her sister, Kenley.

The job? Recruit Ian Holt—or kill him.

Ian's ability to manipulate the dark has drawn an invitation from Jake Tower. But Ian is on a mission of his own. He's come to kill Tower's top Binder: Kori's little sister.

Amid the tangle of lies, an unexpected thread of truth connecting Ian and Kori comes to light. But with opposing goals, they'll have to choose between love and liberty....

Shadow Bound

Available wherever books are sold.

MRV1343R

HEATHER GRAHAM

77615	BRIDE OF THE NIGHT	___ $7.99 U.S.	___ $9.99 CAN.
77486	NIGHT OF THE VAMPIRES	___ $7.99 U.S.	___ $9.99 CAN.
61844	THE KEEPERS	___ $5.25 U.S.	___ $6.25 CAN.
32998	HEART OF EVIL	___ $7.99 U.S.	___ $9.99 CAN.
32939	THE KILLING EDGE	___ $7.99 U.S.	___ $9.99 CAN.
32928	THE PRESENCE	___ $7.99 U.S.	___ $9.99 CAN.
32916	THE SÉANCE	___ $7.99 U.S.	___ $9.99 CAN.
32915	THE VISION	___ $7.99 U.S.	___ $9.99 CAN.
32823	HOME IN TIME FOR CHRISTMAS	___ $7.99 U.S.	___ $9.99 CAN.
32815	GHOST NIGHT	___ $7.99 U.S.	___ $9.99 CAN.
32796	GHOST MOON	___ $7.99 U.S.	___ $9.99 CAN.
32791	GHOST SHADOW	___ $7.99 U.S.	___ $9.99 CAN.
32758	NIGHTWALKER	___ $7.99 U.S.	___ $9.99 CAN.
32676	UNHALLOWED GROUND	___ $7.99 U.S.	___ $8.99 CAN.
32654	DUST TO DUST	___ $7.99 U.S.	___ $8.99 CAN.
32625	THE DEATH DEALER	___ $7.99 U.S.	___ $7.99 CAN.
32527	DEADLY GIFT	___ $7.99 U.S.	___ $7.99 CAN.
31349	THE UNHOLY	___ $7.99 U.S.	___ $9.99 CAN.
31318	PHANTOM EVIL	___ $7.99 U.S.	___ $9.99 CAN.
31303	GHOST WALK	___ $7.99 U.S.	___ $9.99 CAN.
31253	THE EVIL INSIDE	___ $7.99 U.S.	___ $9.99 CAN.
31242	SACRED EVIL	___ $7.99 U.S.	___ $9.99 CAN.

(limited quantities available)

TOTAL AMOUNT	$ _____
POSTAGE & HANDLING	$ _____
($1.00 for 1 book, 50¢ for each additional)	
APPLICABLE TAXES*	$ _____
TOTAL PAYABLE	$ _____

(check or money order—please do not send cash)

To order, complete this form and send it, along with a check or money order for the total above, payable to Harlequin MIRA, to: **In the U.S.:** 3010 Walden Avenue, P.O. Box 9077, Buffalo, NY 14269-9077; **In Canada:** P.O. Box 636, Fort Erie, Ontario, L2A 5X3.

Name: _____

Address: _____ City: _____

State/Prov.: _____ Zip/Postal Code: _____

Account Number (if applicable): _____

075 CSAS

*New York residents remit applicable sales taxes.
*Canadian residents remit applicable GST and provincial taxes.

H HARLEQUIN® MIRA®
™ www.Harlequin.com

MHG0712BL

AUG 2012